Liberating Lana

Teresa Burrell

Silent Thunder Publishing

LIBERATING LANA. Copyright 2023 by

Teresa Burrell.

Edited by L.J. Sellers

Book Cover Design by Madeline Settle

ISBN: 978-1-938680-46-5

Library of Congress Number: 2023918361

Silent Thunder Publishing

San Diego

Dedication

To James Hendershot, a remarkable friend who brought immense joy and support to my brother Philip who was the inspiration for my Tuper character. Your unwavering friendship and countless acts of kindness went far beyond what words can express. Philip often spoke of you as his closest companion, and the love and admiration he held for you were truly profound. I am eternally grateful for the impact you had on his life, making his final years a little easier and a lot less lonely.

Acknowledgments

Thanks to my Montana Consultants:
Clarice Lecy
Mary Ann Walker
Jerome Johnson
Kayla Walker

A special thanks to Marlene Thorne
for submitting the title for this book—*Liberating Lana*.

I always appreciate my great Beta Readers:
Beth Agejew
Vickie Barrier
Denise Bowman
Melanie Cardullo
Crystal Kamada
Sheila Krueger
Linda Langille
Janie Livingston
Joy Lorton
Uma Van Roosenbeek
MaryAnn Schaefer
Denise Zendel

Also by Teresa Burrell

THE ADVOCATE SERIES

THE ADVOCATE (Book 1)
THE ADVOCATE'S BETRAYAL (Book 2)
THE ADVOCATE'S CONVICTION (Book 3)
THE ADVOCATE'S DILEMMA (Book 4)
THE ADVOCATE'S EX PARTE (Book5)
THE ADVOCATE'S FELONY (Book 6)
THE ADVOCATE'S GEOCACHE (Book 7)
THE ADVOCATE'S HOMICIDES (Book 8)
THE ADVOCATE'S ILLUSION (Book 9)
THE ADVOCATE'S JUSTICE (Book 10)
THE ADVOCATE'S KILLER (Book 11)
THE ADVOCATE'S LABYRINTH (Book 12)
THE ADVOCATE'S MEMORY (Book 13)
THE ADVOCATE'S NIGHTMARE (Book 14)

THE TUPER MYSTERY SERIES

THE ADVOCATE'S FELONY
(Book 6 of The Advocate Series)
MASON'S MISSING (Book 1)
FINDING FRANKIE (Book 2)
RECOVERING RITA (Book 3)
LIBERATING LANA (Book 4)

CO-AUTHORED STANDALONE

NO CONSENT
(Co-authored with L.J. Sellers)

Chapter One

Tuesday early morning

I know where you are. Lana's chest tightened as she read the threatening email. Her heart raced as she glanced at the time on her phone: 2:04 a.m. In the silent darkness of her home in Helena, Montana, fear surged through her veins like a jolt of electricity. She always felt uneasy when he sent messages, but this time was different. This time, in addition to the message, she could swear someone had been following her, skulking in the shadows as she rode around town. It had gone on for several days now. Had he really found her this time? Her stomach churned. He had tracked her down like an animal before, but she had simply moved on. This was the first place she'd felt safe enough to make friends and start anew. But if they were already coming for her, it meant one thing: it was only a matter of time until she had to run again. For nearly a year, this had been her safe haven. No, it was more than that. Helena, and her life here, was a place she could finally call home.

Lana leaned against the wall in Clarice's trailer, where she had been sleeping on the sofa since shortly after she arrived in Helena. She sipped her coffee, the bitterness a familiar comfort. At 29, she was a skilled hacker, though few knew her secret past.

Her laptop screen flickered again, the backlights obviously going bad. "Dang piece of crap," she mumbled as she glanced down. Her fingers tapped the keys with practiced precision, a dance she'd known for years. But her eyes darted to the side, an involuntary tic born from fear.

She didn't dare stay in one place too long, always looking over her shoulder, avoiding connections with people. She had learned to live like a dark specter in a world where everyone else seemed to bask in the light.

"Maybe I should just toss you out the window," she mused aloud. She imagined the satisfying crunch of metal and glass meeting pavement.

Lana's computer beeped, signaling she had received another email. She hesitated before opening it, her heart pounding.

Surprise, surprise. You didn't really think you could hide from me forever, did you?

Lana's hands trembled on the keyboard. Had he actually found her, or was this just another scare tactic? If he had, she knew what he was capable of, and she knew he would stop at nothing to get to her.

A knock at the door startled her. Lana froze, her breath caught in her throat. She knew she had to act fast. She quickly shut down her laptop and jammed it into her backpack, which was filled with practically everything she owned. She pulled on her combat boots, grabbed her leather jacket, and peeked out the window, relieved to see Tuper standing there with his black and white border collie. Dually traveled with him almost everywhere he went.

Tuper was an enigma wrapped in a cowboy hat and boots. He was tall and slender, and resembled Sam Elliott, but with a scar down the right side of his face from his eye to just under his chin. He had been her lifeline in this strange new existence. She opened the door.

"Hey, Agony," he said. He'd been calling her that since they first met. In return, she called him *Pops*. He hated that he was getting old and didn't like any reminder of it, but Lana believed he'd gotten used to the handle. Maybe even enjoyed it a little. They had a unique relationship even though they were forty years apart in age. Tuper barely knew what a computer was and didn't even know how to text on his flip phone. He barely knew enough to make a phone call.

"Do you know what time it is?" Lana asked.

"Not exactly. Why? Don't any of your fandangled machines have the time?"

"What are you doing here at two in the morning?"

"I saw the light on. Besides, I knew you'd still be up. You're always on that contraption." Tuper shivered. "Can we come in? It's cold out here."

"Sure." Lana glanced around outside to make sure no one else was there.

"Are you expecting someone?"

"Of course not. But then, I wasn't expecting you either."

Tuper stepped in and closed the door. Lana locked it. Tuper gave her an inquisitive look, then sat down at the table.

"What are you doing out at this hour?" Lana repeated as she reached down to pet Dually.

"Need your help on a case."

"Right now?"

"That machine of yours works all hours, right?"

"Ugh, fine," she said. "The teapot's on if you want something hot to drink."

"Thanks," Tuper said. He stepped into the small kitchen, separated from the dining area by only a counter. When he returned, he sat down at the table next to where Lana had reclaimed her seat.

No one here knew her last name, or anything about her past. They did know she was good at finding things online. As much as she wanted to maintain her secret identity, something about working with Tuper offered a sense of stability in her otherwise chaotic existence. But she hadn't yet trusted anyone enough to let them in. If she ever did reach that point, Tuper would be the one she would tell. In fact, she was tempted to tell him about the email. Yet, if it was real, she didn't want to put him at risk, and she knew he would want to help. Lana downed the last dregs of her coffee.

"Maybe I should just burn it all," she mused, half-jokingly. "Start fresh somewhere else."

"What are you jabbering about?"

Keep it together, Lana. She wanted to tell Tuper, who wouldn't judge her, but she just couldn't. *Nobody can know.* She wasn't alone, but still, the shadows of her past loomed ever closer, threatening to swallow her whole.

She looked up from her computer. "So, what is it you needed?"

"I know a guy who knows a guy."

Before he could finish, Lana said, "Really, Pops?"

"Just listen. The guy thinks his wife is cheating on him, and he wants me to find out."

"I thought you hated those kinds of cases."

"I do, but this is a good friend. He'd do anything for me, so I need to do the same."

"What do you need from me?"

"For starters, I need you to go with me to meet with the husband this morning at nine. We'll figure it out from there."

"You came here to tell me that?"

"No. I stopped because your light was on. I knew you'd be up, and it's cold out there. I wanted a cup of hot tea."

"Whatever, Pops," she said. "By the way, I've got some new info on our latest case."

"Really?" Tuper raised an eyebrow. He leaned forward in his chair, which creaked under his weight. The cowboy hat perched on his silver-haired head matched his well-worn boots. "Let's hear it."

Lana's fingers danced across the keyboard as she pulled up the information she'd gathered. Despite the risks, she couldn't deny the thrill she felt each time she breached another secure server. It was a game to her, one she played with the odds always against her.

"I managed to access the phone records of our shady businessman, Mr. Thompson." She glanced over at Tuper, whose eyes were already sparkling with interest.

"Humph." Tuper leaned back in his chair and sipped his tea. "So, what did ya find?"

"Turns out he's been making frequent calls to a number associated with a known criminal organization. And not just any organization, the Rattlers."

"Those snake-lovin' swine?" Tuper spat, his face contorted with disgust. "That explains a lot about Mr. Thompson."

Lana grinned at Tuper's reaction, but her mind raced as she thought about the implications of their discovery. It was one thing to investigate a corrupt businessman; it was another to tangle with an entire criminal syndicate. She knew all too well the dangers that came with digging too deep into someone else's secrets, especially when those secrets belonged to dangerous people.

"Are you sure we want to go after these guys, Pops?" Lana asked, her voice wavering. "I mean, we're playing with fire."

"We've always played with fire," Tuper replied, his eyes serious, but with a hint of a smile. "Besides, I ain't gettin' any younger. Might as well go out with a bang, right?"

"Only if that bang doesn't take me with you," Lana muttered, her fingers resuming their position ready to type.

Tuper chuckled. "Now, now, don't you worry your pretty little head about that. I know a guy. We'll get through this just fine."

"Whatever you say." Lana rolled her eyes, hiding the smile that tugged at the corners of her mouth. Despite the ever-present shadows of her past, she couldn't help but feel a sense of belonging with Tuper. As they were about to dive deep into the dangerous world of Helena's criminal underbelly, Lana couldn't imagine facing it with anyone else by her side.

Chapter Two

Tuesday Morning

It was still dark when Tuper walked out the door, and Lana closed it behind him. The rickety wooden fence that surrounded the trailer creaked in the wind. The modest home was where she'd found her sanctuary after Clarice and her sister, Mary Ann, had taken her under their wings.

Clarice passed through the dining area into the kitchen. "Was that Tuper just leaving?"

"Yeah. We've been working on a case most of the night."

"I'm surprised he didn't stay for breakfast." Clarice opened the fridge and pulled out a few things.

"He was meeting someone at Smith's."

"I figured he must be up to something. He's never one to miss a free meal." Clarice looked out the window. "They say we might get some snow today."

"Not much though. No blizzard or anything."

"But it won't be long before we can't see the ground again. We seldom get by without a white Christmas."

"I'm looking forward to that."

After a few minutes, Lana closed her laptop and made her way into the cozy kitchen, where the aroma of pancakes and sausage now filled the air.

"Where's Tuper?" Mary Ann entered the room, still in her pajamas.

"Out chasing leads." Lana leaned against the counter. "He's got enough energy for someone half his age."

"Stubborn old coot," chuckled Clarice, sliding a plate of pancakes onto the counter. "He's always up and out before the rooster crows."

Lana smiled, taking in the familiar faces of her makeshift family. She couldn't have survived this past year without them. They had given her a place to call home while she assisted Tuper with cases, never probing into her past. They didn't know where she was from or why she was running, and they didn't pry. Here, she could maintain her secret identity.

"Speaking of cases, did you two manage to track down that missing dog?" asked Mary Ann, as she sorted the stack of mail on the counter.

"Yep. We found the poor thing tied up in some creep's backyard," Lana recalled the earlier rescue. "Tuper gave the guy a piece of his mind, punched him in the face, and left with the dog."

"Good for you guys." Clarice nodded and served up the rest of breakfast.

As they sat down to eat, Lana felt a pang of guilt. She knew how much these women cared for her, yet she couldn't bring herself to share the details of her past with them. It was enough that Tuper had suspicions. She was certain of it, even though he'd never questioned her. She didn't want to put anyone else in danger, and involving them would do just that.

"Anything interesting in the mail?" Lana asked, trying to get her mind onto something else.

"Mostly bills." Mary Ann sighed as she sifted through the stack. "But there's a postcard addressed to you."

"Really?" Surprised, Lana reached for the postcard. The front displayed a picturesque beach scene from San Diego, California.

Lana turned it over. "From Ron Brown." She fought the urge to smile, remembering their brief encounter before he returned to San Diego, after a visit here with Tuper. The kiss Ron gave her before he left still lingered on her lips. He was charming and handsome, but she knew better than to let herself get too close to anyone. It could only end badly.

"Ron, huh?" Clarice's eyes twinkled with curiosity.

"Uh, he keeps in touch," Lana replied nonchalantly. "He's... nice."

"Nice? That's all you've got to say about him?" teased Mary Ann, a grin spreading across her face. "He's actually very handsome and charming as can be."

"Can we not turn this into a thing?" Lana rolled her eyes. "I'm just trying to enjoy my breakfast."

"All right, all right," conceded Clarice with a chuckle. "But if you ever want to talk about this *nice* fella, we're here for you."

"Thanks, guys," Lana smiled, feeling a warmth in her chest she hadn't experienced in years. Despite her secrets and the constant fear of being discovered, she had found something special in this unconventional family. As she ate her meal, surrounded by laughter and love, Lana couldn't help but wonder if maybe, just maybe, she could one day let her guard down and truly belong.

Chapter Three

Tuesday morning 8:30 a.m.

Lana was waiting on the deck when Tuper arrived to pick her up for the appointment with Fenton. He drove up in his beat-up, faded-red 1978 Toyota that looked like it was straight from the junkyard. The body was dented and scratched, and the car's hatchback door was held closed by a rope that tied the handle to the bumper. The door of the old car creaked as Lana swung it open, the rusted hinge protesting its disuse. Dually sat proudly in the passenger seat, but jumped in the back when Lana got in. She sat down and started examining the contents of her backpack.

Tuper peered over the top of his silver-rimmed aviator sunglasses at her. "Got everything you need, Agony?" Tuper drawled, adjusting his hat.

"Of course, Pops." Lana secured the clasp of her backpack with a satisfying click. "You know I'm always three steps ahead of you."

"Humph."

Tuper in those sunglasses reminded Lana of Clint Eastwood in one of his cowboy movies. She smirked, amused by the thought. "Where did you get those glasses? They're so *not* you."

"Louise gave them to me. She says they make me look fashionable."

"And we both know how important that is to you."

"That's what I told her," Tuper smiled. "Let's go."

As they drove through Helena, Lana couldn't help but glance nervously out the window, checking between the rearview mirror and the passing scenery. Her heart raced every time she saw a car that stayed behind them too long. She knew Tuper had noticed her constant vigilance. It was hard to miss when she nearly jumped out of her skin at the slightest provocation. But he never pried, respecting her privacy.

"I wish we didn't have to do this today," Tuper said, breaking the silence. "I hate this sort of thing."

"So, why are we doing it?"

"Because my friend Brad Bergstad asked me to. The guy is a good friend of his, and when Brad asks for help, I give it. Brad has been in my life since he was a kid. His pa and I go way back."

"What is *this* exactly?"

"The guy thinks his wife is cheating on him. Pretty common these days."

"Doesn't make it any less sad." Lana sighed, fidgeting with her fingers.

"I guess." Tuper glanced at her, concern etching lines on his weathered face. "You all right there, Lana? You seem more jumpy than usual."

"Nothing I can't handle, Pops. Just... you know, life stuff," she replied evasively. She appreciated Tuper's concern, but she couldn't risk telling him the truth.

"All right," Tuper finally said, nodding his understanding. "But you know I'm here for ya, right? Whatever it is."

"Thanks, Pops," Lana whispered, her voice thick with emotion, something she seldom showed. She knew he meant it, in his own cantankerous way. She cleared her throat. *Cowgirl up!* She was getting too soft.

As they parked outside the office building where their client worked, Lana gave herself a mental pep talk. This was her life now, helping Tuper solve cases while staying under the radar. It wasn't perfect, and it certainly wasn't easy, but it was better than the alternative.

"Ready to catch a cheater?" Tuper asked.

"Absolutely." Lana's voice was steady and strong.

"Let's do this," Tuper declared. They exited the car, ready to tackle another case together. As they walked across the parking lot, Lana couldn't help but steal another glance over her shoulder, then shook it off. She was probably overreacting. It wasn't the first time the man from her past had made her think he knew where she was when he didn't. He loved to play mind games.

As they entered the office building, they were immediately met with suspicious stares from the other occupants. It was clear they were out of place. Tuper's weathered cowboy hat and Lana's combat boots stuck out like sore thumbs in the corporate environment. But Lana didn't mind. She felt unique and empowered, knowing that even though she didn't fit in with the rest of society, she was her own person.

They took the elevator up to their client's office on the fourth floor. As they rounded a corner, Lana spotted a familiar figure in the hallway, his profile looming in the distance. She gasped.

Lana tugged Tuper's arm and pulled him back before the man spotted them. Lana peered around the corner and stared at the figure. If it was who she thought, he could identify her. She held her breath.

"Are you okay?" Tuper asked.

When the man turned and took a step in their direction, she saw his entire face and breathed a sigh of relief.

Tuper gave her a concerned look.

"I'm fine. Sorry."

Tuper nodded and they continued to their client's office without further incident.

Chapter Four

Tuesday morning 9:00 a.m.

Tuper and Lana knocked, then stepped into the huge office.

"I'm Tuper and this is Ag... Lana."

"Henry Fenton." He was short, round and balding. Pointing to the chairs in front of his desk, he added, "Please sit." Tuper and Lana took their seats, and before either could say anything else, Henry blurted out, "Angel's been lying to me."

"Angel's your wife?"

"Yes."

"How do you know she's been lying?" Tuper asked.

"Lots of little things." Henry paused. "And a few big ones."

"Such as?"

"When she gets a phone call, she leaves the room. If I ask who she's talking to, she ends the conversation. She's been having more *spa* days." He made quotes in the air. "She's been coming home late after nights out with her *girlfriends*." Again, with the air quotes.

Tuper listened intently, taking in the details and filing them away in his memory, but not taking notes. Lana pulled out a notepad from her bag and started writing things down.

The man's expression changed, shifting from pain to anger as he shared more details about his wife's behavior. He seemed torn between wanting to believe her and ready to catch her in the act. His eyes moved between Tuper and Lana as he struggled to recall the events that had led him to suspect his wife was having an affair.

"I mean, I asked her if everything was okay and she said it was, but I'm sure she was hiding something from me." Henry looked away for a moment before continuing. "A few weeks ago, I found a button on our bedroom floor that I don't think was hers. Angel seemed so nervous when I found it. She swore up and down that it was off a pair of her pants, but she didn't voluntarily produce the pants and I didn't push." His words echoed through the large office, his voice rising and falling as he recounted his grievances. The only other sound was Lana's pen scratching in her notepad as she methodically took notes. Tuper nodded along sympathetically.

"I'm sure there's something else going on," the man finished quietly.

"You mean something besides the lying or what she's lying about?" Tuper asked.

"She's been less affectionate. She used to be so open and loving." Their client paused.

"In what way?" Tuper asked.

"She just doesn't seem to love me as much. I don't blame her, really. I'm not much to look at, and she's younger than me, and far more attractive."

"I'm still not sure what you're saying."

Henry sighed and drifted off into thought.

Lana blurted, "Has she stopped having sex with you?"

Tuper gave her a scornful look, but he admired her frankness.

"Not entirely, but it's not as often. I miss her." Even in his pain, his voice was laced with love and heartache for his wife.

"What else have you noticed that is different?"

"She doesn't want to cook for me. I know Angel doesn't like to cook, but she used to do it anyway. Now, she only cooks if she has to. And she spends more time on her phone. I've caught her in the middle of the night on her phone, sitting in the dark in the den."

"She was talking to someone?" Tuper asked.

"No. I think she was texting."

"Did you ask her?"

"She denied it and said she was playing a game because she couldn't sleep."

Tuper was getting exasperated. He needed real details. "Do you think she's having an affair with someone you know?"

"There are a few possibilities, like Adam, the next-door neighbor. He always flirts with her. And there's the mechanic we go to. She's been having a lot of car trouble lately. I offered to buy her a new car, but she refused. The one she has is only two years old, but she claims it needs maintenance. She also works out at the gym far too often. So, it could be someone there." Henry struggled to keep his voice steady. He spoke with a tinge of desperation, his words punctuated by sighs and pauses as he searched for suspects. He continued to name possibilities, some of them realistic, others seemed far-fetched.

"Do you have a photo of your wife?" Tuper asked.

Henry reached into his desk, pulled out a large manila envelope, and handed it to Tuper. "There's a photo of her as well as her car. I took a picture of the license plate so you'd have that. There's also a schedule of regular activities and the names and addresses of those places. You know, the gym, her hair salon, her nail salon, stuff like that."

"That'll be helpful." Tuper stood. "We'll be in touch. And if you think of anything else, please give me a call."

When they left the office, Lana reached out. "Let me see the envelope. I want to see what she looks like."

"Wait until we get to the car."

Tuper stood on the sidewalk for a minute, zipping up his jacket and feeling uneasy. He glanced at Lana. "These cases leave a sour taste in my mouth."

Lana gave him a questioning look. "Really? Would it be different if it was Henry doing the cheating?"

"No. If a person wants to cheat, let them cheat. Man or woman. It isn't the worst thing in the world. But she could be a little more discreet."

"Of course, you'd think that, Pops." Lana adjusted her scarf. "I'll be digging up dirt on Angel from behind my computer screen." She grinned, but there was steel in her eyes.

"Yeah," Tuper replied gruffly. "But while you're hackin' and crackin', I'll be out here in the cold, talkin' to people. You know, the old-fashioned way. I've got a few contacts around town that might have some info on Angel."

Lana rolled her eyes. "Yeah, I know. You know a guy," She sighed, but then her expression softened. "Just stay out of trouble."

"Trouble?" Tuper chuckled, fingering the scar down the right side of his face. "I haven't seen real trouble since before you were born."

"Whatever you say, Pops." Lana smirked. "Take me home and I'll get crackin', as you put it. I'll start with social media. It's amazing what people will share without a second thought. And if that doesn't turn up anything, I can always try to access her phone records and emails. People have no idea how they expose themselves. They think they're being so secretive and yet they do things that are so obvious."

"Do you ever stop jibber-jabbin?" Tuper tipped his cowboy hat. "I'll see if any of my buddies have heard anything about Angel or her family."

When they reached the car, Lana slid into the passenger's seat. Tuper had barely closed his door when she said, "Open it."

Tuper took his time, fiddling with the envelope. Then he held it up and waved it nonchalantly in the air. "You know, this is the first bit of anything we have to go on."

Lana grabbed the envelope and opened it. "You can be so irritating. I think it's your favorite sport."

She pulled out a photo of a gorgeous blonde woman standing next to Henry. Even though his wife was wearing flat sandals, she was three inches taller than him. "Wow!" Lana said. "She's a knockout. I can see why he'd be suspicious." She handed the photo to Tuper. "Why do you suppose she married Henry?"

Tuper smiled as he studied the photo. "I'm sure it was love at first sight."

"For him, maybe."

Lana continued to peruse the paperwork. "Oh, this is good."

"What?" Tuper asked.

"Just thinking about her name."

"Angel?"

"Yes—Angel. Why do I get the feeling she isn't?"

Chapter Five

Tuesday afternoon

Tuper adjusted his cowboy hat as he sat in his truck, eyes trained on Angel Fenton as she left her house. He had chosen a spot down the street, just out of sight from her front door. With a deep breath, Tuper geared up for a long day of tailing Angel and speaking with people he didn't really want to talk to.

As Angel drove away, Tuper started the engine. "Time to see what you're hidin'."

He followed her at a safe distance, making sure not to draw attention to himself. Her first stop was a small café. He went inside and got in line, with two people between Angel and him. He ordered tea and took a seat. Carrying two cups, she sat down at the back of the café only a few tables away.

Within minutes, a man around thirty-five entered and walked directly to Angel's table. He was tall and broad shouldered, with dark hair and stubble-covered cheeks. He wore a brown leather jacket, with jeans that fit snugly, and the easy confidence in his stride made others in the café look up with curiosity. A subtle scent of cologne lingered in the air as the man moved closer to Angel's table, masking the smell of coffee and baked goods.

Tuper observed their interaction for a while, but nothing seemed out of the ordinary until the man took her hand, wrapping both of his around hers. Intrigued by the exchange, Tuper followed when they left. He trailed behind them as they walked a block, ending up outside a small apartment building. Most of the way, the man had his arm around Angel's shoulder, then he opened the door for her and she stepped inside.

Tuper wanted to take a closer look, so he ducked into an alley across the street and waited for them to come out. After an hour, Angel emerged with the man behind her. As they said goodbye, the man kissed her lightly on the cheek, before going a separate way.

Tuper walked toward his truck. He was in front of Angel and made it back just in time to continue tailing her. She went to a bookstore, the gym, and back home. Nothing more seemed out of the ordinary.

Tuper drove back to the café to see if he could learn anything else. He approached the counter and struck up a conversation with the barista. "Say, I saw a woman in here earlier today, long blonde hair, blue eyes. Name's Angel Fenton. You know her?"

"Sure do." The barista paused for a moment. "She comes in pretty often, usually meets with a guy named Mitch. They seem close... maybe too close."

"Interesting." Tuper filed that piece of information away. "Thanks for your help." He tipped his hat and left, heading to the bookstore where he'd followed Angel earlier.

Tuper had a friend who worked at the store, and she was behind the checkout counter. "Hey there, Sally," he greeted her with a charming smile. "Got a minute?"

"Always for you, Tuper." She grinned and leaned on the counter.

"Looking for info on a woman named Angel Fenton. She was in here earlier today."

Sally frowned, thinking back. "She comes in every Tuesday afternoon and spends a lot of time in the self-help section. Today, she bought a book called *The Pain in Keeping Secrets from Your Loved Ones*. Odd, huh?"

"Very," Tuper agreed. "Has she ever come in with anyone?"

"No. Always alone."

He thanked Sally and left the store.

It was late afternoon when Tuper returned to his car, piecing together the information he'd gathered. Angel's choice of reading material added to his suspicions.

His next stop was a bar in the same area as the apartment Angel and the man had visited. Tuper had friends that frequented the place, and there was a chance Angel might be a regular as well.

He pulled out his phone as he walked toward the local bar. Then he ambled into the dimly lit room, the smell of stale beer and cigarette smoke hanging in the air like a fog. He scanned the room, looking for familiar faces, people who might have the information he wanted. He spotted a rowdy group of friends—some he'd known for years—huddled around the bar. He approached them with a grin.

"Hey there, boys," Tuper called out, slapping one of the men on the back. "Mind if I join you, David?"

"Sure thing, Tuper!" David signaled to the bartender. "Get my friend what he wants."

"I'll have a Sprite," Tuper said.

As they drank, Tuper casually brought up Angel Johnson Fenton, trying to gauge their reactions. "Ya' know, I met a gal named Angel recently," he said. "Pretty thing, but she seems a bit secretive. Any of you boys know her?"

A couple of the men exchanged glances, then one spoke up. "Angel? Yeah. I've seen her around. She's got connections in high places. But she keeps her cards close to her chest, if you catch my drift."

"Interesting," Tuper mused. "Any idea who those connections might be?"

"She's married to some rich guy. That's all I know."

"Any of you know any more about her?"

"I know she's out of your league," David said. They all laughed. "But she comes in here occasionally, so maybe talk to Joe, the bartender. He might know something."

"Thanks, fellas." Tuper walked over to the end of the bar to speak to Joe.

"Hi, Toop."

"Hey, Joe. How's the wife and kids?

"Expensive."

Tuper laughed. "That's why you don't marry 'em."

"What can I do for you?"

"I understand you might know something about a woman named Angel Johnson Fenton."

Joe eyed him warily for a moment before saying, "I'm not one to gossip, but she comes in here once in a while with a young man who I know isn't her husband."

"Do you think it's an affair?"

"They're pretty cozy, but no outward displays. I figure they're just being careful, or maybe they're just friends. It's hard to tell and none of my business anyway."

"Do you know the guy's name?"

"No. But he's about thirty-five, well built, and I guess by most standards, good-looking."

"I think I know who yer talkin' about."

"You working on something big, Tuper?"

"Nah. Just tryin' to help out a friend."

Chapter Six

Tuesday afternoon

Meanwhile, Lana hunched over her laptop at the dining table, fingers flying across the keyboard as she hacked into Angel's social media accounts. She started with the basics: Facebook, Instagram, X. On the surface, everything seemed normal—vacation photos, check-ins at local restaurants, and the occasional inspirational quote. Lots of photos with her husband. But Lana knew better than to take things at face value.

Digging deeper, she employed a custom script she'd written to scour the hidden pockets of the internet for any trace of Angel's digital footprint. Lana found several encrypted chat logs and an unlisted email account under a pseudonym. At last, the decryption software completed its task, and Lana eagerly opened the now-accessible files. She quickly scanned through them, searching for any information that could help their investigation. Her pulse jumped as she uncovered compromising photos, confidential documents, and cryptic messages.

"Gotcha," she whispered, grinning with satisfaction. With a few more keystrokes, she cracked the encryption on the chat logs and began sifting through them for relevant information.

Lana squinted in concentration as she navigated Angel's accounts. She had accessed private messages and uncovered interesting chats, but now she faced a tougher challenge—breaking into Angel's cloud storage account, where she hoped more crucial evidence was hidden.

"Dang," Lana said as she encountered a multi-layered security system. Her pulse quickened, adrenaline fueling her determination. This was the kind of challenge she lived for. She took a deep breath, calming herself before diving into the complex code.

Come on, Lana, she coached herself. *You've cracked tougher systems than this.*

Her fingers danced over the keys, expertly typing lines of code to bypass the firewalls and encryption. As she maneuvered through the security measures, her mind raced with strategies, evaluating each potential weakness in the system and exploiting it.

Tuper would never understand the intricacies of what she was doing, but that didn't matter. They each had their own methods of investigation, and together they made quite a team. He had called to let her know that Angel was with another man but then had to leave abruptly without giving her any details.

Finally, after 25 maddening minutes, Lana found herself inside Angel's cloud storage account. But her victory was short-lived when she discovered the files she wanted were protected by yet another layer of encryption. Frustration bubbled up, but she pushed it down, reminding herself that she thrived under pressure.

"All right, let's see if this decryption software works its magic." Lana uploaded the program she'd developed years ago when she was committing cybercrimes. She was still hacking into sites, but now she did it for the greater good, or so she told herself. She was still invading people's privacy, but this was different. Those cybercrime days were long behind her even though the skills she'd acquired were invaluable now.

As the software worked through the encrypted files, Lana allowed herself a moment of pride in her abilities. Overcoming challenges like these reminded her of why she loved it — in spite of the risks it posed. The thrill of navigating the digital world, outsmarting security measures, and uncovering hidden secrets was intoxicating.

"Come on, come on," she urged, her impatience growing as the decryption process inched forward. Lana's heart thudded in her chest, anticipation building.

Finally, she had what she wanted. She couldn't wait to share her findings with Tuper, knowing that together they were one step closer to unraveling the mystery that was Angel Fenton.

Lana's expertise in hacking was nothing short of remarkable. Her father had trained her, but she'd surpassed the master at a young age. Hours and hours of practice instead of hanging out with friends and living a normal teenage life had cost her dearly, but now she was an expert. She had honed her skills in the shadows, becoming one of the best on the dark net. By now, there was little she couldn't accomplish with her customized tools and extensive knowledge of programming languages, encryption algorithms, and network infrastructures.

As she sifted through the messages, Lana's sharp eyes caught a pattern. Angel frequently exchanged late-night texts with Mitch, their conversations filled with innuendos and suggestive emojis—lots of hearts back and forth. The evidence, combined with Tuper's findings, painted a damning picture of Angel's unfaithfulness.

"Mitch, you slime ball," she hissed. She felt sorry for Henry Fenton, as much as she could for a rich guy who should've known better. But she kind of liked their client and thought maybe he deserved better than the web of deceit he'd found himself entangled in. But Lana also knew that the truth, no matter how painful, was better than living a lie.

She picked up her phone and called Tuper. "Hey Pops. I got something you need to see."

Chapter Seven

Tuesday evening

The sun dipped below the horizon, casting long shadows across Helena's rugged landscape. Lana stood on the porch of the mobile home, squinting as she took in the vibrant orange and purple hues that painted the Montana sky. She breathed in the crisp December air, catching a whiff of smoke from a nearby chimney. Moments like these made her appreciate the refuge she'd found in this small town.

"Are you ready for dinner?" Clarice called from inside, her voice ringing through the screen door. "We're having pot roast tonight!"

"Sounds delicious." Lana tore her gaze away from the sunset and stepped back into the cozy living room. The warmth of the house enveloped her, chasing away the evening chill. Mary Ann sat on the couch giving herself a manicure. Tuper lounged in his favorite recliner, watching an old Western on TV while absentmindedly stroking the scar on his right cheek.

"Have a seat, Lana." Tuper nodded toward the empty spot next to Mary Ann. "You've been parked in front of that computer all day. I'm startin' to think you don't like us."

"Just doing what you asked me to, Pops." Lana settled onto the couch with a grin. "And I had a few things to take care of for myself."

"Must be important if it kept you away from this wonderful company," Mary Ann teased, her eyes twinkling behind her reading glasses.

"Nobody can resist our charm for long," Clarice added, emerging from the kitchen with a steaming platter of pot roast. The rich aroma filled the room, making Lana's stomach grumble.

"I admit it, you guys are irresistible," Lana conceded with a chuckle. "I'm lucky to have found my way into this little family."

"Let's eat before the food gets cold," Tuper said.

As they gathered around the worn dining table, the conversation flowed easily, filled with laughter and good-natured teasing. Lana marveled at how effortlessly she fit in with these people who were so much older than her, and raised so differently than she was but didn't judge her for her shortcomings; they simply welcomed her with open arms and treated her like family, something she hadn't experienced in a long time. Actually, never.

"By the way, Pops," Lana said between bites, "I went through that envelope we got from Henry. He gave us a lot of good information, including his wife's phone number. Her persona doesn't seem to fit her name though."

"What's her name?" Clarice asked.

"Angel," Tuper said. They all laughed.

"There's other helpful information in there as well," Lana continued. "You already know he included her regular schedule, names of places she frequents, her gym, her hairdresser, even her measurements." Lana knew he hadn't read it, but he would act like he had, so she embellished a little.

Tuper's head shot up. "What?"

"I thought that might get your attention."

Clarice and Mary Ann laughed.

"I've already checked her phone records. Now, I'm working on finding out who the numbers belong to, especially the frequently called ones."

"Of course, you are." Tuper shook his head. "You know, if a person is gonna cheat, they ought to be good enough at it to not get caught."

"Sure, Pops." Lana smiled, then summarized the information she'd found for Clarice and Mary Ann. She'd shown Tuper the encrypted texts when he first arrived. "It's not definite they're having an affair, but those messages between her and Mitch are pretty incriminating."

"Couldn't they just be friends?" Clarice asked. "I haven't heard anything that conclusive."

"That's possible," Lana said. "I'm trying to keep an open mind."

"No way," Tuper said. "No guy could be *just friends* with a woman who looks like that and not want to nail her."

"Not every guy is like you Tuper." Lana shook her head. "And not every guy wants to nail every woman he meets."

"Maybe not, but every guy who meets *that* woman wants to nail her. Trust me."

"You're such a dog, Pops."

Chapter Eight

Wednesday early morning

The next morning, Lana sat at the kitchen table, sipping coffee and browsing through social media posts on her encrypted laptop. The sun streamed in through the window, casting a warm glow on the worn vinyl floor. She couldn't help but be reminded of her childhood home— or more specifically, the one vivid memory that had haunted her for years.

"Hey, kiddo." Tuper walked into the kitchen, wide-awake. "You're up early."

"Couldn't sleep." she rubbed her eyes. Her mind drifted back to when she was eleven, huddled in front of her father's computer, learning how to crack passwords and bypass firewalls. Hacking had been exhilarating at first, like having a secret superpower, but it wasn't long before the consequences started to catch up with her.

Tuper poured himself a cup of tea, then sat down across from her. "Whatcha workin' on?"

"Nothing important," Lana lied, quickly closing her internet tabs. "Just... checking the news." She hoped Tuper wouldn't notice the slight tremble in her voice. Recalling her days with a hacking group, exposing corporate secrets and toppling corrupt institutions had left her shaken.

"I see," Tuper said. "Ya don't need to worry about that Rattler gang case anymore. I got rid of it."

"What do you mean?"

"I turned it over to a cop friend of mine. He'll take care of it."

"Good, then we can concentrate on Fenton."

Tuper sat for a while discussing the Fenton case. When he finished his tea, he got up from the table. "I need to call a guy."

"Of course." Lana waited for him to leave the room. Once she was alone, she allowed herself to wallow in memories for a few more minutes before shaking her head and refocusing on the present.

"Enough of that," she muttered under her breath, closing her laptop with resolve. She had left that world behind, and she would do everything in her power to ensure it stayed that way—no matter how much she would miss the thrill of the chase.

In that moment, Lana's phone buzzed, displaying a text message from an unknown number.

I told you I know where you are. Now, do you believe me?

Lana felt a chill run down her spine and her heart raced. It was one thing for him to have her old email address. It was another to have her phone number. How had he gotten it? Nothing about the message felt right. She knew she couldn't ignore it, but she also couldn't risk sharing it with Tuper or the others.

"How did you find me?" she whispered, staring at the screen.

Lana wrestled with her next move, wondering if her past had finally caught up with her. She jumped up from the table and started pacing back and forth between the living room and dining area. *How could this have happened?*

"Would you stop pacing?" Clarice said from her armchair, where she tried to focus on a novel. "What is going on with you?"

"Sorry, Clarice," Lana halted her movement. She glanced at Tuper, who had just returned and taken a seat at the dining table. She sat down across from him and checked her email again, pounding on her laptop keys. She had nothing new from *him.* She was both relieved and frustrated.

"What did that machine ever do to you?" Tuper scratched his head with a calloused hand.

"What?" Lana looked up.

"I don't know who peed in your corn flakes, but something's got you riled. Care to tell us what it is before you break that thing?"

Clarice walked over and stood next to Lana, putting a hand on her shoulder in a comforting gesture. Lana wanted to blurt out everything, but decided that wasn't wise. However, she needed to let them know someone was after her. If he had her email and phone number, he could easily know her address as well. The more she thought about it, the more she realized they could all be in danger, and her friends needed to know so they could protect themselves. Maybe they would want her to leave. Maybe she should just do that and not say anything.

"What makes you think something's wrong?" Lana stalled, still not sure what to say.

"Because you're not your usual annoying self." Tuper glared. "You're not chattering like a magpie, and you're beating up on that contraption you love so much."

"Lana," Mary Ann called softly from her stool at the counter. "Are you in some kind of trouble?"

Lana's chest tightened at the sound of Mary Ann's concerned voice. Taking a deep breath, she decided to explain what had happened.

"I need to tell you something," she began, her voice wavering slightly. "I'm... I'm in a bit of trouble."

Tuper scowled. "What kind of trouble?"

"Nothing I can't handle," Lana said quickly, not wanting to worry them too much. "But it's important that you know someone might be... looking for me. You know, just in case."

"Who's looking for you?" Mary Ann asked gently

Lana hesitated. "A man named... a man from my past. He's dangerous, and I think he might have found me."

"How do you know?" Clarice asked.

"Someone sent me an email and a text message claiming they know where I am." Her voice trembled. "They know my email address and phone number, so it's possible they've found out where I live too."

Silence filled the room as everyone digested the information. Finally, Tuper asked, "Do you know who sent the messages?"

"I think so."

"Care to share who that is so we can help?"

"I'm not sure I'm ready for that."

"What can we do?" Clarice offered, her eyes shining with resolve.

"Right now, the best thing you can do is just be careful." Lana was grateful for her friends' support, but unwilling to put them in harm's way. "I'll handle this guy."

Clarice repeated her earlier request, her tone firm. "What do you need us to do?"

"I don't know." Lana sighed, feeling overwhelmed by the possibilities. "Maybe I should just take my things and leave. Start over somewhere else."

"Not on my watch," Tuper grumbled.

Clarice nodded in agreement, and Mary Ann walked over to put her hand on Lana's other shoulder, giving her an encouraging smile.

"Whatever you decide, we are here for you," Clarice said. "But I don't think you should leave. Let us help you."

Lana was filled with relief that she had their support, no matter what she decided to do next. But their support only made her more determined to not risk their lives any further.

As if on cue, her laptop chimed. Her gut fluttered as she turned toward the screen. There it was—an encrypted document that confirmed her suspicions. Jack Peterson had tracked her down.

"Cheese and crackers," she said out loud. She glanced back at her friends, their faces etched with concern. "I need to figure out how he found me and what he wants."

"Are you goin' after him?" Tuper's gruff tone betrayed his concern for her safety.

"More like trying to stay one step ahead of him." Lana looked at each of her friends in turn, seeing the fear and determination in their eyes. "I won't let him hurt any of you. I'll do whatever is necessary to keep that from happening."

Chapter Nine

Wednesday morning

Lana sat with her laptop in the cozy dining area that had come to be her sanctuary. Her hands cramped from typing furiously and swiping through data she'd gathered. As she clenched and unclenched them, Tuper walked in.

"Dang it," she said faintly. "How did he find me?"

Tuper ignored her comment and asked, "Any progress?" His weathered face bore a mix of concern and annoyance.

"Maybe." She glanced up. "I found something that might link this guy to my location."

"Lana, I think it's time you let me help. Who is this guy and how does he know you?"

She hesitated. She hadn't spoken of this in so long, and the less Tuper knew, the better off he was. She didn't want to involve him in her crimes. On the other hand, he couldn't help her without more information.

She sighed. "His name is Jack Peterson, and he used to be my father's business partner."

"Used to be?"

"Before my dad died in a terrible accident."

"What happened?"

"He died in a fire when his home—my childhood home—burned down."

"I'm so sorry," Tuper said.

"No need to be. I've accepted it and moved on. My father wasn't the best role model a girl ever had. He gave me a few skills I needed to survive and provided a nice home with anything material I ever wanted — but he was a crook. Don't get me wrong; I loved him very much. Especially as a child, when I worshipped him. I wanted to be just like him—until I got to know him better."

Tuper wasn't good at showing emotional support, so Lana wasn't surprised when he changed the subject. Although, Lana detected concern in his wrinkled eyes.

"What did you find?" Tuper squinted at the monitor.

Lana pointed at the document on the screen, then noticed something new and gasped. "Oh no!"

"What is it?"

"See here? This is an email exchange between Jack and Brock Shero. It has coordinates that match Helena, Montana." Lana's voice shook.

"Why does that name, Brock, sound familiar?"

"Because you met him. He's the firefighter I was seeing a few months ago."

"Could be a coincidence." Tuper folded his arms across his chest.

"Seriously, Pops? You think this is just a coincidence?" Lana snapped, glaring at him. "This isn't some random person I'm dealing with; it's Jack freaking Peterson, my father's old partner! Do you have any idea what will happen if he finds me? And Brock. I was actually starting to like the guy. That jerk."

"But that means this Jack guy has known where you are for a while. At least he knew you were in Helena."

Lana took a deep breath, trying to compose herself. "But maybe he didn't have the exact address. I never brought Brock to the house."

"That was smart."

"I don't know how smart it was. As usual I was suspicious. That's the way I live my life these days. But I still let Brock learn more about me than I should've."

"You're right. This isn't a coincidence." Tuper raised his hands defensively.

"What did you say?"

"This isn't a coincidence." Tuper repeated.

"No, the part before that, when you said I was right. I wasn't sure you actually said it."

Tuper ignored her sassy remark. "We just need to be sure before we do anything about it."

"What do you propose?"

Tuper stood. "I'm gonna talk to Brock."

Lana jumped up and grabbed her jacket. "Not without me."

Chapter Ten

Wednesday noon

Lana had only gone out with Brock Shero a couple of times so she didn't know where he hung out. Consequently, before they left the house to look for him, Tuper made calls to some buddies and got information about his likely whereabouts. He was known to frequent a bar on Montana Street. Although Tuper wasn't much of a drinker, he was familiar with most bars in town, including this one.

Lana and Tuper pulled up in front of the bar. "Jack knows I'm in Helena, and he's somehow tied to Brock." Lana felt a mix of curiosity and fear. "Do you suppose he sent Brock here, or did he find him and recruit him?"

"Don't know," Tuper said. "Let's find out."

They walked inside and she breathed in the familiar smells of a dive bar—beer, sweat, and liquor. Once Lana's eyes adjusted to the dark room, she looked around for Brock.

"There he is," Lana said. "At the end of the bar."

Tuper nodded, a gesture of agreement that communicated more than words.

They walked in Brock's direction, and Lana sensed Tuper's body tensing beside her. Brock spotted them coming. Tuper pushed his hat back to meet Brock's gaze, a look of determination on his face.

Brock stood and nonchalantly strolled toward the back of the bar. They followed. Brock glanced back once and picked up his pace, but the gap between them narrowed as Lana and Tuper moved faster. They reached him just as he stepped outside and followed him into the alley. The smell was even worse with a musty odor of spilled beer and urine.

"Brock Shero," Tuper demanded. Brock kept walking. "Stop! Now!"

Brock glanced back.

"I wouldn't go anywhere if I were you," Tuper said, making sure Brock saw his gun. "I don't wanna have to shoot you in the back."

Brock turned around and shrugged. "Since you put it that way."

"Come here," Tuper said.

Brock closed the few feet between them. Lana stepped toward him.

"Hi, Lana," Brock's six-foot-four sculpted body cast a huge shadow in the afternoon sunlight.

"Hi, Lana?" She moved in closer, until she was right in his face. "That's what you have to say to me?"

"What do you want me to say?"

"All right, Brock," Tuper growled, his scarred face menacing. "Start talkin'."

"Wh..what do you want from me?" Brock stammered, sweat beading on his brow.

"Jack Peterson," Lana spat, her boots scuffing the gravel beneath her feet. "What's your connection to him?"

"Put the gun away first."

Tuper hesitated, then acquiesced. "Start talkin'."

"Look, I barely know the guy." Brock shook his head. "I just did some work for him — nothing illegal."

"Tell us everything," Tuper demanded, his tone leaving no room for argument.

"There's not much to tell. A guy called me and said he was referred by an agency that knew a mutual friend. He said he was your father and that you'd left without a word, and he wanted to make sure you were alive and well. He offered me a lot of money to find out where you were living."

"Did it occur to you that he might want to know my whereabouts so he could hurt me?"

"I checked him out with my friend, and he knew the agency, and it all seemed legit."

"What if this guy wanted to kill me?" Lana shouted. "Does he?"

"I don't know if he wants me dead, or he wants to kidnap me, hold me hostage, imprison me, or whatever," she stammered, "and you didn't know either. I think he might have already killed someone, so he's capable of anything."

"Like I said, it all seemed harmless. He was very convincing, and I really needed the money."

"What? You needed to buy a fancy new truck or something?" Lana's hands clenched into fists, nails digging into her palms.

"No. I needed it to help my grandmother. She has Alzheimer's, and she required extra care that we couldn't afford. Everything extra from my salary went to help her, but it wasn't enough."

For a second, Lana felt sorry for this big, vulnerable man. But it didn't last long. He was a fool to be taken in. But she couldn't be too critical. After all, she'd been foolish too.

"Every day, I'm looking over my shoulder, scared that one wrong move could expose me," she whispered fiercely. "When Jack finds me, I'll lose everything I've worked for — my new life, my friends, my family."

"I'm sorry, Lana. I know it's not much, but eventually I told him I couldn't find where you lived, even though I did know your address." Brock looked sheepish and ashamed. "The only thing I gave him was your phone number. I never took the money either. I really liked you, and I was hoping we could get closer, but then I realized it's not the kind of betrayal you come back from."

"So, how did he find me?"

"I don't know. I guess he found another *fool* to do his bidding."

She had nothing more to say. It no longer mattered how Jack had found her, just that he had. And it wouldn't be long before he had Clarice's address. She glanced at Tuper, who offered a reassuring nod, his eyes filled with anger. She knew he wanted to take Brock on, but that was the last thing she wanted to see. Brock was taller, had a lot more muscle, and was half Tuper's age. The old man was a scrapper, but she didn't like the odds.

"Let's go," Lana said. Tuper didn't move. "Come on. Please." She stared hard, pleading with him. He followed her to the car without a word.

Chapter Eleven

Wednesday early afternoon

Lana and Tuper both thought it was a good idea to contact JP and ask him to find out if Jack Peterson was home in southern California. After their confrontation with Brock, they knew Jack was close on her tail. Lana was pretty certain Jack would eventually show up himself, but there was also the risk that he would have her kidnapped and brought to him.

Lana called JP's number. She had helped him out on more than one occasion, so she was certain he would be willing to help her.

"Hi, kid," JP said when he answered. "Is everything okay?"

"We're all good, but I need your services."

"It would be tough for me to get away right now, but if you or Tuper need me, I'll see what I can do."

"You don't have to come here. I want you to investigate someone in Del Mar."

"Sure, Little Bit, just tell me what you need."

Lana didn't want to divulge too much, but he needed to know enough to stay safe. "You probably already know that I've been on the run. Not from the law," she quickly assured him. "It's not that I haven't done anything criminal, because I have, all in cyberspace. But I've never been caught, so I'm not running to avoid prosecution. There are other reasons why I had to hide out, and people I had to hide from, and..."

"Lana." JP interrupted her. "It doesn't matter what you've done. I owe you plenty of favors, so just tell me what you need."

" A man named Jack Peterson, who lives in Del Mar, has been trying to find me ever since I left California. He will stop at nothing to get me back in his clutches. And he has evidence of my hacking that could put me in prison for a long time." The thought made her shudder. "He was involved too, but that's not the way it would be presented. I have no evidence against him, so he could set me up to take the fall. Consequently, I was afraid to fight him, so I left. You don't need to know the specifics—unless you do—then I'll tell you, but for now that's probably enough to go on."

"What exactly do you want me to do?"

"Oh, sorry. I want you to find out if Jack is in Del Mar, or if he has left the area. And if he has left, is he here in Helena?"

"I should be able to do that. What else?"

"I'd like to know what he's up to, so see what you can find out. He knows I'm here in Helena. He sent me an email at an old account so I wasn't too concerned at first, but then he sent me a text. And he got my phone number from a source here in Helena that he hired. The guy, Brock Shero, swears he didn't give him my home address, but I don't know whether to believe him."

"Anything else?" JP asked.

"I'll text you Jack's name and address and any other pertinent information. I'll also send you a photo so you'll recognize him. I found one online that should be fairly current."

"That'll work. I'll get on it right away."

"I sure appreciate this."

"One more thing," JP said. "Does Ron know? Because if you don't want him to, I won't use him on the investigation."

"It's okay. Just give me a minute to call and tell him myself."

"Will do."

"JP, please be careful. This man is dangerous. He has a lot to lose."

"Don't worry, Little Bit, I never drop my gun to hug a grizzly."

Lana smiled. She loved JP's quaint sayings. As soon as she hung up, she called Ron.

"This is a welcome surprise," Ron said.

"Thank you, but I called to let you know that I'm having a bit of trouble."

Before she could say more, Ron asked, "What is it? Can I help?"

"Sort of. I'm sure you know I'm living here because I've been running from something in my past. It may have caught up with me."

"I'll catch the next plane and ..."

"No. I don't want you in danger too. I just asked JP to do some snooping around. The man who is after me lives in Del Mar. The best way you can help is to work with JP. The last thing I need is to have you here where I would worry about you too."

"Are you sure?"

Her response was adamant. "Do not come here." In a softer tone, she added, "But, Ron, please be careful. I don't know to what extent this man will go."

When he finally assured her he wouldn't come, she hung up and sent the information to JP. Then she walked into the kitchen and put on a pot of coffee. Before sitting down again to the task at hand, she stretched her back and flexed her hands to get them ready for a long keyboarding session.

When Tuper walked in, Lana was in front of her laptop, preparing to dive into Jack Peterson's digital world. The scent of strong coffee brewing filled the air.

"You sure about this, Agony?" Tuper asked, his cowboy hat casting a shadow over his concerned face. "It seems pretty risky to me."

She glanced up at him. "I have to do this, Pops. It's the only way we'll get answers. Besides, this is the fun part." It was also scary, but she pushed forward, knowing hesitation would leave her vulnerable.

Before she began, she contacted Ravic, a fellow white hat hacker she'd met in the underground when she was a novice. His calm demeanor always helped steady her nerves when she was pushing her limits. They had formed an unexpected friendship in the digital abyss. They'd never exchanged photos, phone numbers, or any other identifying information. She knew nothing about his personal life, and she assumed he knew nothing about hers. She wasn't even sure of his gender, but she guessed he was male by his tone. It was clear they both valued their anonymity more than anything else. In this world, he was Ravic and she was Cricket. Whenever someone started to pry into personal matters, it always signaled danger; they both knew this. Lana left a message on Ravic's account.

It suddenly hit her that she trusted this stranger more than anyone she had ever met in the real world. Even Tuper, Clarice, and Mary Ann didn't know her most dangerous secrets. But Ravic had been watching over her almost from the beginning, like a cyberspace guardian angel. He had warned her that people were using her and that she needed to bail before they dragged her under, but instead she had trusted Jack and her father. When she had finally been ready to make the move, Ravic was the one who'd helped her.

Cricket—*Are you busy?*

Ravic responded quickly—*Always* available for you.

Cricket—*I* know this is a lot to ask, but can you do me a favor?

Ravic—*W*hat do you need?

Cricket—*I*'m going into a sensitive area. I could use some cover.

Ravic—*Are you trying to return more money?*

Cricket—*N*o. (Smiley face emoji.) More personal, emails and social accounts. I need to cover my tracks. He could follow.

Ravic—Script Kiddie or black hat?

Cricket—*M*ore of a brown hat. Lana inserted a smiley emoji. A black hat Wannabe. Knows enough to be dangerous. Are you in?

Ravic—Absolutely. Give me a second to set things up.

Lana breathed a sigh of relief, knowing Ravic's expertise would minimize the risk of being caught. As she waited, she couldn't help but think about the consequences of not confronting Jack. The potential danger he posed to her and her loved ones weighed heavily on her mind, fueling her urgency. Her thoughts were interrupted by a ding on her laptop.

Ravic—*I'm ready. Let's do this.*

Lana gave Ravic with the information he needed. As they worked together, their chat, a mix of technical jargon and reassurances, provided Lana a sense of camaraderie with Ravic. It was comforting to know that even in her darkest moments, she wasn't completely alone. No one else she knew could share this moment with her. The exhilaration was greater than the thrill of bungee jumping or parachuting.

"Got it," Lana whispered triumphantly as she broke through Jack's digital defenses.

Cricket—*I'm in.*

Ravic—*Send me the coordinates.*

Cricket—*Done*

Ravic followed her into the accounts, scrambling her trail.

Ravic—*Right behind you.*

Lana's fingers sailed across the keyboard as she sifted through Jack's emails, her heart pounding in her chest, completely enveloped in a different world. She lost track of time and was startled by the sound of Tuper's voice.

"Remember, we're just looking for answers," Tuper reminded her, leaning over her shoulder to catch a glimpse of the screen. "Don't get lost in the rabbit hole."

"Trust me, Pops, I'm focused." She kept scanning messages, her eyes darting back and forth. But as time ticked by, her sense of urgency grew stronger.

Cricket—*Ravic, are we still clear?*

Ravic—*Clear as day. Just keep going. You're doing great.*

Tuper paced behind her, footsteps thudding softly on the vinyl floor. She knew he was worried, and she couldn't blame him. The stakes were high, and one wrong move could bring her entire world crashing down.

"Come on, come on." Lana's frustration mounted as she dug deeper into Jack's secrets.

"Humph," Tuper said. Empathy was not his strong suit.

Lana took a deep breath, feeling the weight of their shared determination. With renewed focus, she continued her search, knowing that the truth—and the confrontation with Jack Peterson—was only a matter of time.

Chapter Twelve

Wednesday afternoon

When Ravic asked for a break, Lana sat back and took a deep breath. She noticed the postcard she had just received and her thoughts drifted to Ron Brown. She had met him only a few months ago when Ron came to see Tuper, and she couldn't help but be drawn to his warm smile and captivating eyes. The fact that he lived in Southern California, not far from Jack Peterson, was both intriguing and concerning. She shook off the thoughts and focused on her task.

"Hey, Pops." Lana glanced over at Tuper, who was watching her intently. "I contacted JP. He'll check to see if Jack is still at home."

"Good move. JP's the best," Tuper said. "Did you tell Ron too?"

"Why would you ask that?"

"Humph," was all he said.

"I did, but only because he'll be working with JP."

"Young love," Tuper said with a snort. "Or is it just old-fashioned lust?"

"Don't make it weird, Pops," Lana groaned, rolling her eyes.

"Ain't nothin' wrong with lust. It's always worked for me."

Lana shuddered. "Now, you *are* making it weird."

Tuper snorted again, his eyes twinkling with amusement. "Stop daydreaming about your boy toy and get back to work."

Lana shook her head and resumed her task. The quiet hum of the computer filled the space as she navigated the intricate world of code and data that most people couldn't begin to comprehend. The ticking of the wall clock seemed to echo louder in the quiet room, underlining the urgency of her actions.

Ravic—*I'm back.*

Lana gave him a thumbs up and continued her search.

Tuper got restless and stepped outside with his dog, Dually, then returned and asked, "Any luck?"

"Shh," Lana whispered, her concentration unwavering. "I'm almost there."

As she typed, a pop-up window appeared on screen. A shiver of excitement shot up Lana's spine. This might be it—the file she'd been searching for. She took a deep breath before opening it, preparing herself for whatever secrets it might unveil.

"Found something?" Tuper leaned forward.

"I think so." Lana scanned the document. "There's just so much."

Lana's voice trembled slightly. "I knew they had a lot going on, but I never realized the full extent."

Tuper scratched his chin thoughtfully. "That explains why he's so hell-bent on finding you. He must think you know something he can use."

"Or that I'm just like my father." A sad thought. "He probably wants to exploit me for his own gain. Or kill me."

"He'll have to get past me first," Tuper growled.

"Thanks, Pops." Lana fought back tears of anger and composed herself. "I need to dig deeper. There has to be more here."

"You sure you know what you're doin'?" Tuper asked. "Ain't this dangerous?"

"More than you know," Lana shot back, her heart pounding as she continued to dig through Jack's digital labyrinth. When she saw the look on Tuper's face, she added flippantly, "Did you know the national bird of Uganda is the grey-crowned crane?"

Tuper shook his head. "Who cares?"

As Lana delved further into the maze of information, she felt the weight of her past pressing down. The connection between Jack and her father seemed more tangled by the second, and she had to unravel it before it ensnared her completely. Only then could she hope for a real future.

Lana's eyes widened as she stumbled upon a recent email in Jack's inbox. The subject line read *Arrival in Helena,* and the sender's name was redacted. Her heart jumped as she opened the message.

"Dang it!" Someone working with Jack had just arrived in Helena, and she had little doubt they were looking for her.

"Something wrong?" Tuper asked, sensing her tension.

"Jack—or someone he sent—is here. In Helena."

"All right. We need a plan." Tuper's expression tightened.

"First things first," Lana said. "I need to find out who this person is and where they're staying." She started hacking into the local hotel registries. "Once I find them, I'll approach and demand answers."

"Or not," Tuper countered.

Lana ignored his remark and sent Ravic a message saying she could take it from here.

Ravic—*Okay, Cricket. Let me know when you need me again.*

Cricket—*Thanks, I will.*

As Lana searched, her mind raced with possible scenarios and outcomes. What if this person attacked her? What if they weren't willing to talk? How far would she have to go to get the information she needed?

"Found them." Lana announced. "Looks like our visitor is staying in room 207 of the Residence Inn."

"Are you sure about this, Lana?" Tuper asked. "Confronting them directly might not be the best idea."

"Trust me, Pops," Lana said, her determination unwavering. "I've been hiding and running for too long. It's time to face this head-on."

"Then I'm comin' with ya."

"Absolutely not!" Lana protested. "This is my fight, not yours."

"Like hell it isn't!" Tuper's eyes flashed with anger. "Yer family. We take care of family."

Lana hesitated, touched by Tuper's protective instincts but afraid to put him at risk. Finally, she relented with a sigh. "Fine. But we do this my way. We stay calm, and we stay focused."

"Humph."

Lana took that as agreement.

As they left the safety of Clarice's home, Lana couldn't help but feel a mixture of fear and excitement coursing through her veins. Confronting Jack—or his associate—would be dangerous, but it was a risk she had to take. The truth was finally within reach, and she wasn't going to let it slip away.

Chapter Thirteen

Wednesday evening

Inside the hotel lobby, Lana sat nervously at a table near Tuper, her flashy grunge look contrasting with the subdued decor. She tapped her foot on the floor, betraying her unease. Tuper, ever the calm presence, leaned back in his chair, cowboy hat tipped slightly forward as he studied the room with a watchful eye.

"Relax," Tuper said.

Lana clenched her hands as she watched the black SUV pull up just outside the window. The wind picked up just as Jack Peterson stepped out. The sight of him sent a shiver down her spine. He checked his reflection in the car window, then ran his fingers through his greying hair and adjusted his collar. His piercing blue eyes scanned the parking lot. A wry smile crossed his face as he zipped up his jacket and strode toward the entrance.

The hotel doors swung open, ushering in a gust of wind that sent papers flying from the reception desk. Jack entered, his stride purposeful and steady as he locked eyes with Lana and Tuper. Lana's breath caught in her throat, and Tuper's hand instinctively went to his side.

Jack turned away and checked in at the counter, then strode over as if he was meeting old friends.

"Jack," Lana managed to say, her voice quivering. "What do you want from me?"

"Nice to see you too, Lana." Jack replied smoothly, as he pulled out a chair and sat down, uninvited. He leaned back casually. "I've been looking for you."

"Clearly," Tuper interjected. "Tell us why you're following Lana. What do you want from her?"

"Ah, Mr. Tuper, the man of many questions," Jack said with a smirk. "My dear Lana, I noticed you didn't bother to change your name. How cavalier of you." When Lana didn't respond, he continued. "But I see you weren't brave enough to use your last name. What's the matter? Are you ashamed of it?"

"Yes. I am ashamed of it. Very ashamed."

"But it could get you a long way. Speaking of which, I have a business proposition for you."

"Business? With you?" Lana scoffed, shaking her head vehemently. "No way. I'm not interested in anything you have to offer."

"Is that so?" Jack's tone shifted, sounding more sinister. "I think you'll find my offer quite... compelling."

Lana glared at him, trying not to show fear. "I don't care. I won't work with you."

Without a word, Tuper placed a steadying hand on Lana's shoulder. Then he turned his attention back to Jack. "What is this proposition of yers?"

"Let's just say it involves some old friends and a certain set of skills Lana has been hiding," Jack replied.

"Enough with the games!" Lana snapped, unable to contain her frustration. "Tell us what you want or go away!"

"Fine." Jack leaned forward, locking eyes with Lana. "Your father and I had unfinished business, and I believe you can help me complete it. You have a choice to make—either you cooperate and work with me, or I will ruin your life here in Helena. I'll destroy everything you hold dear and ensure that your future is filled with misery and despair."

Lana's heart thumped as she stared back at him, torn between wanting to run and standing her ground. She could feel Tuper's grip on her shoulder, a silent reminder that he was there to support her no matter what decision she made.

"Your father," Jack drawled, a smirk playing at the corners of his mouth. "He always had a way of getting out of tight spots, didn't he? A real Houdini."

Lana clenched her fists, trying to hold onto the anger and not let it be swallowed by fear. "You don't know anything about my father," she spat.

"Ah, but I do." Jack leaned back, his eyes gleaming with a dark satisfaction. "I know more than you think, Lana. And if you want to find out the truth, well... maybe it's time we worked together."

"Cut the crap," Lana snapped. "Why have you been pursuing me all this time? What do you really want?"

"Isn't it obvious?" Jack spread his arms wide. "I want what your father had—his knowledge, his skills. Lana, my dear, you're the key to unlocking all of that."

"By exploiting me like you did my father?"

"Your father was a willing partner," Jack countered, his voice dripping with disdain. "But when he turned soft, I needed someone to take his place. Someone just as skilled and perhaps even more... malleable."

"Like hell," Lana growled, fury surging through her veins. "You'll never control me, Jack."

"Perhaps not," Jack conceded, his eyes narrowing. "But I've come too far to turn back now. And there's something you should know, something your dear old dad never told you."

"Nothing you say can change anything." Lana refused to let him get under her skin.

"But what if I told you..." Jack paused as if savoring the tension in the air. "That I'm not the only one who's been lying to you?"

Lana's heart skipped a beat, but she refused to let him see her falter. "What are you talking about?"

"Your father, Lana," Jack whispered, with a wicked grin. "He lied to you right up until his departure. He lied to all of us. Even his last act was a lie."

"What are you saying?"

"His death was not what you think. What if I told you it wasn't an accident?"

"Are you suggesting my father killed himself?"

Jack shrugged.

The revelation hit Lana like a punch to the gut, her world suddenly spinning out of control. *Was it possible?* Could her father have taken his own life? *No.* He had problems, but he wouldn't do that to her. And certainly not that way.

"Impossible," she stammered. "My father wouldn't do that to me. Not after my mo…. No. He wouldn't. He couldn't. He was smoking in bed and dropped his cigarette. The doctor said so."

"Did he?" Jack taunted, his laughter echoing through the hotel lobby.

The idea that her father might have killed himself, then let his body burn up in a fire ignited a fierce internal conflict. Part of her wanted to flee, to distance herself from this man and the dangerous past he represented. But another part couldn't help but be drawn in by his tantalizing premise, the possibility that her father hadn't died the way he said—even if it meant facing the demons she'd run from for years.

"Listen here, you snake." Tuper cut in, his voice steady but laced with fury. "You don't get to play games with her emotions. You either tell us what you know or you leave."

Jack's grin widened. He was clearly enjoying the turmoil he'd caused. "I'll tell you everything you want to know, but only if Lana agrees to work with me."

"Doing what?" Tuper asked.

"What she's best at."

"Nope," Tuper said. "Too dangerous."

"No more than it has ever been. There's no physical danger, but there's always a risk of getting caught." Jack stared into her eyes. "But that's the thrill, isn't it, Lana? That's what keeps your heart pumping."

In that moment, Lana felt as though she were standing on the edge of a precipice, about to take a terrifying plunge. The thought of working with this man made her skin crawl, but the prospect of learning the truth about her father was too compelling to ignore.

"There's so much you don't know about your father," Jack said.

"Why should I believe anything you tell me?"

"You don't have to. I'll lead you to what you want to know. You'll discover it for yourself."

"Fine," she whispered. "I'll think about it."

"That's good enough for now, but don't take too long."

"If I do this, I'll need some evidence that this is not a bluff."

"Fair enough." Jack's smile stretched even wider, his eyes alight with victory. "Now that we have an understanding, I'll leave you to discuss the details. We'll be in touch soon."

"The only understanding we have is that I'll think about it."

Jack stood, winked at her, and sauntered out of the hotel lobby, leaving Lana feeling as though she'd just made a deal with the devil himself.

"What are you thinkin'?" Tuper scolded.

"I don't know, Pops," Lana admitted. "But I need to know what really happened to my father. I've never quite been comfortable with the findings about his death. But mostly, I thought telling him I'd think about it would buy us some time."

As they sat in the dimly lit hotel lobby, still reeling from their confrontation with Jack, Lana couldn't shake the feeling she'd just stepped onto a path with no return—one that would force her to confront the shadows of her past, regardless of what horrors awaited her there.

Chapter Fourteen

Thursday early morning

By five a.m., Lana was already dressed and at her computer—running on very little sleep. The thought of working with Jack overwhelmed her, and she wondered if she'd made the right decision. Deep in thought, she jumped when someone knocked on the door. Lana glanced out the window and saw Tuper's car, then heard Dually thump his tail against the door. When she opened it, the dog dashed in, rubbing his body against Lana. She reached down and scratched his head.

"You startled me," Lana said to Tuper. "Although, I'm not sure why since it's not unusual for you to show up this early."

Tuper walked in and locked the door behind him. "Got the hot water on?"

"Yes, but you missed Clarice so there won't be any breakfast. She left for work about twenty minutes ago."

"That's too bad."

"You can make yourself some toast if you want."

"I'm good. I'll hit Smith's a little later."

They stood in the living room talking. Finally, Lana blurted, "I'm thinking about leaving, finding another place to settle in, and telling Jack to pound sand."

"I know what you do is illegal, but you hack all the time. So, what bothers you about working with him?" Tuper shrugged. "I don't blame you, mind you. The man's a snake. I'm just wonderin' if there's more."

"I hack, but it's for a good purpose. He wants to hurt people and steal from them." She paused. "But you're right, it's more than that." She took a deep breath. "I never believed my father's death was an accident."

"You think your father was murdered?"

"Not only that, I always thought Jack had killed him."

"You still think so?"

Lana nodded. "Now, he's implying my father took his own life, but I think that's a cover-up for his own actions and to throw me off his scent." She started pacing. "Jack's a blood sucker, and no matter how you look at it, he drove him away. Jack is the reason my father is gone. I'm not sure I can stand to be around him, or even talk to him, much less work with him. So, I'll only do that for as long as it takes to find out the truth. The other option is to run again."

"Listen, Agony." Tuper leaned against the wall, arms crossed over his chest. "I know you're scared. Hell, I'd be too if I was in yer shoes. But runnin' away won't solve nothin'."

Lana stopped abruptly and spun to face him, her eyes flashing with defiance. "You don't know what it's like, Pops. To be constantly hunted, never knowing when your past will catch up with you."

"Maybe not," Tuper admitted, pushing off the wall and taking a step closer. "But I've seen enough in my life to know that the past has a way of catchin' up with all of us, one way or another."

Lana looked away, unable to face him. She felt vulnerable, a trait she hated to feel or exhibit. She knew her fierce independence was both her greatest strength and her Achilles heel—a shield she used to protect herself from the traumas that had shaped her life.

"Look," Tuper said softly, then waited until Lana met his gaze. "You've got a chance here to face this head-on, to find out the truth about your father. If you keep runnin', you'll always be lookin' over your shoulder, wonderin' what might have been."

Lana clenched her fists. "And what if it's all just a trap? What if Jack's lying and there's nothing but idle threats?"

"Then at least you'll know," Tuper said gently. "But you can't let fear rule your life, Lana. You're stronger than that."

"Am I?" Lana whispered, her voice cracking with uncertainty. "Sometimes I feel like I'm just one step away from breaking."

"Hey." Tuper placed a reassuring hand on her shoulder. "We all have rough moments. But you are one of the toughest people I know. You don't buckle under for anyone. Don't start now."

For a moment, Lana wavered, torn between the instinct to run and the desire to fight back. Finally, she lifted her chin. "All right, Pops, let's do this. Let's find out the truth about my father—no matter what it takes."

"Atta girl. So, what's next?"

Lana marveled at the strange turn of events that had brought her to this point. She was ready to face whatever challenges awaited. Deep down, however, she knew the road ahead wouldn't be easy.

"I'm going to contact JP and have him look into my father's death. Then I'll find anything and everything that's new about Jack Peterson."

Chapter Fifteen

Thursday morning, San Diego, California

JP Torn stood outside Charles Storm's former residence, holding the police report he'd received from a friend at the Sheriff's Department. The report included the fire investigator's report. He determined the fire started in the proximity of the body, and that Lana's father had likely fallen asleep while smoking, inadvertently starting the fire that consumed him and his home. The origin of the fire was determined to be in the bedroom, so "smoking in bed" was their best guess. The body was burned beyond recognition.

The black charred remains of the house served as a morbid reminder of the tragedy that had occurred more than three years ago. The windows were broken, and its walls crumbling. The neighboring lawns were neatly kept with emerald green grass and vibrant floral blooms that provided a stark contrast to the destroyed house. Nothing had been done to the property since the fire, which didn't happen often in California. JP made a mental note to ask Lana why. Then he realized she was Storm's only heir and since she was in hiding, there was no one to take care of it.

As he scanned the report, he couldn't shake the feeling something wasn't quite right. Perhaps it was because Lana was skeptical, so he was looking for something beyond what he was reading. He needed to question the neighbors and friends about the incident, hoping to uncover any discrepancies or suspicious activity.

"Hey there," JP called out to the next-door neighbor who was tending her garden. "I'm investigating the fire that happened here a few years ago. Mind if I ask you a few questions?"

"Not at all," she replied, wiping dirt from her hands. "What do you need to know?"

"Were you living here at the time of the fire?"

"I've been here for twenty-seven years."

"Did you know the family well?"

"As well as any neighbor does, I suppose. The Storms were wonderful people."

"How long did they live there?"

She thought for a moment. "Charles moved in when Lana was about nine or ten, maybe twenty years ago." She thought again. "Yeah, that's about right. We had lived here about seven years before they moved in. It was right after Charles's wife died. She committed suicide in their old home. I'm sure that's why they left it. Charles never talked about it, but I heard the scuttlebutt from a friend who used to work with her."

"Are you still friends with the woman who told you?"

"Oh yes, Pearl and I play whist together once a month."

"Whist?"

"It's a card game. We're both from Minnesota, and we learned it growing up. It's hard to find anyone around here who knows the game. My husband and I play with

Pearl and her husband. We used to play couple against couple, but now we play the guys against the girls. It's more fun that way."

"Did you notice anything unusual leading up to the fire?" JP studied the neighbor's reaction.

She furrowed her brow in thought. "Nothing out of the ordinary,"

"Can you remember if anyone visited Charles that day or the few days prior to the fire?"

"One of the few people who ever came around was his business partner, Jack. I met him a couple of times over the years, but I didn't really know him. And I don't know his last name."

"That's all right. I know who he is. When was he there?"

"It was so long ago, but I think it was a day or two before the fire. He left in a huff."

"What do you mean? Were they fighting?"

"I don't know for sure, but Jack didn't look happy. He yelled at Charles as he was leaving. I only know that because I had just pulled into my driveway when Jack stormed out of the house yelling."

"What did he say?"

"Something like, 'I'm not going to forget this.' Then he got into his car, slammed the door, and drove off."

"Interesting," JP mumbled, making a quick note in his notepad.

"You said Jack was one of the *few* people who came around. Who else visited Charles?"

"He had a good friend, Robert, who came around for years, but I couldn't tell you much about him. Sometimes he brought his wife for backyard barbeques, but most of the time, he showed up alone."

"Do you know his last name?"

She shook her head. "Sorry."

"Is there anyone else in the neighborhood who may have seen something?"

"Maybe Eugenia Roberts across the street," the neighbor suggested. "She's always keeping an eye on things, if you know what I mean. Her husband is always getting on her case because he says she's too nosey." She smiled wryly. "Eugenia spends a great deal of time in her kitchen, and the truth is, she doesn't miss much."

"Thank you for your help," JP said. "By the way, would you mind giving me Pearl's phone number and address?" He had a nagging suspicion she might know more.

The neighbor wrote it down for him, then he walked across the street to talk to Mrs. Roberts

A spry woman in her mid-to-late seventies greeted him with a smile. Eugenia looked to be about four-foot-eleven and JP guessed her weight at about a hundred and ten pounds, soaking wet. She had a good view of Charles's house from her large kitchen window, and she was eager to share what information she had.

"Were you home when the fire started?"

"I was. I didn't see it start, but I was awakened by the sirens. We're lucky the whole neighborhood didn't burn down."

"How long have you lived here?"

"Nearly forty years. We moved here when the house was only a few years old. We're not the ones who have lived here the longest though. The Millers were here before us. They live just over there, cattycorner from us." She pointed at the house sitting diagonally across the street, two doors down from the Storms.

"What kind of man was Charles Storm?"

"He was a good neighbor, and he raised his daughter by himself. Her mother committed suicide, you know?" The old woman shook her head. "Poor little girl. She was a good kid, kept to herself mostly. Didn't seem to have many friends. She spent most of her time with her father. He took her everywhere, probably trying to make up for the mother. Lana was..." Eugenia hesitated. "I'm not sure how to put this. She was a little odd."

"In what way?"

"She dressed funny, a hippie sort, and as I said, she never had friends over like most normal teenagers. And she carried her laptop everywhere she went. I'd go over there sometimes and take them cookies I'd baked, and she was always on her computer. I know kids spend more time on those machines nowadays, but she was worse than most. I guess it's not a surprise because her father was a computer guy too from what I've heard. I don't think the boy was though."

"What boy?"

"Charles's stepson, Lana's half-brother. He was living with them when they moved in, but he left as soon as he turned eighteen, which was only a few months later. I don't think he and Charles got along."

"What makes you think that?"

"They yelled at each other a lot. I'd hear them going at it almost every night. Then the kid would stomp out and not come home until late."

Chapter Sixteen

Thursday, San Diego, California

JP crossed the street to the Miller house, where he was invited inside.

"Thanks for agreeing to meet with me," JP began, his tone casual. "I'm trying to learn more about Charles and Lana Storm. Did you know them well?"

"Sure did," Mrs. Miller said, nodding. "They were nice folks, always willing to lend a hand. It was such a shame when their house burned down."

After listening to a dialogue back and forth between the old couple about how wonderful Lana and her dad had been, JP asked, "Did you ever notice anything strange or unusual about them?"

Mr. Miller scratched his chin thoughtfully. "There was that time Charles borrowed my ladder to fix something on his roof. He was up there for hours, but I never could figure out what he was working on."

"Interesting," JP mused, scribbling in his notepad. "Anything else come to mind?"

"Only that the daughter, Lana, was quite the character," Mrs. Miller said. "She used to come over for dinner occasionally with her father. She was such a sweet girl, always so polite."

"Sweet and polite, huh?" JP tried to reconcile that image of Lana with the fierce, independent woman he knew her to be now.

"Unusual?" Mr. Miller was still focused on that question. He exchanged a glance with his wife. "I suppose there was that fire three years ago. Their house went up in flames. That didn't happen every day."

"Ah, yes, the fire." JP scribbled in his notebook. "What do you think happened?"

"Accident. They say he fell asleep smoking," Mr. Miller said.

"Though some people in the neighborhood say it could've been arson." Mrs. Miller sipped her tea.

"Only you, Mary Lou," her husband grumbled. "You're the *some people*."

JP decided to change the subject before he had them arguing. He had a feeling she would circle back to it anyway. "Did you know Charles's stepson?"

"Only saw him a few times," Mr. Miller said. "He left shortly after they moved in, and I haven't seen him since."

"Do you know his name?"

"I can't remember it." She looked at her husband but he shook his head. "I saw him the night of the fire, you know?"

"Now, Mary Lou, you can't be sure of that," Mr. Miller countered.

"I know what I saw." She crossed her arms.

"What did you see?" JP asked.

"I couldn't sleep, and the dog wanted out, so I took him out on the front lawn. After he did his business, I sat down on the step and watched that young man walk up and go into that house."

"Did you see him leave?"

"No. I went inside after a few minutes so I didn't see anything else."

Mr. Miller shook his head.

"How soon after that did the fire start?" JP asked.

Mrs. Miller thought for a second. "An hour or two later, I think."

"Are you sure it was the stepson?"

"No. She isn't sure," Mr. Miller interjected. "It was dark, and he was wearing dark clothes. There's no way she could've seen his face."

"I didn't have to see his face, because I recognized his walk. It was definitely him. I notice the way people walk. Everyone has their own, and his is unusual."

"Did you tell the police or the fire investigators about the stepson?"

"*He* wouldn't let me." She nodded her head toward her husband.

"Because you could've gotten that poor boy in a lot of trouble when you didn't really know anything," Mr. Miller said.

JP nodded, making another note. "Do either of you remember Charles's friend, Robert?"

"Yes." Mr. Miller nodded, his eyes distant as if recalling a memory.

"Chain smoker, that one," Mrs. Miller added, her nose wrinkling in distaste. "Always had a cigarette hanging out of his mouth."

"Interesting." JP made a mental note of the detail. "Anything else you can remember about him?"

"Can't say there's much more to tell." Mr. Miller shrugged. "Only met him a few times. Didn't really know him."

"Thank you for your help." JP got up from his seat. He figured the Millers had given him all the information they had about Lana's past, and now he was armed with two more leads.

"Best of luck, dear," Mrs. Miller called after him as he headed out the door.

As JP walked out, he felt a growing sense of urgency. Lana was in danger. He stepped outside the Miller's house, the evening air providing a much-needed respite from the stuffy living room. He pulled out his phone and sent a text to Lana.

JP—*Do you know anything about your dad's friend, Robert?*

As he waited for Lana's response, JP inhaled the scent of freshly cut grass and the faint aroma of a neighbor's barbecue. The sun was setting, casting an orange glow over the quiet suburban street.

His phone buzzed with a new message.

Lana--*Robert Jensen. He was my dad's best friend. They were really close, practically like brothers. Robert always had this crazy obsession with vintage cars, especially Mustangs. He owns a garage in town where he restores them. He's a bit of a loner. Chain smoker, too.*

JP--*Did they ever have any arguments?*

Lana--*None that I can recall. But I was just a kid and not that interested in my dad's friends. Besides, my dad kept a lot of secrets from me, even though we were close.*

JP—*Thanks. Please send me the name of Robert's garage and any addresses or phone numbers you have for him.*

Lana responded with the details for the garage.

Lana—*If that isn't enough, I can find a cellphone number for him, but it might take a little time.*

JP—*Thanks. I'll start with this.*

Lana—*Thanks, JP. I appreciate your help.*

JP—*Anytime, but be careful, and remember, a dead snake can still bite.*

JP pocketed his phone. He hoped Robert Jensen held the key to unraveling the mystery of the fire, if there actually was a mystery. Then there was the stepbrother. He wondered why Lana hadn't mentioned him. He wanted to ask her, but he decided to gather a little more information before he did. She must have had a personal reason for not volunteering it.

As he walked to his truck, JP reviewed the information he now possessed. Robert Jensen: vintage cars, a garage in town, and a close friendship with Lana's father. Lana's stepbrother: may have been at the scene of the fire and didn't get along with Charles. These were the pieces of the puzzle that could lead him to the truth. But what was missing? What did it all mean? And how did it connect to Lana's pursuer?

JP called the number Lana had given him for Robert's garage and made an appointment to meet him at a coffee shop the next morning before work. But that still gave him time this evening to try and catch Pearl, the woman who lived in the house next door to where the Storms had lived twenty years ago before Lana's mother died.

Chapter Seventeen

Thursday late afternoon, San Diego, California

JP walked up the quiet suburban street. As he approached the house, the smoke from the chimney smelled like cinnamon or pumpkin pastries. He knocked on the door, and an elderly woman answered.

"Good evening, ma'am. My name is JP, and I'm investigating a case that involves Lana Storm."

"I'm Pearl. My friend told me you might come calling. I remember Lana well. Sweet girl, but she went through so much." Pearl's eyes clouded with sorrow as she recalled the past. "Come in, dear."

As they sat in the cozy living room, JP noticed old photo albums and memorabilia scattered around, a testament to a lifetime of memories.

"Pearl, can you tell me about what happened when Lana's mother passed away?" he asked gently.

Pearl sighed. "It was horrible. Poor Lana found her mother hanging in the garage. She was only ten years old at the time. The poor child screamed so loud it chilled me to the bone. It took her father hours to console her."

JP grimaced, imagining the trauma Lana must have experienced. No wonder she had grown up to be so fiercely independent and guarded—she'd learned early on that life could throw devastating curveballs.

"Did you ever hear any theories as to why her mother did it?"

Pearl hesitated, then said, "Many people thought it was because of Lana's father—his constant disappearances and secretive behavior. They believed she couldn't handle the uncertainty and stress anymore. But I think there was more to it than that."

"Go on," JP urged, leaning forward.

"Her mother was a lovely woman, but there was always something... off about her. Almost like she was hiding something too. Maybe it was guilt, or fear, but it weighed heavily on her. I think that, combined with her husband's behavior, ultimately pushed her over the edge."

JP processed the information as he glanced around the room, taking in the old photographs and trinkets of a life well lived. He wondered what secrets hid within these walls. Everyone had them.

"Thank you for your time, Pearl," JP said, rising. "You've been very helpful."

"Please, find out what happened for Lana's sake. She deserves some peace," Pearl's eyes filled with empathy.

As JP walked back to his truck, he felt an uneasy stirring in his gut. The case was growing more tangled by the moment, and Lana's safety hung in the balance. He hoped he could find what Lana was looking for.

JP's mind raced as he climbed into his car, the weight of Pearl's words settling upon him. That poor little girl finding her mother like that. He couldn't imagine the pain she had suffered. He didn't really want to talk to

Lana right now, wasn't sure what he should say. So, he called Tuper.

"I just had an enlightening talk with an old neighbor about Lana's mother." He updated him on the conversation with Pearl, then started the engine.

"That poor woman," Tuper said. "It's never easy to lose someone like that. So, what did you find out?"

"Her theory is that Lana's mother was hiding something, feeling guilty or afraid, and that her husband's actions pushed her over the edge. Apparently, Lana isn't the only one her father kept secrets from."

"Secrets are like wildflowers, my friend," Tuper said with a chuckle. "They sprout up everywhere, whether you want 'em to or not. The trick is knowin' which ones are worth pickin'."

JP couldn't help but smile at Tuper's analogy. Despite the tension surrounding the case, the old cowboy always managed to find a way to lighten the mood.

Chapter Eighteen

Thursday, earlier that afternoon, Helena

Clarice stood behind the counter at Nickels, wiping down the polished wood as she scanned the room. A tall man with greying hair and piercing blue eyes sauntered in, looking around as if searching for someone. Then his gaze landed on Clarice. He approached the counter, and leaned against it casually.

"Hi there." He offered a warm smile that didn't quite reach his eyes. "I'm Mike."

"Nice to meet you, Mike." Clarice felt an odd sense of unease, but decided to brush it off. She couldn't help but notice how handsome he was, despite the strange feeling she got from him. "I'm Clarice."

"Beautiful name for a beautiful woman." His voice was smooth like honey. "What's a lovely lady like you doing in a place like this?"

"Working, obviously," Clarice teased, trying to lighten the mood. She couldn't deny that the attention was flattering. "It pays the bills."

"I'd be happy to help pay those bills if it meant more time with you." His eyes locked onto hers.

"Is that so?" Clarice asked coyly, surprised by her own flirting. Something about Mike intrigued her, and she couldn't quite put her finger on it.

"Absolutely." He leaned in a bit closer. "In fact, I think I could use a drink right now. Care to join me?"

"Maybe later." Clarice was torn between suspicion and attraction. "I still have work to do."

"All right. But don't forget my offer." Mike winked, and took a seat at the bar with a confident swagger.

Clarice kept drying glasses behind the bar while Mike leaned against the end of it, flashing a roguish grin as he regaled her with stories of his travels.

"... then the camel just took off, leaving me stranded in the middle of the desert!" he exclaimed, feigning horror.

Clarice laughed, shaking her head in disbelief. "Oh, Mike, you must be pulling my leg!"

"Would I do that?" he asked innocently, a soft look in his eyes.

"I do believe you would," she teased, giving him a playful push. "But I have to admit, your stories are certainly entertaining."

Mike continued to hang around, occasionally getting up to take a phone call or use the restroom. When he returned, Clarice asked, "Are you a local?"

"I am now. I've only been here a few weeks, moved from California."

"That's quite a change. What brings you to our little piece of paradise?" Clarice thought she detected skepticism in his expression. "Or haven't you discovered the paradise part yet?"

He smiled. "There are lots of things I like about this place, the beautiful countryside, the huge starlit sky.

You know, I never understood why people call Montana 'big sky country' until I came here." Another charming grin. "It's true: the sky looks so much bigger than at home. I guess it's because you can see so far and nothing blocks it. And I'm amazed at the number of stars up there. I've never seen so many stars."

"It is a beautiful place." Clarice glanced at the window. "The winters are way too cold and hard to maneuver, but the rest of the year is lovely."

"I have to agree with you. It has been colder than I expected. I'm not looking forward to my first blizzard."

"They're not any fun. But you still haven't told me why you moved here."

Clarice's question hung between them as Mike stared off into the distance, seemingly lost in thought. Finally, he spoke, his voice a whisper: "I wanted to get away." He looked up at Clarice, his tone pained. "There was too much stress at home... too little time for me. Then my wife divorced me, and I had too much time to myself. I needed to find someplace where I could just *be*... and Montana seemed like the perfect place."

Clarice nodded in understanding. She knew what it was like to feel overwhelmed with everything going on in life. She reached out and touched his arm in a gesture of comfort.

"You found a good place to land," she said gently. "And if you need anything while you're settling in, don't hesitate to ask."

Mike smiled gratefully and thanked her, assuring her that he'd keep her offer in mind. Then he stood and started to walk away. A second later, he turned back and, with a twinkle in his eye, said, "You know what? I think I'll take you up on your offer after all. How about joining me for that drink later?"

Clarice hesitated, then said, "Meet me back here after work, about five maybe?"

"Five is fine, but are you sure you want to stay here where you've worked all day? I'd like to take you to a nice restaurant or anywhere you want to go."

"Maybe another time. Tonight, right here is good."

"Your call."

~~~

Clarice finished her shift and sat down on the other side of the bar. She had worked a double shift because someone had called in sick, and she was tired. She wished she hadn't made plans to meet Mike but changed her mind when she saw him. He had arrived five minutes early, and his face lit up with a warm smile as she joined him.

"You're prompt," Clarice said. "I like that."

"My dad taught me to always be punctual, and my mother taught me to never keep a lady waiting."

"Sounds like smart parents."

"Okay, I have a confession to make," Mike said.

"Already? We've only known each other a few hours." Clarice made light of it. *Here it goes.* She expected him to say he wasn't really divorced, or he was dying, or something crazy. She braced herself for the worst.

"The truth is I chose Montana because my friend lives here. I'm house sitting for him right now while he's out of the country."

"Why wouldn't you tell me that in the first place?"

"Because it seemed more romantic and dramatic if we had a chance encounter. He told me to come to this bar and find you. He was trying to set us up, I'm sure. I
~~~

kept meaning to bring it up, but we just started talking and it slipped my mind."

"What's your friend's name?"

"Darren Black. You do know him, right?"

"For sure. Darren's a character. He comes in here all the time."

"He would've introduced us, but like I said, he's out of the country right now."

They talked about their lives, their histories, and where they'd come from. Clarice found herself sharing stories she never thought she'd tell anyone else. There was something special about this man that made her want to open up to him in a way she hadn't experienced before.

Eventually, the topic shifted to Montana and all the things they loved about it—the vast open spaces, the wildlife roaming free in the national parks, and of course the starry night sky. When their conversation wound down, Clarice decided it was time to go and thanked Mike for joining her for drinks. They exchanged numbers and made plans to meet again soon as they walked out.

As Clarice drove home under a blanket of stars, she reflected on what a nice evening she'd had. It had been a while since she'd had a man in her life. It felt good.

Chapter Nineteen

Thursday evening

Tuper watched as Mitch left his apartment, then followed him from a safe distance. Rain had started to fall, reminding Tuper that he needed new windshield wipers. He tracked Mitch through the streets of Helena, until they reached Angel's house. Mitch boldly parked in the driveway, not very smart for an adulterer. Tuper parked on the street, watching as Mitch dashed from his car through the rain and rang the doorbell. When Henry appeared, Tuper's heart dropped into his stomach, afraid the men would have a physical confrontation. Tuper started to exit his car, ready to intervene, when to his surprise, Henry invited Mitch inside.

What the heck? Tuper closed his door, turned up the heat, and called Henry. "I think you ought to know something about your houseguest."

"What?"

"Are you alone right now?"

"I'm in the den, by myself. What's going on?"

"I have reason to believe the man who just entered your home is the man Angel is having an affair with."

Henry burst out laughing. He tried to explain, but his mirth interfered. Finally, he said, "Mitch is Angel's brother."

Tuper was stymied and started to question what he had witnessed with his own eyes. "Are you sure they're not both playing you?"

"I'm sure." Henry was still chuckling under his breath.

"I'll keep lookin'." Tuper hung up before he embarrassed himself further. He replayed every move in his mind, wondering if all their little touches could've been innocent.

~~~

Meanwhile, Lana hunched over her laptop, with Dually at her feet. She tried to busy herself with anything that didn't remind her of Jack Peterson. They had to resolve the Fenton case, so she turned to her search of Angel's personal data. The familiar hum of the computer mixed with the sound of rain tapping against the window created a soothing soundtrack for her mission.

"Come on, Angel," Lana whispered, as she hacked into Angel's phone records and social media accounts. "Let's see if you're playing Henry for a fool."

She was momentarily set back when Tuper came in. Dually ran to greet him at the door. Tuper scratched the dog's head. "Thanks for watching him for me."

"Anytime. I love having Dually around," she said. "How did it go?"

"Fine," Tuper grumbled and sat down at the table across from her. "You find anything?"

"Nothing worthwhile yet."

A series of numbers and symbols flashed across the screen, then moments later, Lana found what she was looking for: a list of contacts and recent call logs. The
~~~

number of deleted messages and late-night phone calls stunned her. "Hey, Pops!" Lana called, not taking her eyes off the screen. "You might want to see what I got here."

Tuper stood and walked around the table, his brow furrowed. He leaned over Lana's shoulder, to stare at the data on the screen. "It looks like a bunch of chicken scratch to me."

"While the rooster's away, the hen will play." *What had she just said?* "Ick. Now you've got me spouting Tuperisms. Here's the thing: Angel's been deleting messages and making calls at odd hours of the night. Also, there's a lot of calls and texts to numbers that are not in her contact list." Lana clicked on a string of messages to reveal their content.

"Still don't look like much to me."

"Something's definitely up."

"Could be innocent." Tuper stepped back. "Maybe she's planning a surprise party for Henry or something."

"Or maybe she's cheating on him." Bitterness creeped in as she recalled her own past experiences with betrayal. Lana shook her head, unwilling to let the thought fester. "Either way, it's our job to find out."

"Just don't get too attached to any one theory."

"Please, Pops." Lana snorted, rolling her eyes. "You know me better than that."

"Exactly why I said it," Tuper replied.

"Wait a minute. What happened tonight? Did you follow Mitch?"

"Right to Angel's house. Only Henry was there and... "

Lana looked up. "Tell me. Tell me. Did little ol' Henry squish Mitch like a bug?"

"Henry invited him inside for dinner. Seems Mitch is Angel's brother."

What? Lana's mouth dropped open. "Are you sure that's not part of a bigger scam?"

"Henry's convinced, but it sure wouldn't hurt if you did some research."

Before Tuper finished his sentence, Lana was already on it. Tuper joined Clarice in the living room while Lana searched. Once she knew what she was looking for, it didn't take long to verify the information.

"OMG!" Lana exclaimed.

"What have you got?" Tuper hurried back to the dining room.

"They're siblings, all right. Born to the same parents, the same day, thirty minutes apart. Mitch is not only her brother, he's her twin."

"I'll be a monkey's uncle."

"We were sure on the wrong track with that one. Maybe she's not cheating on Henry."

"Just 'cuz she ain't cheatin' with Mitch, don't mean she ain't cheatin'."

Chapter Twenty

Late Thursday night

The rain had stopped, Clarice and Mary Ann had gone to bed, and Tuper was dozing in the living room recliner. Lana was done with the Fenton case for the night. She couldn't concentrate on the shenanigans of an unfaithful wife when she had real troubles of her own. Lana hunched over her laptop, the soft keyboard clicks creating a rhythm that echoed through the room. She looked up to discover Tuper leaning against the doorway, watching her work.

"Any luck?" His grave voice broke the silence.

Lana paused, squinting at the screen. "I gave up on the blonde bimbo and her rich husband to concentrate on Jack. I'm finding more connections between him and my father, but nothing concrete yet. It's like they're ghosts."

"Maybe it's time to take a break." Tuper pushed off the doorframe and took a few steps into the room. "You've been at this for hours."

"Can't," Lana snapped, then sighed, rubbing her temples. "I just... I need answers."

Tuper nodded, then pulled up a chair and sat beside her, scanning the information on the screen. Lana wondered why he bothered. She was pretty certain he didn't understand any of it.

"Sometimes you gotta trust your gut, kid."

"Trust doesn't come easy to me, Pops," Lana confessed. "Even my own gut has been letting me down lately."

"I know." Tuper leaned back in his chair. "Took me awhile to learn how to trust too. When I was young, I tried to do everything on my own, but life has a way of showing us that don't work." He paused, lost in thought for a moment. "I had a family once, but I was different than them. I didn't want to live my life with all those rules. Besides, I was young and thought I knew everything, like most kids. So, I ventured out on my own, nearly got myself killed more times than you can imagine. I learnt pretty quick not to trust anyone. One day, I had someone come to my rescue when I least expected it."

Lana looked over at him, curiosity piqued. "Did he save you from the bear?"

"That's a story for another day." Tuper smiled. "What I'm sayin' is it's time to let me help *you*."

"You've been helping."

"Not like I could."

"I don't want you mixed up in this any more than you already are."

"It's too late for that."

"You don't know how bad this really is." Lana shook her head. "And you're not the one with a crazy guy after you."

"Sure enough. But remember you got us—me, Clarice, and Mary Ann. We're your family now."

Lana mulled over Tuper's words, then forced a smile and went back to work. She pounded away for some time, then spotted something intriguing. "What's this?"

"Found something?" Tuper leaned forward.

"Maybe," Lana said cautiously, scanning the contents of the document. "It's a list of transactions, and my father's name is all over them."

Tuper furrowed his brow. "What kind of transactions?"

"Offshore accounts, shell companies, the works." Lana's voice trembled. "Jack and my father were partners in crime. Literally."

Tuper scratched his chin. "That explains why he was so hell-bent on finding you. He must think you know something he can use."

"Or that I'm just like my father." Lana closed her laptop. "We both know he wants to exploit me for his own gain."

Chapter Twenty-One

Early Friday morning

The inviting aromas of freshly brewed coffee and sizzling bacon filled the air at Smith's Cafe. The dark sky and chilly temperature outside made the café even more inviting. Locals huddled around tables scattered with newspapers, coffee cups, and half-eaten meals, their lively conversations blending into a familiar hum.

Lana sat across from Tuper, amused by his latest adventure, her boots tapping rhythmically against the chair leg. She sipped her coffee, enjoying the simple pleasure of a good breakfast shared with someone she cared about. For a moment, she pushed everything else out of her head.

As Tuper recounted his tale, Lana's gaze wandered toward the door. The bell above it jingled, announcing a new arrival. Lana stared at the person who entered. Grant Simmons, a man she'd hoped to never see again. Her mouth tightened and her spoon clattered to the table. She froze, her breath catching in her throat.

"You okay?" Tuper asked.

"Uh... yeah." Lana looked away from Grant, trying to avoid eye contact. She gripped her cup tightly, knuckles turning white. "Just thought I saw someone I knew, but

I was wrong." She forced a tight-lipped smile, but deep down, a knot formed in her stomach, and her heart raced with dread.

"Hey, Lana," Tuper said softly. "You sure you're okay? You look a little pale."

"I just remembered I need to take care of something really important." She bolted to her feet, knocking her chair back in the process. Her heart raced as she tried to make a swift exit without drawing any more attention to herself.

As she hurried out, she scanned the room, hoping to avoid Grant at all costs. However, fate had other plans. As she neared the door, Grant stepped out from behind another guy, and accidentally bumped into her. The impact caused Lana's phone to slip from her hand and clatter to the floor.

"Sorry about that." Grant bent down to retrieve the fallen device. He held it out to her, and Lana snatched it from his grasp, barely able to contain her annoyance.

"Thanks," she muttered through gritted teeth, her eyes downcast. Lana pushed past him and strode toward the exit.

"Wait!" Grant called after her.

Lana heard Tuper step between them. "Leave her alone," he growled.

Outside the café, Lana leaned against the brick wall, taking deep breaths to calm her racing heart. Thoughts swirled in her head like a tornado: Why was Grant here? What did he want? How had he found her?

Despite her fear, Lana knew she couldn't avoid confronting her past any longer. If she didn't deal with Grant now, there was no telling what might happen to her and those she cared about. Her resolve hardened, and she decided to face him head-on.

As he emerged from the café, she called his name. "We need to talk."

"Sure thing, Lana." He tried to sound casual, but she noticed tension in his voice.

"Cut the crap!" Lana folded her arms across her chest defensively. "Why are you here? How did you find me?"

"I didn't mean to scare you." He rubbed the back of his neck, nervously. "I just... I needed to see you. To talk to you. That's all."

"About what?" Lana's suspicion mounted with each passing second. This wasn't like Grant. He'd never cared for heartfelt reunions or long, emotional conversations. No. Something else was going on, and she intended to find out what it was.

"Fine." Grant looked around nervously, then lowered his voice. "I think someone's after us, Lana. They know about our past, our... activities."

A cold sweat broke out across her forehead. Lana glanced over toward the café. Tuper had exited and was keeping an eye on them.

"Who?" she demanded. Lana tried to keep her voice steady as she fought against the wave of panic threatening to consume her. "Who's after us, Grant? And why now?"

"I don't know." He ran a hand through his disheveled hair. "But I've been getting these weird messages, and I think they're connected. That's why I came to find you. We need to figure this out together, Lana. Before it's too late."

Despite the urgency in his voice, Lana couldn't bring herself to fully believe him. Grant had always been unpredictable, and she knew how easily he could manipulate others for his own gain. What if this was just another of his games?

"Tell me the truth, Grant," she said, her voice wavering with a mix of anger and fear. "Is this really about someone coming after us, or is there something else you want from me?"

"Look, I swear, I'm not lying to you." He reached for her arm. "This is serious."

Lana pulled away. "Give me one good reason why I should trust you." Her heart pounded in her chest. "After everything we've been through, everything you've done—why should I believe you now?"

"Because." He met her gaze with a rare sincerity that made her briefly question her own doubts. "Despite it all, I still care about you. And I don't want anything to happen to you or those you care about."

As Lana stared into his eyes, searching for any hint of deception, she felt the weight of their shared past pressing down like a heavy burden. She wanted to trust him, to believe that he had changed and that they could work together to protect themselves and their friends. But she was terrified of what might happen if she let him back into her life. "Was that a threat?"

"Of course not."

"Give me some time," she finally whispered, pulling herself away from his intense gaze. If what Grant said was true, then it wasn't just her safety at stake. Her friends were in danger too. "I need to think about this. I'll be in touch when I'm ready."

"I'll text you, then you'll have my contact information."

"You have my cell number?"

"Of course," he said, sounding arrogant. Then he added, "Please be careful, Lana. We're both in danger here."

"What do you really want?" Lana asked, still questioning his motives.

Grant raised his voice. "Damnit, Lana, we're in trouble."

As the confrontation unfolded with Grant, Lana could feel the tension rise in her body. Her fists clenched and her jaw set. Her voice wavered slightly as she interrogated him. But his answers weren't satisfactory and Tuper must've been concerned because he stepped forward and placed a protective hand on her shoulder.

"All right, that's enough. Why don't we all take a step back and cool down?"

Lana shot him a grateful glance. "You're right, Pops," she said. "I need some time to think." She turned back to Grant.

"Don't take too long," Grant said.

"You don't scare anyone, punk." Tuper glared at her ex.

"You might want to rethink that, old man." Grant stepped toward Tuper.

Lana grabbed Tuper's arm and led him away. As they put distance between them, Lana felt her posture slowly relax, her breaths coming more easily. By the time they reached the car, she was back to normal.

"I know this is tough for you, but confronting Grant like that might not be the best approach," Tuper said. "On the other hand, if you'd like me to take him down a peg or two, I'd be glad to."

Lana stared at her boots, her fingers tracing the scarred leather. "I know, Pops," she said. "But I can't keep running from my past. I have to face it, sooner or later."

"True." Tuper tipped his cowboy hat back. "But you gotta be smart about it. Think about what you want to say and how you're gonna handle it. Remember, you've got people coverin' yer back, always."

A small smile tugged at the corners of Lana's mouth as she looked up at Tuper. "I appreciate that, Pops."

"Anytime, Agony," Tuper replied, his own lips curving into a warm smile. "By the way, Henry Fenton called today, wanting to know if we've found the goods on his wife yet."

"I'll work on it tomorrow."

They drove in silence the rest of the way home. Lana's mind was filled with questions and fears. She glanced back at Tuper. She'd have to tell him everything soon, to lay her secrets bare and hope that he would understand. But first, she needed to find out the truth—if not for herself, then for the people she had come to call family.

Chapter Twenty-Two

Friday morning, San Diego, California

As he climbed out of his truck, JP squinted against the bright sun. The day was clear with just a slight chill in the air.

"Let's hope this fella's got something useful." JP adjusted his Stetson, then entered the quaint coffee shop, where the aroma of freshly ground beans wafted through the air. He was here to meet Robert Jensen, Charles's best friend, and hopefully find the key to unraveling the mystery surrounding Lana's father's death.

JP quickly spotted Robert seated in a booth near the back. The man looked to be in his early sixties, a tall, lanky man with blond hair and a deep bronze tan. JP strode over and extended a hand, introducing himself. "I'm JP Torn. We spoke on the phone yesterday."

"Good to meet you." Robert shook his hand firmly. "I appreciate you looking into Charles's death. I just can't shake the feeling that something isn't right about how it supposedly happened." Robert had kind eyes that seemed to harbor a deep sadness.

"Me neither." JP slid into the booth across from Robert. "That's why I'm here. I want to find out the truth. I understand you and Charles went way back?"

"Since we were kids." A nostalgic smile tugged at the corners of Robert's mouth. "We were practically brothers, always getting into some kind of trouble. We did everything together. We started our first business together, started our families around the same time, even made a pact to quit smoking together."

JP raised an eyebrow. "How'd that work out for you two?"

"Pretty well, actually," Robert replied. "Though there were times when the cravings would come back with a vengeance, and we'd have to remind each other of our promise."

"Sounds like you had a strong bond." JP empathized with him. "Must be hard to lose someone who was such a big part of your life."

Robert sighed, his eyes misting. "It is." Sunlight filtered through the window, creating shadows across Robert's face. "That's why I want to help you get to the bottom of this. If there's any foul play involved in Charles's death, I need to know."

"Agreed," JP said. "Perhaps you could walk me through the last days before Charles died."

Robert nodded, then took a quick breath before diving into the details. "Charles had been working more than usual for months, leaving little time for us to hang out. I was one of the few, probably only, person he spent time with outside of his work. For him, I think, I was a bit of an escape."

"And you were okay with that?"

"Absolutely. Whenever we did anything, it would take Charles a little time to unwind, but when he would finally relax, he'd enjoy himself."

As Robert talked, JP made mental notes of anything that could be a lead, occasionally jotting something down in his notebook. The conversation flowed, punctuated by sips of coffee and sporadic pauses as Robert collected his thoughts.

Finally, Robert said, "That's about all I know, but I'm not sure how any of it can help."

"You're helping me understand the man. That's always worthwhile." JP decided it was time to dig deeper. "Did Charles ever talk about his work with you?"

"He tried not to. That was the glory of our relationship. He didn't have to. Although, on occasion he would share his frustrations, but never any details. He mentioned a few times that he was quarreling a lot with his business partner."

"Did you know Jack Peterson?"

"Not well, but I've been around him a fair amount over the years. He's... an *interesting* man."

"Interesting?"

Another hesitation. "He's a smart guy, quite the charmer, actually."

"You're choosing your words carefully. Is it fair to say you didn't like him much?"

"I didn't know him well enough to like him or not like him. But I didn't trust him." Robert suddenly opened up. "He was shifty, an *Eddie Haskell* kind of guy—always saying the right thing in front of people, but someone you didn't dare turn your back on."

"Do you think he had anything to do with Charles's death?"

Robert blinked a few times. "I have no real reason to think that, no evidence of any kind."

JP stared at the empty coffee cups, his thoughts churning. Something gnawed at the back of his mind—a detail that seemed inconsistent. A moment later it clicked.

"Robert," JP began, leaning forward and locking eyes with Charles's best friend. "You mentioned that you and Charles made a pact to quit smoking. Did he ever break that pact?"

Robert frowned and rubbed his chin in thought. "Not that I know of, at least not until the night he died. We both struggled at first, but we stuck it out."

"Think back," JP urged. "Did you ever see Charles pick up a cigarette after you guys quit?"

Robert's brow furrowed with concentration. "There was one time, a couple of months before the fire. We were having a drink, and Charles really wanted a cigarette. I talked him down, and he swore he hadn't had any since our pact, then he promised he would call me if he got tempted again."

"Did he?"

"A couple of times he called for no apparent reason, and I think it was because he was fighting the urge. But that's not what we talked about. Then he'd say, 'I'm good now' and end the conversation."

"How long before the fire did you make the pact?"

"Six months and twelve days."

JP's gut tightened with suspicion. If Charles hadn't broken the pact, then the fire that claimed his life hadn't been started by his own cigarette. "Robert, do you know if Jack Peterson was aware of your pact?"

"Jack knew about it," Robert confirmed. "Actually, he was there when we shook on it. He even joked that he'd hold us accountable if either of us slipped up."

JP's suspicions grew stronger. "Robert," JP said, "I need you to be honest with me. Do you think there's any chance that Jack Peterson could have had a hand in the fire that killed Charles?"

Robert hesitated before answering. "I don't know, JP. I'd hate to think so, but as I said earlier, I don't trust him. It's hard to imagine someone you know taking another man's life, and saying it out loud is a little frightening. I just can't wrap my head around it. But I'll say this much, if there was foul play, I'd keep him at the top of the list."

"I want you to think hard about anything else you might know about Jack and Charles's relationship," JP said, his voice heavy with resolve. "Any disagreements they may have had, any shady business dealings, anything that might suggest a motive for foul play."

Robert nodded, his face pale. "They bickered with each other all the time. As long as I can remember, it wasn't a comfortable relationship. Two days before Charles died, we met for drinks. He said Jack had stopped by the night before and they'd had quite a fight. Charles even called Jack 'a real ass.'"

"Did Charles say what the fight was about?"

"No. Just that Jack was furious about a business decision and stormed out."

"Do you know if that happened often?"

"Over the years, Charles had mentioned arguments, but this one seemed worse than the rest." Robert pondered for a moment. "I guess I never liked Jack much," he finally admitted. "But to tell you the truth, I don't think Charles did either."

"Why did he keep working with him?"

"Because Charles had too much time and money invested in their business to walk away."

"What exactly did they do?" JP asked.

"He managed other people's money. Made financial investments for clients. As I said, Charles didn't talk about his work much. I know he spent a lot of time on his computer and he made a very good living. Anything to do with technology has never been my thing, so I didn't question him much and I wouldn't have understood it if he told me."

"The report says Charles likely fell asleep smoking and dropped his cigarette. Considering the stress he was under, doesn't that seem plausible to you?"

"Except for one thing," Robert said.

"What?"

"I don't believe Charles started smoking again. He promised he would call if he couldn't handle it, and Charles never in his life broke a promise to me."

Chapter Twenty-Three

Friday late afternoon, San Diego, California

JP walked down the alley, making a crunching sound on the gravel. His gaze lingered on the burnt remains of Charles Storm's house, the charred timber a haunting silhouette against the sky. Everything in the reports seemed to point to an accident. The fire marshal had found no signs of arson. There was no evidence that indicated foul play. Yet, JP couldn't shake the nagging feeling that there was more to the fire than met the eye, including the weaselly Jack Peterson and Lana's disbelief that it was an accident. JP couldn't help but wonder if he was projecting too much. He would keep kicking rocks until he had them all turned over.

JP adjusted the brim of his Stetson, then pulled out his cellphone and called his friend and part-time investigator, Ron Brown.

"Hey, Ron, I need your help," he said, his voice low and urgent.

"Sure. Whatever you need."

"Remember, I told you I was helping Lana investigate the death of her father?"

"Yeah. Lana called me as well."

"I'm working on a hunch here, but his death may have not been an accident. And if it wasn't, Jack Peterson could be involved."

"Jack Peterson?" Ron's surprise was evident. "Isn't that the guy who's stalking Lana in Montana?"

"That's the one. I need you to look into the relationship between Charles and Jack, both personal and business. See if you can find any dirt on Peterson. I'll keep digging from my end."

"I'm on it," Ron said, then ended the call.

As JP slipped his phone back into his pocket, he noticed a young man leaning against his car in front of the house. A cigarette dangled from his mouth, and his eyes were red-rimmed and tired. He looked to be about thirty-five and had a certain air of someone who had been around the block a few times. His dark hair was short, but not military-short, and he wore jeans and a t-shirt that hung casually from his thin frame.

"Excuse me," JP called out, approaching the stranger cautiously. "You wouldn't happen to know anything about the fire that happened here, would you?"

The young man flicked ash onto the ground, squinting at JP suspiciously. "Who wants to know?"

"Name's JP Torn, private investigator." He flipped open his wallet to reveal his identification card. "I'm looking into the death of Charles Storm. You knew him?"

The man hesitated, his gaze darting between JP's face and his ID card. "Yeah," he finally admitted. "Charles was my stepdad. I'm Danny Atterbury."

"Sorry for your loss, Danny," JP said sincerely.

"I'm still deciding how much of a loss it was."

JP wasn't sure what to make of that, although from what he'd heard, there was no love lost between Danny and Charles.

"May I ask what you're doing here?"

"I could say it's just a coincidence, that I was visiting a neighborhood friend. But you probably wouldn't believe me."

"Probably not, and certainly not now."

"I heard someone was asking questions and snooping around. I wanted to get the deets straight from the source."

"Fair enough. I'm trying to figure out what really happened here."

"I thought that was all settled. Charles fell asleep, dropped his cigarette, and will forever remain in flames."

"You didn't like him much, I take it."

"You could say that, but mostly I didn't like the way he treated my mother. He killed her."

JP was surprised, wondering if the man was delusional. "I heard she committed suicide."

"Same thing. She did it because of him. I'm sure of that."

The young man had just moved up on his list of suspects. "What can you tell me about that night? Did you see or hear anything unusual?"

Danny took a drag from his cigarette, releasing a stream of smoke as he considered the question. "I wasn't living here," he explained, "I had already moved out of the house. I left as soon as I graduated from high school."

"Why did you move out?"

"It's no secret I didn't get along with Charles. Looking back, I see that some of it may have been my fault. I was young and impetuous, but I never quite trusted him. I saw some shady stuff going on."

"Like what?"

"He was a techie. And I'm convinced he used it to get information he shouldn't have. That's why he was able to make so much money. He wanted me to learn the technical part, even told me how fun it was to get into people's social media and stuff. I guess he thought that would entice me to learn, but I was never interested."

"One of the neighbors said you came by the house that night. What were you doing?"

"I was hoping to move back home, but Charles said a flat no, so I left. I talked to my friend, Finn, who lived next door at the time, and he said he heard an argument earlier in the evening."

JP's interest was piqued. "Any idea who it was with?"

"Jack Peterson. Finn said Jack and Charles had some disagreements earlier in the week. Something about money, he thinks. Finn hung out at our house a lot and saw Jack and Charles arguing several times, so he wasn't surprised when he heard them, but he said this fight was epic."

"Peterson, again," JP murmured. "Would you mind giving me your friend's name and phone number?"

"Sure." His tone softened. "I'd like to help Lana if I can. She was a good kid." He scrolled through the contact list on his phone. "I should've kept in touch with her. I feel bad that I wasn't there for her. I know she didn't have it easy after our mother died." Danny showed JP the name and phone number of his friend, Finn Castle.

"Thanks." JP wrote the info in his notebook. "If you remember anything else, please give me a call." He handed the young man a business card then walked away, his mind racing.

It seemed the more he uncovered about Charles Storm's death, the more tangled the web became. But one thing was clear—Jack Peterson appeared to be at the center of it all.

Chapter Twenty-Four

Friday evening

Clarice dressed for her date with Mike. He'd sent her a beautiful bouquet of flowers earlier. Despite her wariness, she couldn't help but be intrigued and flattered by his attention. She adjusted her necklace in the mirror, a delicate gold chain with a small pendant. She smoothed the fabric of her shimmery blouse, taking a deep breath to calm her nerves.

"Clarice, you look gorgeous!" Lana exclaimed, entering the room. "Mike is one lucky guy."

"Thanks, Lana," Clarice blushed. "I'm really looking forward to tonight. He's different than the guys I usually date."

"In what way?"

"He's a businessman who looks like he just walked out of a magazine. But he's also down to earth and fun. And he's so darn charming."

"Have fun and don't be nervous," Lana said.

"Thank you," Clarice said gratefully. "I do believe I will."

As she headed for the front door, Tuper and Dually walked in. "Don't you look like a million bucks. Hot date?"

"A guy named Mike. You don't know him."

"I know a guy named Mike."

"Of course, you do. Not the same guy."

"My Mike's a nice guy."

"I'm sure he is." Clarice walked toward the door.

"There's a lot of weirdos out there. Who is this guy?

"Don't worry, Toop. He's a friend of a friend. I'm in good hands." She dashed out.

Clarice drove to Lucca's on Last Chance Gulch, where they had agreed to meet. When she arrived, Mike met her at the door.

"Clarice, you look stunning." Mike said as she entered the restaurant. His eyes lingered on her appreciatively. "I'm one lucky man tonight."

"Thank you." Clarice blushed at his compliment, thinking that's exactly what Lana had said earlier. "You clean up pretty well yourself." He was dressed impeccably in a tailored suit that showed off his strong build. Something about the way he looked at her made her feel both excited and uneasy.

As they walked to their table, his hand brushed hers, sending a shiver down Clarice's spine. It had been a long time since she had been on a real date. She hoped this was the beginning of something special.

Chapter Twenty-Five

Friday night

Lana paced the hardwood floor of the dining room, the tapping of her feet echoing through the small space. Her mind was a storm of thoughts and worries. Images of Grant's pleading eyes earlier that day blended with memories of their time together—back when they were partners in crime, before everything had fallen apart.

"Dang it," she murmured, running a hand through her hair. For Grant to come to Helena, he must've had a good reason. But she couldn't shake the gnawing fear that he had brought danger with him—the kind of danger that could threaten not only her life but also the lives of those she cared about. This was a whole different kind of enemy from Jack.

As she paced, Lana's thoughts drifted back to the beginning, to the time when she and Grant had been inseparable, living on the edge and chasing the thrill of the next big score. They had been young, reckless, and insanely talented when it came to hacking. And to be able to share that thrill with someone you loved. It all seemed so perfect. But it was like an addiction, always seeking a bigger score, a bigger challenge. It hadn't been long before they set their sights on a higher target: organized crime.

Together, they had hacked into the digital networks of the most dangerous criminal syndicates, obtaining information that resulted in swindling hundreds of thousands of dollars. At first, the thrill and the money made it seem worth it. But then, reality had set in—the realization that they had made powerful enemies who would stop at nothing to find them and make them pay.

"Grant, what have you brought with you?" Lana whispered to herself, staring out the rain-streaked window. A flash of lightning illuminated the room, casting an eerie glow.

"Hey, Lana," Tuper's gruff voice called from the doorway, startling her from her thoughts. "You've been pacing for a while now. You want to talk about it?"

Lana hesitated, then slowly nodded. She knew she couldn't keep this secret from Tuper any longer, not if there was a chance that her friends' lives were in danger.

"Grant and I used to be partners." Her voice was barely above a whisper. "We hacked into some dangerous people's systems, stole a lot of money, and made powerful enemies. Now I'm worried that he might have brought those criminals here with him. Or that he might be after me himself. He was pretty angry when I left."

Tuper's eyes narrowed as he took in the new information, his jaw clenched tightly. "What do you think we should do?"

"I don't know." Lana's chest tightened. "I need to find out if he's really changed, like he said. But if I confront him, those dangerous people might come after all of us."

"Listen," Tuper said gently, placing a hand on her shoulder. "We'll deal with this together, all right? Just don't be doin' anything reckless."

"Okay," Lana agreed, taking a deep breath to steady herself. "I won't act without thinking it through first."

"How about you don't act alone?"

"I don't know if I can promise that, but I'll think about it."

Tuper gave her a look and walked out.

Lana leaned against the cool glass of the dining room window, watching the sun dip below the horizon, casting orange and pink hues across the sky. The vibrant colors contrasted sharply with the dark thoughts swirling in her mind. Her fingers tapped rhythmically on the windowsill as she considered the consequences of being turned in to the police.

Jail time. A shiver ran down her spine at the thought.

Lana's thoughts turned to Clarice, Mary Ann, and Tuper. The fear of losing them tore at her heart. The thought of them learning about her past and turning away from her was almost too much to bear. But most of all, she didn't want to put any of them in danger.

She sighed heavily, torn between her desire to confront Grant and fear of the backlash. In the quiet of the room, Lana allowed her thoughts to drift back to the time she spent with Grant before everything went wrong. They'd had moments of genuine happiness, romantic adventures, and shared laughter. Despite her better judgment, she couldn't deny that she still harbored feelings for him. But those emotions were inextricably tangled with the darker memories of their crimes and the danger they'd brought upon themselves.

Damnit! Why had Grant come back now?

As if responding to her thoughts, a soft knock sounded at the door. She turned to find Tuper standing in the doorway.

"Hey, kiddo," he said gently. "You all right? You've been holed up in here for an hour."

"I'm fine, Pops." Lana forced a smile, though her voice wavered. "Just... thinking."

"About Grant?"

Lana nodded, struggling to find the words to express her turmoil. "I don't know what to do, Tuper," she admitted. "Part of me wants to confront him and demand answers. But I'm terrified of what might happen if I do—and what might happen if I don't."

"Whatever you decide, I have your back."

Lana looked into Tuper's eyes, searching for reassurance, and found it in the unwavering loyalty reflected back at her. The weight of the decision settled on her shoulders.

"Thank you, Tuper." Her voice was stronger this time. "I think... I need more time to figure this out."

"Do you have the time? Or will Grant take action?"

"I don't know. He can be menacing, and if others have followed him, we might be out of time."

When Lana sighed, Tuper said, "Why don't you take some time to clear your head before you get back on that machine? Maybe relax on the porch. I'll fix you a cup of tea."

Lana feigned a shocked look. "You're bringing *me* tea? You're scaring me, Pops," she joked. Before Lana could say more, her phone rang. She looked at the caller ID.

"Aren't you gonna answer it?" Tuper asked.

"It's private." Lana didn't want Tuper to get more involved in her problems. She could handle Jack on her own.

"Humph," Tuper said and walked away.

Lana stepped outside to the back deck and took the call. "What do you want, Jack?"

"I want your decision."

"It's only been two days," Lana pleaded.

"What is there to think about? You'll either do it, or your friends will pay the price, one by one."

"Don't try to bully me, Jack. You know I'm tougher than that."

"We'll see."

When Lana say Clarice drive up, she said, "Goodbye, Jack." She hung up the phone and waited for her on the deck. They walked inside together with Clarice chattering about what a wonderful time she'd had.

Chapter Twenty-Six

Saturday morning, San Diego, California

Danny's friend, Finn Castle, lived in a small apartment in Linda Vista. JP and Ron drove over together. Finn was very cooperative, open to whatever questions they had to ask. He was a tall, stocky man with thick black hair, a squared jaw, and bright green eyes. Danny had apparently schooled him on what they wanted because when he answered the door, he invited them right in. "I remember Lana. Cute kid. I'm glad to help."

JP glanced at Ron, and they stepped inside. Finn led them into his living room, where he had already arranged two chairs. He sat in a third chair opposite them and waited for them to begin.

"Thank you for agreeing to see us," JP said. "We hope to find out more about the fire at the Storms' house."

"I'm glad to help."

"Thank you," JP said. "Danny told us you heard an argument between Charles and his business partner, Jack. What can you tell us about that?"

"It was two nights before the fire. I was in my room, which was directly across from Charles's den. I heard arguing, so I opened my window." Finn blushed, then shrugged. "Danny had moved out and asked me to keep tabs on things. Jack was angry and waving his arms around. Charles kept trying to calm him down, but it didn't work."

"Did you catch any of their conversation?" JP asked.

"Something about money." Finn scratched his chin. "Jack accused Charles of not holding up his end of some deal, then he stormed out. He was furious."

"Did you hear anything else? Did Jack mention anyone else?" JP asked.

Finn shook his head. "I didn't hear any names, and last I saw, he was heading for the street."

"What did Charles do after Jack left?"

"Nothing. He just let him go." Finn looked thoughtful for a moment. "Charles seemed distracted after Jack left. He kept pacing around his den and looking out the front window, like he was expecting someone. But no one ever showed up." Finn paused before adding, "It was strange."

"Did Jack say anything when he left?"

"On the walkway, he turned briefly and shouted, 'You're finished!' Or at least that's what I think I heard."

"Thanks." JP stood and handed him a business card. "If you think of anything else that could be helpful, please call me."

Outside, Ron asked, "Where do we go from here?"

"Let's get back to my office and go over everything we have," JP suggested. "Maybe we're missing something, a connection tying Jack to Charles's death."

As they pulled away in JP's truck, Ron stared into the rearview mirror. "We're being followed," he said, his voice urgent. "Someone was watching us. He jumped into his car and now he's right behind us."

Glancing in the mirror, JP saw a blue sedan keeping pace, not speeding up or slowing down. He furrowed his brow. "Do you recognize the car?"

Ron shook his head. "I've never seen it before."

JP made a sudden turn onto a side street. The car followed. He did the same several more times, until the vehicle was no longer behind them.

"I think we lost him," Ron said, breathing a sigh of relief.

"I don't know. That was too easy." JP mulled it over. "I think he wants us to know we're being watched."

Chapter Twenty-Seven

Saturday morning, Helena, Montana

Lana was overwhelmed. She wanted to run—to protect her friends and herself from the dual threats of Jack and Grant. But she had already pulled Tuper too far into it, and he could be in more danger if she disappeared. No matter what she did, Jack still had a grip on her life that he could use as a weapon against anyone close to her.

Lana decided to focus on their other case so Tuper could get Henry Fenton off his back.

As Lana dove deep into Angel's online life, she wondered if her pleasure in the task was the same thrill a peeping Tom got. She always felt a pang of guilt for violating someone's privacy, but her sense of accomplishment in doing something few others could was exhilarating. And as the mystery surrounding Angel's actions thickened, Lana's curiosity overcame any hesitation.

"Secrets have a way of coming out, Angel," Lana murmured. "Believe me, I know."

The rain outside intensified, hammering against the windowpane as if reflecting Lana's determination. Somewhere beneath Angel's layers of secrecy, the truth was waiting to be found.

Too many things looked suspicious, but nothing that was concrete evidence of Angel's infidelity. "Come on, come on..." Lana whispered, heart pounding in rhythm with her keystrokes. Time seemed to stretch as she chipped away at the encryption, determined not to let it stand between her and the truth.

Finally, after what seemed like hours, the barrier crumbled. Lana grinned triumphantly as the decrypted messages flooded her screen. "Gotcha!" A fierce grin stretched across her face. But it vanished quickly when she realized she was looking at a pattern of doctor appointments.

Oncologists? Radiologists? Maybe this wasn't about infidelity. She bypassed another firewall and additional security measures.

Finally, more medical records loaded onto the screen. She scanned the information hungrily, searching for answers.

Angel had stage two breast cancer and a mastectomy scheduled. "Oh, Angel."

For a moment, the noise in the room disappeared, replaced by the weight of sympathy that settled on Lana's chest. The poor woman wasn't a cheater. *But why was she keeping it a secret from her husband? Why did she go to such lengths to hide her doctor's appointments?*

"Angel, why haven't you told Henry?" Lana asked the empty room, feeling an unexpected connection to this woman whose life she had invaded. Lana knew how difficult it was to trust, but keeping a secret like this could only lead to more pain.

"Hey, Pops," she called to Tuper in the living room. "I found something, but you're not going to like it."

"Is it about Angel?" Tuper hustled over to the dining table.

"Yeah." Lana glanced down at the flash drive in her hand. "But it's not what we thought. She's got stage two breast cancer, and she needs a mastectomy."

"Dang." Tuper scowled. "That poor woman. We're gonna have to tell Henry."

"Uh, not we—you. That's not in my job description."

Chapter Twenty-Eight

Saturday afternoon

As Clarice stepped out of Nickels Bar after her shift, she saw Mike leaning against a silver Lexus sedan rental car in the parking lot. Her heart leapt at the sight of him. They'd had such a great date the night before, and he'd been a perfect gentleman.

Wearing a friendly smile, Mike approached her. "How about if I take you to a late lunch?"

"I'd really like to go home and shower first."

"You look great. And by the time you do all that, we'll be starving. We don't need to go anywhere fancy."

"All right." She wanted to spend more time with him before he realized she wasn't the youngest or prettiest woman in town. Her insecurities kicked in. *Mike is handsome, sophisticated, and worldly. I'm just a small-town girl. He'll tire of me quickly.* She pushed them away.

"Great. Where would you like to go?"

"You decide."

"I've heard about this place in Montana City that's supposed to have the best burger around."

"There's plenty of burger joints closer," Clarice said.

"I know, but it's only about fifteen minutes away, and there's something I want to show you."

Clarice was tired, but she was also thrilled that Mike had stopped by to take her out. She relaxed and chatted with him as they drove to the restaurant.

After lunch, they got into Mike's Lexus and he said, "I know you're tired, but if you don't mind, I'd like to show you something. It won't take long."

"Sure," Clarice said. "What is it?"

"You'll see in a minute. I'll explain when we get there."

After a short drive, they arrived at an abandoned barn near the outskirts of town. Once out of the car, Clarice began to wonder if this was a mistake. "What is this place?"

"I know it looks ominous, but it has real potential."

"It looks to me like it should just be torn down. What could you possibly do here?"

"I did a lot of construction when I was younger, and I'm looking for something I can get involved in. Real hands-on project."

"This will take a lot of hands," Clarice said, trying to keep it light. "Do you plan to live here?"

"No. Just trying to bring a little culture to the area." He opened the rusted metal door. It screeched from disuse. They stepped inside. The air was thick with dust, and cobwebs draped across the corners like sinister curtains.

"I'll tell you about my vision for this main space in a moment, but first I want you to see the office. It's so special." Mike led her to a small room in the back that was dimly lit, with only a single chair and a table.

Confused, she turned to him. "How is this special?"

"Sit down, Clarice." Mike's voice was suddenly so cold it sent a shiver down her spine.

"What's wrong with you?" Fear bubbled up, and she stepped back toward the door.

"Sit down, Clarice," Mike commanded again, pulling a stun gun from an ankle holster.

Clarice froze, feeling her stomach drop as she realized the gravity of her situation. *Who was this man?*

She tried to walk away, but Mike grabbed for her arm. She sidestepped and moved toward the exit, her chest heaving with terror. Mike blocked her way and grabbed her arm, yanking her back to the musty-smelling chair. Its wooden legs creaked in protest as they scuffled until she was pinned in place. He tightly wound a length of rope around her wrists and ankles, trapping her in the chair. He gritted his teeth as he tugged to make sure it held her securely.

Clarice scanned the room for escape routes, but there wasn't even a window. Jack stood between her and the only opening, the door they came in. Her heart pounded in her chest and her thoughts raced around in her brain. She had to find a way out.

Bound and helpless, Clarice wriggled in the chair, trying to loosen the tight knots. Sweat trickled down her brow as she strained against the ropes, feeling them bite into her skin. Her pulse pounded in her ears, drowning out all other sounds.

"Mike, why are you doing this?" she asked, her voice trembling with fear and desperation. She desperately hoped that somehow there was a misunderstanding, that the man she believed she knew wouldn't do this to her, but she knew better. *How had she been so naïve?*

"Mike?" Jack snorted derisively. "That was just a convenient cover to gain your trust. You can call me Jack."

"Jack? So, it was all a lie? The friendship, the flirting, the interesting conversations? All of it?" She couldn't hide the bitterness in her voice. Betrayal laced her words, and her heart ached at the thought that someone she had trusted could be so deceitful.

"Of course, it was," he replied, his cold blue eyes devoid of remorse. "It was simply a means to an end. I needed you close, Clarice, so I could get to Lana."

"Lana? But why?" Clarice's thoughts were in a flurry as she tried to make sense of the revelation. She couldn't remember Lana ever mentioning someone named Jack. Then she remembered the message Lana got. Someone was after her. *Was this the same man?* Questions swirled around in her head like a whirlwind, but one thought remained clear: she needed to find a way to escape this nightmare.

"Please, let me go," she begged, her voice cracking. "I won't tell anyone about this. I promise."

"Sorry, dear," Jack said with a sardonic smile. "You're not going anywhere until Lana does what I need her to do."

As she struggled against her restraints, Clarice's thoughts shifted from her own predicament to Lana's safety. If Jack was willing to go to these lengths, what might he do to Lana?

"I don't know what Lana has done to you, but I'm sure it can be worked out." Clarice knew her pleas would do no good, but she had to try.

"I don't plan to hurt her. I need her. But I will hurt *you* if she doesn't do what I ask."

"Please, Mike... Jack, I don't believe you're the kind of man who could hurt anyone."

He let out a belly laugh. "You'd be wrong there, sweetheart. I've hurt plenty of people and I don't intend to stop now." He stepped toward her with an evil smile. "Oh, I can be nice when it suits me, but sometimes, the only way to get what I want is by taking risks and playing dirty."

"Let me talk to Lana. I'll get her to do whatever you need." Tears streamed down Clarice's cheeks. She knew she couldn't rely on this dangerous man for mercy. He was a sociopath, and her chances of survival seemed slim.

"No," Jack countered coldly.

Clarice's mind jumped from one plan of escape to another, each more desperate than the last. Her fate, and Lana's, lay in their own hands. Her heart pounded in her chest as she stared at Jack, recalling the details of how he'd deceived her and orchestrated this terrifying ordeal. She instinctively tugged at the ropes binding her to the chair, but the knots held fast. Her fear morphed to anger and surged through her veins, fueling her determination to break free.

"What do you want from Lana?"

"Ah, Clarice." Another chilling grin. "I'm simply here to collect on a debt. And I need Lana to help me do that. You, my dear, are the bait."

Jack pulled a small black phone from his pocket, keyed in a number, and held it to his ear. Clarice's breath hitched as she realized he was calling Lana.

Chapter Twenty-Nine

Saturday late afternoon

Lana was home alone, glancing through a magazine and taking a break from the insanity that had become her life. Abruptly, her phone rang and shattered her peace of mind. It was Jack. She debated answering it, but she knew he would just keep calling.

"Hello, Lana." Jack's voice was smooth, with a hint of malice. "I've got your dear friend here with me. Say hello, Clarice."

No! "Please, Lana," Clarice choked out. "Don't trust him."

The sound of Clarice's terrified voice almost broke her. "Where are you?"

"Montana—"

Before Clarice could finish, Jack apparently yanked the phone away from her and came back on the line. "Here's how this will go down," he said. "You're going to help me finish what we started, or else your friend will suffer the consequences. You know what you have to do. You have three hours."

What? "You know I need more time than that!"

"Why? Have you gotten rusty?"

"It's harder now, Jack. There's more security, and it could take days."

"This poor girl could starve to death by then, but have it your way. Clarice will get no food or water, and I don't think she's very comfortable, but take your time."

A heavy silence filled the house as Lana tried to figure out what to do. She should've expected this, and now it was too late. He already had her friend. *Could she actually save Clarice from this nightmare?* Lana's first instinct had been to beg Jack to let her go, but she knew it wouldn't do any good. And she refused to give him the satisfaction of hearing her beg.

"Fine. I'll move as fast as I can, but you'd better keep Clarice healthy and unharmed, or I swear I'll make you pay."

"Very well," Jack replied, with a sinister sound in his voice. "You know what I'm after. Once I get it, your friend will be released unharmed."

"I mean it, Jack. It does take more time than it used to. Give her food and water, or I promise, I will find you."

"Brave words," Jack replied, with a hint of amusement. "Let's see if you can back them up. And if I see that Tuper guy, or anyone else, sniffing around, the deal's off, and Clarice won't be the only friend you lose."

Lana hung up, feeling both relieved and terrified. She would do everything in her power to save Clarice, but she also understood the ruthlessness of the man who held her captive. Lana thought about all the people who would be hurt if she complied with Jack's request.

Lana's heart pounded in her chest as she thought about Jack's threats, his voice cold and menacing on the other end of the call. The air in the small trailer seemed to grow thick, making it difficult to breathe. She glanced around the room, from one familiar object to another: the chipped coffee mug that belonged to Mary Ann, the worn couch where she and Clarice had spent countless evenings talking and laughing together.

Lana agonized as she weighed the risks of helping Jack against the safety of her loved ones. If she gave in to his demands, who knew how far he would take it and what damage he would cause? But if she refused, would she be able to live with herself, knowing she could've saved Clarice but didn't?

Her grip tightened on her phone, and she resisted the urge to throw it against the wall. She knew she couldn't trust Jack, but she couldn't shake the image of Clarice, helpless and alone, probably tied up. Angrily swiping at the tears that threatened to spill from her eyes, she knew she had no choice but to comply with Jack's demands.

Lana took a shuddering breath and wiped her eyes. She seldom cried. She had learned to stifle her feelings at a very young age. She glanced at the framed picture of her with Clarice, Mary Ann, and Tuper—all smiling and carefree, their arms draped around one another. This makeshift family had given her a sense of belonging she hadn't had since her mother died.

She sat down at her laptop and started Jack's scheme. With each click of the keys, Lana felt her soul grow heavier, wondering if she was making the right choice. But as she envisioned her friend's face—filled with warmth, compassion, and unwavering support—she knew there was no other option. For Clarice, she would risk everything. But could she do this alone? She had to try.

~~~
~~~

The stale air in the barn hung heavy with tension, as Jack paced back and forth.

"Please." Clarice whispered, her voice cracking with desperation. "Please, just let me go."

Jack sneered, stopping for a moment to glance down at her. "Your fate isn't really in my hands anymore." He waved the phone. "It's up to your little friend, Lana. If she does what I need, maybe I'll consider letting you live."

Fear washed over her like a tidal wave. "Please," she tried again, tears streaming down her face. "I have people who care about me. They're waiting for me to come home."

"Everybody has someone who cares about them, sweetheart," Jack replied coldly, resuming his pacing. "But that doesn't change the fact that your life is hanging by a thread, and it's all up to a girl you barely know."

Clarice's mind raced, searching for any way out of this nightmare. She scanned the dimly lit room, finding no solace in the ominous shadows cast by the single stream of light that came through the broken boards in the wall. It only served to emphasize the hopelessness of her situation.

Every minute felt like an eternity, as Clarice's thoughts turned inward. Why had she been so trusting? What had made her believe that Mike—or Jack, as she now knew him to be—was a good person? Was it her own naiveté and need for attention that had led her so easily into his trap? *I'm such an old fool.*

As the seconds ticked by, the oppressive atmosphere of the barn seemed to close in around her, heightening her sense of vulnerability.

Chapter Thirty

Saturday late afternoon

Lana was frantically working on her computer when she heard a car engine. She looked out the window and saw Tuper and Dually drive up. When he knocked, she yelled at him to come in.

"Hi, Tuper," she mumbled, not looking away from her laptop until Dually nudged her arm. She petted him, giving him the attention he was seeking.

"Whatcha doin'?"

"It's nothing. Don't worry about it." She tried to sound nonchalant.

"Doesn't look like nothin' to me," Tuper pressed. He stepped into the cramped space and leaned against the cluttered countertop. "Are you okay?"

"Sure." She tried to sound perky.

"Agony, what's wrong?"

"I'm fine."

"No, you're not. Something's wrong." He looked over her shoulder at the screen filled with code. "Mind tellin' me what you're doin', kiddo?"

Lana sighed, then gave in. "I'm working on something. I can't say much, but it ain't good."

"Any word from Jack?"

Lana jerked her head up and stared at Tuper. "What have you heard?"

"Nothin', but looks to me like you have. Somethin's not right. You sound bummed, you called me Tuper instead of Pops, then you had a weird reaction when I asked about Jack. What's goin' on?"

The trailer smelled faintly of coffee and lavender, a combination that spoke of both Clarice's presence and her absence.

"Where's Clarice?" Tuper tipped his head.

"Out." Lana tried to shield her screen from Tuper's view. *Not that it would matter,* she thought. *He wouldn't understand it.* She dug her feet into the worn linoleum as if bracing for impact.

"Out where?" Tuper persisted, his scarred brow furrowing with suspicion.

Lana bit her lip and clenched her fists. She knew Tuper wouldn't let it go, and the truth weighed heavily on her chest. She stopped typing and took a deep breath. "Jack kidnapped her," she finally admitted, her eyes filling with guilt and fear.

"Dammit!" Tuper slammed his palm against the countertop, causing the hanging coffee mugs to rattle. "Why Clarice? What does he want?"

"I have to do something for him. Something I shouldn't." She told him about Jack's phone call.

"Why didn't you call me immediately?"

"Because I'm scared, Pops!" Lana shot back, her voice cracking. "I'm scared of getting attached to people, then losing them! You, Clarice, and Mary Ann... you're the closest thing I have to family, and I can't bear the thought of anything happening to any of you. I know what Jack's capable of. He threatened to kill Clarice if I told anyone. And he threatened to kill you if he finds you snooping around."

Tuper's expression softened, and he reached out to place a reassuring hand on Lana's shoulder. "We're gonna find her, kid. I promise." He swallowed. "But we've gotta work together, and that means no more secrets."

"Okay." Lana nodded and wiped away a stray tear. "I'll explain what Jack wants me to do, then we'll come up with a plan to find Clarice."

When she finished, she added, "If I do this, a lot of people will lose their life savings. And if I don't, he could kill Clarice."

"Why doesn't he hack it alone?"

"He can't. It takes three people and someone to spearhead it. That was my father's job because his skills were more advanced than Jack's. That's the spot he wants me to fill."

"Can you?"

"Yes. And the first part, I can do on my own."

"Are you as good as your father was?"

"Better. I surpassed him many years ago."

"You said it takes three people. Who's the third?"

"He didn't say."

"So, let's find Clarice," Tuper said.

"All right." Lana stood to stretch her legs. "When I asked her where she was, she said 'Montana,' followed by kind of a hissing sound. Like she was saying something that started with an S. But that's all she got out before Jack took the phone back. What do you suppose that means?"

"Could be Montana Street," Tuper suggested. "Lots of places to hide."

"Maybe." Lana sat back down at her laptop. "But that doesn't narrow it down much. There's Montana Sulphur, Montana Steel, Montana State Capitol, Montana Silver, Montana Solar, Montana Sign Co. There are just too many options. It could even be Montana City. We need more to go on."

"And we need more help, someone we can trust." Tuper pulled out his flip phone. "I know a guy who might be available."

As he stepped outside to make the call, Lana's mind returned to thoughts of Clarice. The fear of losing her gnawed at Lana's insides, threatening to consume her.

Focus! She started a browser search.

Tuper returned, his face grave. "My guy is out of state. Sorry."

"Right." Lana nodded, determination settling over her like armor. "We'll keep looking, asking around."

"We need trained eyes to help."

"You mean the police?" Lana tensed. "That scares the heck out of me. It could mean life in prison for me, but if you think that's the only way."

"Actually, I'm not sure there's much they could do. We need someone we know and can trust. Someone who has experience in surveillance and can protect himself. And someone to follow up on any leads we might get."

"You're thinking JP and Ron, aren't you?"

"Yep."

Lana pulled out her phone and called JP.

"Hi, kid," JP said when he answered. "We don't have a whole lot for you yet, except that I think we're being followed."

"I'm calling about something else. Clarice is in trouble. Jack Peterson is holding her hostage."

"Dang! What can I do?"

"We need help. Can you come here?"

"Of course."

"Maybe Ron too?" Lana felt guilty for her surge of excitement about seeing Ron.

"He's right here with me. We'll get on the first plane out."

Lana looked at the web page she had just loaded. "There's a flight out in a little less than two hours. It gets in pretty late, but one of us will be there to pick you up. Do you want me to book it?"

"Absolutely. That'll give us time to pack a few things and get to the airport."

"I'll text you the flight information."

Mary Ann walked in just as Lana was hanging up.

"What flight information? Is someone going somewhere?"

"JP and Ron are coming here."

"That's nice." Mary Ann looked from Lana to Tuper, obviously sensing something was wrong. "What's going on?"

"Clarice is being held hostage," Lana blurted, then wished she had used more tact.

"No!" Mary Ann screamed.

Tuper put his arm around her and led her to a living room chair as she sobbed and hurled questions at them. Tuper explained what had happened, then added, "You need to calm down because we need your help to find her."

Mary Ann took a deep breath, then reached for a tissue and blew her nose. Between gasps she asked, "What can I do?"

"I need you to go to Jack's hotel and watch to see if he comes or goes."

Lana looked at Tuper. "Are you sure? Wouldn't that put her in danger?"

"No. Because she's going to do everything exactly as I tell her. Aren't you, Mary Ann?"

Mary Ann nodded. Lana delved back into her search.

"You cannot go inside the motel," Tuper cautioned. "And you cannot confront him. He may not come back or he may not even be registered there anymore. Either way, he'll be trying hard not to lead us to Clarice."

Lana stopped typing. "He's still registered at the Residence Inn, but that might be a ruse. I'll check to see if he's registered somewhere else too."

"Good idea," Tuper said. "In the meantime, we need the Residence Inn covered. Can you handle that, Mary Ann?"

She sighed and nodded.

"Can you do it without exposing yourself or confronting Jack? Because if you do, you'll be putting Clarice in more danger, as well as yourself."

"I can do it."

"Damn straight you can." Tuper squeezed her shoulder. "Let's get to it. We've got a friend to save and a snake to deal with."

Chapter Thirty-One

Saturday night

"We've got to cover all our bases," Lana said, as she, Tuper, and Mary Ann brainstormed ideas at the dining room table. "I'll check for online activity related to Clarice and see if we can find anything that way."

"Good idea." Tuper tapped a gnarled finger against his forehead. "I'll get out and talk to some folks. Montana Street is a big place, but I'll see what I can do."

"It's not Montana Street," Mary Ann said.

"What do you mean?" Lana asked.

"It's Montana Avenue."

"She's right," Tuper said.

Mary Ann clarified her thinking. "If Clarice was talking about North Montana, she might just call it Montana. But the road splits around Breckenridge and becomes South Montana Avenue. Most likely, she would say that, not Montana South."

"True," Tuper said. "But she didn't have time to say much, so maybe the S sound she made was for south. I'm just not sure where to start searching." He glanced from Lana to Mary Ann. "When did either of you last see her?"

"This morning when she left for work," Lana said.

"Same here." Mary Ann nodded. "She started early this morning so she got off about two, maybe even one."

"Then I'll start with Nickels Bar. Maybe someone saw her leave or knows where she went after work."

"All right, Pops." Lana gave him a look. "You sure you don't want me to come with you?"

Tuper shook his head. "I can handle it. Besides, you've got your computer stuff to do for Jack, in case it comes to that, right?"

"Unfortunately." She glared at her laptop as if it had personally offended her.

"You don't happen to have a photo of Clarice, do you?"

"I've got plenty on my phone, and I could send you one if you didn't have that thirty-year-old flip phone."

Mary Ann jumped up and headed for her bedroom. She returned, carrying a printed snapshot and handed it to Tuper.

"Thanks," Tuper said. "Let's go."

Mary Ann grabbed her keys and followed him.

"Remember, if you need help... " Lana said.

"Agony, I've been doing this longer than you've been alive." Tuper's tone was gentle but firm. "Trust me. I can take care of myself. And I'll let you know if I find out anything."

"Okay." Lana nodded, though her brow remained furrowed. "Just be careful, all right? Both of you."

"Always." Tuper tipped his hat, then strode out, leaving Lana alone with her thoughts and the hum of her laptop.

~~~

As Tuper walked past two men puffing away on cigarettes outside of Nickels Bar, the scent of smoke and
~~~

whiskey filled his nostrils. The smell immediately reminded him of a time in his life when everything was filled with possibility and yet still simple. People are much different now, he thought as he opened the door to the bar. He scanned the room, eyeing each of the patrons with a sternness that made them look away. He stepped up to the counter and cleared his throat to get the barkeep's attention.

"Kitty, have you seen Clarice?"

"Not since she left." Kitty was a stocky woman with short-cropped hair and a scar on her neck. "About fifteen minutes after her shift ended at one."

"Was she alone?"

"She left alone, but I saw her talking in the parking lot to that guy, Mike, she just started dating. Why?"

"What does he look like?"

"Tall, handsome, a little grey in his hair, amazing blue eyes, and always wears a suit."

"Dang." Tuper thanked Kitty, then glanced down the counter at a few regulars. "Any of you see Clarice this afternoon after she left here?"

People murmured amongst themselves, then, a guy in the corner spoke up. "She was leaving just when I was coming in. She was with that suit. He's been hanging around her lately."

"Do you know where they went?"

"I heard them mention lunch, but didn't catch where."

"Thanks." Tuper started to leave, but Kitty called out after him. "Is Clarice in some kind of trouble?"

Tuper tensed. "I'm not sure, ma'am. I'm just trying to help her out." He walked away, his stomach churning with worry. In the parking lot, Tuper called Lana.

"You got something?" she asked.

"You know that fellow, Mike, Clarice went out with?"

"Yeah?"

"It's Jack. She left with him this afternoon."

"That snake. He set her up."

"Seems so." Tuper looked around and saw Clarice's burgundy Pontiac Supreme with the spoiler. "Her car is still here in the parking lot. We'll pick it up later. Right now, I'll hit the restaurants on South Montana. If someone saw her at lunch, maybe they can tell us something."

"Good plan."

"It's a plan. Probably not a good one, but I can't just sit still."

Tuper hung up and drove to South Montana where he methodically checked each restaurant, scanning the customers, and showing her photo to the employees. He rushed from one establishment to the next, his frustration mounting with each disappointment.

Where are you, Clarice? A sinking feeling settled deep in his gut, but he couldn't give up.

As the rain began to fall again from the dark night sky, Tuper's search grew more urgent, fueled by the knowledge that they were running out of time. He feared that Clarice was in some dark place, alone and scared to death, maybe even getting soaked.

Tuper hurried back to his car, his heart heavy. He pulled out his phone, keying in a number he knew by heart, and waited for the call to connect.

"Norm, it's Tuper. I need your help. My friend, Clarice, is missing, and I'm running out of time."

"Clarice from Nickels?"

"That's the one. Can you ask around, check if anyone's seen her?" Tuper gave him a few more details about where she was last spotted.

"Of course, Tuper. I'll do my best."

"Thanks, Norm." Tuper ended the call and stowed the phone back in his pocket. He took a deep breath, steeling himself for a long night.

Chapter Thirty-Two

Saturday night

Back in the trailer, Lana hunched over her computer, switching between working on Jack's scheme and searching for clues that might lead to Clarice. The tension in her neck and shoulders ached, but she couldn't slow down, let alone stop. Her only comfort came from Dually who lay by her feet providing a warm sense of security.

"Come on, come on," she whispered as she worked. The weight of Clarice's life on her shoulders threatened to crush her.

"Think, Lana, think," she urged herself, pausing to rub her temples. A sudden thought struck her, and she raced to search through old messages between Clarice and herself.

As Lana continued her search, a ping from her computer caught her attention. It was a notification from one of Clarice's social media profiles. She had been tagged in an older photo by someone named *Montana*. A chill ran down Lana's spine. Was it just a coincidence, or did this person hold the key to finding Clarice?

She called Tuper to update him as she searched for *Montana's* contact information.

"Hey, Pops," she said, feeling excited. "I stumbled on something that might help us." She gave him the name and address.

"Good work," Tuper replied. "Before I go, I think I'll check with Mary Ann. After that, I'll pick up the guys at the airport. I'll let you know what I find out."

~~~

Tuper was close to the Residence Inn, so he decided to drop in and check on Mary Ann instead of calling. She was parked in a back corner, but she had a good view of the front entrance.

Tuper parked next to her red Honda Civic and switched cars without getting too wet.

Mary Ann seemed pleased to have the company.

"I think I'm in a good spot," she said. "I can't see the side door, but even if he came out that way, he'd have to get to his car. And in this rain, I figure he wouldn't want to walk too far."

Tuper studied the setup. In the dim light of the parking lot, he could just make out Jack's SUV, its black paint reflecting the wet pavement like a sinister mirror. The lights from the motel were bright enough that they could easily see if someone got inside the car, driver or passenger.

"Good thinkin'," Tuper said. "But I stopped to ask about somethin' Lana found on Fastbook, or Facejerk, or whatever it's called."

"It's Facebook." Mary Ann smiled for the first time since she'd heard about Clarice. "But Lana already called me about it. There is a woman we know who goes by Montana, but I can't imagine there's any connection. She's eighty-five and bedridden. Her granddaughter
~~~

gave her a tablet a few years back and taught her how to work Facebook so she could connect with people."

"I can't imagine how she'd fit into this whole mess."

Mary Ann shrugged. "She doesn't live far from here. You could run by her apartment, but I'm sure she's asleep by now."

"I think I'll do just that."

Mary Ann gripped the steering wheel tightly. "We'll find her, won't we, Tuper?"

"You bet we will."

Tuper left and drove to the address Lana had given him. The rain had stopped, at least for the moment, making it easier to see. He circled the block twice looking for a car that might belong to Jack. Since they had just seen his SUV at the hotel, he was looking for another rental, but found none. From there he drove to the airport.

The rain intensified, splattering against the windows of Tuper's beat-up car as he pulled up to the baggage claim area at the Helena Regional Airport. The pungent smell of wet leather and dog hair filled the air inside the cab, a scent Tuper had come to find oddly comforting. He adjusted his cowboy hat and peered through the windshield, scanning the doors for JP and Ron.

"Dang rain," he muttered. "Not the best welcome for out-of-towners."

Tuper finally spotted two men exiting the small airport. JP, wearing his signature Stetson hat, walked with an air of quiet confidence. Beside him, Ron hunched his shoulders against the rain, his expression hard to read.

Tuper honked his horn to get their attention. By the time they reached his car, their clothes were soaked from the downpour.

"Thanks for coming, boys," Tuper said sincerely, as they climbed into the backseat. "We sure need your help."

"Of course." JP's voice was steady despite the late hour and his wet clothes. "You know we'd do anything for you and Lana."

"Let's just hope we're not too late," Ron added.

Chapter Thirty-Three

Late Saturday night

Lana's phone buzzed with an incoming call from Jack. She hesitated, knowing that hearing Clarice's voice would only make this situation more real, more urgent, but she had to do it.

"Are you done yet?" Jack asked.

"No. I told you this would take some time."

"Your friend doesn't have much time. She's cold, hungry, and scared. And it's very dark here, and I'm about to leave. You might want to hurry up."

"Let me talk to her," Lana demanded, her voice cracking as she tried to keep her emotions in check.

"Fine." He was cool and composed. "But remember, one wrong word and it's over for her." Lana heard him give Clarice the same warning, only he added that he would kill Mary Ann, Tuper, and her if she even attempted to tell where she was.

As Clarice's voice came through the line, Lana felt a mixture of relief and desperation wash over her. They exchanged brief pleasantries, then Clarice asked, through chattering teeth, "How is Tuper holding up? I know he plays poker a lot when he's upset, and I'm sure he's upset now."

That struck Lana as odd, but she went along. "He's doing okay, gambling a little, but not off the deep end."

"Just don't let him dig out his lucky hat from that storage place. That means he's really lost it."

Clarice was trying to give her clues, but Lana didn't know what any of it meant. "I won't. Are you okay? You sound cold."

"I am, but I'll make it. Give Mary Ann my love."

In the background, Jack snapped, "That's enough."

Assuming Jack had the phone now, Lana warned, "You'd better get Clarice something to keep warm. If she gets pneumonia, she won't make it. She has a poor immune system. And if she doesn't live, I'm not doing one single thing for you."

"Yeah, yeah."

"I mean it, Jack. I will not do one thing to help you, and I'll send everything straight to the feds."

He scoffed. "You won't do that because you'll implicate yourself."

"You don't know me anymore, Jack. I'm not the selfish little girl I used to be. I have people who love me, and who I love, and it's amazing what a person is willing to do for their loved ones."

"Lana," he said, speaking slowly. "You're running out of time."

"I'm working as fast as I can."

"You'd better be."

"I know you, Jack. I wouldn't try to buffalo you. I'm not an idiot."

"We'll see. Keep in mind that time's running out, Lana." Jack's voice was low and menacing. "Don't forget what's at stake here." He hung up.

Lana paced the small trailer, her mind racing. A knock at the door startled her. She opened it to find Tuper and JP standing outside, all soaking wet.

Lana looked behind them for Ron, but didn't see him. "Come in and get warm and dry."

The men stepped in and took off their wet coats.

"He's comin'," Tuper said.

"Who?" Lana asked.

"Ron. That's who you're lookin' for, ain't it?" Without letting her answer, he went on. "He's bringing the rental car."

"Good."

"Are you okay?" Tuper asked. "You seem upset."

"Let me get you something hot to drink, then I'll explain."

Lana went in the kitchen and turned the teapot on. She poured JP a cup of coffee she had brewed earlier. When she returned, Ron was in the room. Their eyes caught one another's momentarily. Time seemed to stop for a second, until Tuper interrupted.

"Okay, Lana, spill. What's going on?"

Trembling, Lana recounted what had just happened—the threatening call from Jack and the ultimatum he'd given her. Her friends listened intently, their expressions tight with stress. "He let me talk to Clarice for a minute, and she was so cold, she was shaking. I could hear it in her voice."

"That jackass," Tuper said.

"I think she was trying to tell us where she is."

"What exactly did she say?"

Lana repeated Clarice's remark about Tuper playing poker. "It was a weird thing to say, right? It sounded like code to me."

"It is. Clarice knows I never gamble when I'm upset, especially poker. Can't focus." Tuper swallowed hard.

"Did she say anything else?"

"She said not to let you dig your lucky hat out of that storage place."

"Clarice is in Montana City in an old barn." Tuper sounded certain.

"How did you get that from what she said?" JP asked.

"Montana City makes sense," Lana said. "Because that's your favorite place to play poker. That would explain her first comment. But why a barn?"

"Because I used to keep a bunch of stuff in an old barn. I never used a storage place."

"Was it in Montana City?"

"No, but she went with me there once to get my old hat."

"To go gambling?"

"No." Tuper sounded irritated. "But that old barn is torn down, so it can't be there. It must be another barn in Montana City."

"Okay," Ron said. "I'm completely lost."

"She mentioned my gambling to tell us it was Montana City. She mentioned the 'lucky hat' to tell us she was in a barn. She specifically said it was in a storage place, but I never used a storage place. I used an old barn."

"So, what do we do now?" JP asked.

"As much as I hate to leave Clarice out there all night, there ain't much we can do in the dark and rain." He turned to Ron. "I'll take you to relieve Mary Ann, if you're all right with that."

"Wherever you need me," Ron said.

"Then I'll take Mary Ann to pick up Clarice's car at Nickels. She keeps Clarice's extra key with her. JP, you get some sleep 'cuz we're startin' real early in the morning. We don't want to miss a minute of daylight."

Lana made Ron a thermos of coffee to get him through the night, then he and Tuper left.

~~~

The storm raged on as Tuper navigated the slick roads with a not-so-steady hand. He glanced over at Ron. "You ready to take over watchin' Jack's hotel?" he asked gruffly.

"Absolutely," Ron replied. "Just tell me what I need to do."

"Just keep an eye on the hotel entrance and on Jack's black SUV." Tuper gave him the license number. "If you see him, call me immediately He was with Clarice when he called Lana, so he ain't at the motel, which means he has some other vehicle. He probably rented another car, but we don't know when he might show up."

"I'm sure he wouldn't leave a paper trail with an Uber or taxi."

As they pulled into the motel's parking lot, they spotted Mary Ann hunched in her car, eyes locked on Jack's vehicle. The rain pelted against her windshield, creating a chaotic pattern of droplets. Tuper rolled down his window, letting the cool air and dampness invade the car.

"Ron's here to relieve you," he called out, his voice barely audible over the drumming rain.

"Good." She sighed, her body sagging with exhaustion. Then she bravely added, "I'm okay if you need Ron somewhere else."
~~~

"We're good. You take a break," Tuper advised, his concern genuine. "Ron will handle it from here."

With a nod of gratitude, Mary Ann exited her car and handed the keys to Ron. "Don't lose sight of him," she warned, her voice laced with worry.

"I won't," Ron promised, as he settled into the driver's seat.

Tuper and Mary Ann drove toward Nickels Bar, the rain blurring Tuper's vision as the wipers struggled to keep up with the deluge. He gripped the steering wheel tighter, his knuckles white.

"Dang this rain," he said. "Makes it near impossible to see anything."

"Slow down a bit, Toop," Mary Ann cautioned gently. "I'm just so scared for her."

"She's okay right now," Tuper said. "Lana talked to her a bit ago. She said to tell you she loved you and that she's okay. Clarice even gave some hints that might help us find her." Tuper explained about the gambling and the barn, but left out the part about Clarice being cold.

As they pulled into Nickels' parking lot near Clarice's car, the rain continued its relentless assault.

Tuper stepped out of the car, rain pelting his hat and running down the brim, as he surveyed the darkened building. Nickels Bar stood silent and unassuming, its neon sign casting an eerie glow onto the slick pavement. The storm seemed to echo the turmoil within him, a relentless tempest of worry and determination.

Tuper checked Clarice's car before letting Mary Ann get inside. "Go home and get some sleep. We'll need you again tomorrow."

"We're not going to let him win, are we, Toop?" Mary Ann asked.

"Not on my watch!"

~~~

Inside the trailer, Lana hunched over her laptop, her eyes aching from staring at the screen. She tapped her foot impatiently against the leg of her chair. She had started working on Jack's scheme, but her heart wasn't in it. Instead, she was focused on finding him and saving Clarice.

"Come on," she said under her breath, her fingers soaring across the keyboard as she hacked into every possible surveillance system, GPS tracker, and security camera feed she could think of. "Show your face." The soft tapping sounds echoed in the dim room. Her green eyes darted across the screen at the lines of code and encrypted information unfolding before her.

"Come on, Jack," she said. "Where are you hiding?"

As if in response, a new string of information flickered into view, revealing the location of a motel and rental car, both registered to Jack.

A triumphant smirk played upon Lana's lips as Tuper returned home. "Got him," she announced. "He's at the Hilton DoubleTree, Pops. And he has a second rental car. You're looking for a silver Lexus with license plate Y43-MCP."

Tuper nodded. "Good work. Call Ron and let him know. And set an alarm for four, in case I don't wake up. We're goin' after that snake tomorrow."
~~~

Chapter Thirty-Four

When the alarm went off at four, Lana was already awake, thinking about her next move. She had tossed and turned for the few hours she'd been down, unable to block out the images of Clarice in a cold, dark barn by herself. Lana rolled off the sofa, strolled past JP asleep on the floor, and went straight to her laptop, still open on the dining room table. Before she sat down, she remembered she was supposed to wake Tuper, then headed down the hall to Clarice's room where Tuper had slept.

Just then he opened the door. "Anyone else up yet?"

"Just you and me."

Lana walked back and sat down, trying to be quiet, but Mary Ann soon meandered into the dining area.

"Good morning," she said. "I'll put coffee on." She offered to make breakfast too, but Lana and Tuper both declined. When JP came into the kitchen to get coffee, shortly thereafter, she offered again and got the same response. "Okay, but I'm making sandwiches for you all to take along."

No one objected.

"So, what's the plan?" Mary Ann asked.

"We decided that Ron would switch to the new motel and watch for any sign of Jack," Lana said. "JP will stake out the edge of Montana City to watch for Jack's vehicle. Tuper's headed into the town to find empty barns. And I'll stay on the computer trying to narrow down the list of warehouses. And I'll work on Jack's stuff in case we have to be ready for him."

"What can I do?"

"Get some more sleep. If this goes on very long, we'll need you to relieve people."

"I am awfully tired, but I'm not sure I can sleep."

"Can you try?" Tuper chimed in.

"I will, but promise me you'll wake me up if I can help."

"We promise," Tuper said.

"Okay. I'll finish making sandwiches and pack you guys each a lunch. You have to eat."

Lana went back to her laptop. "We've got to find that barn or warehouse."

"Yep," Tuper agreed. "I'm goin' to Montana City right now."

"It's awfully early. Will anyone be up at this hour?" Lana asked.

"I know a guy."

"Of course, you do," Lana said. "I'll search public records for farms that have been abandoned or just empty for quite a while."

"Good." Tuper pulled on his boots and adjusted his hat. Mary Ann handed him a lunch bag, then gave one to JP. Tuper started for the door. "You can follow me, JP. You know what exit to take, right?"

"Sure do," JP said.

~~~
~~~

Driving the blue Hyundai rental car, JP followed Tuper and exited the highway just before entering the small town as he'd been instructed.

The entrance to Montana City loomed in the darkness a picture of eerie desolation. A weathered wooden sign, its paint peeling and letters barely legible, creaked as it swayed in the early morning breeze. An abandoned gas station with shattered windows sat nearby, its rusty fuel pumps standing like silent sentinels, guarding the remnants of a bygone era. JP parked next to it, the engine idling softly, waiting for any sign of Jack's rental car. He had a perfect view of the highway.

Silver sedan, Y43-MCP, he reminded himself.

The sound of laughter brought JP's attention to a group of rowdy teenagers emerging from a nearby wooded area, their voices echoing in the quiet morning air. He observed them for a moment, taking in their carefree demeanor, and couldn't help but feel nostalgic for simpler times when the world felt less treacherous.

He shook off the distraction and refocused on the entrance to Montana City. There he sat, watching and waiting.

Chapter Thirty-Five

Sunday morning

Montana City welcomed the gentle patter of raindrops on quiet streets, remnants of the storm that had passed through in the night. The first blush of dawn illuminated the Victorian-style buildings lining Main Street. At five in the morning, the air was cold and crisp. A large public park with several hiking trails beckoned those who sought respite from the city's confines, but it was still too early for anyone to venture out.

As the town slept, Tuper walked downtown, his worn cowboy hat shielding his eyes from the drizzle. He had his flip phone in his pocket, the old-fashioned gadget a testament to his resistance to change. His hip held his holstered pistol at the ready.

The urgency of his search for empty barns where Clarice could be hidden weighed heavily on him as he walked along Main Street, looking for cafés or coffee shops that might be open. His best bet was to talk to locals. As the town began to stir, Tuper approached a small diner. The smell of fresh coffee and frying bacon drifted through the air, drawing locals in from the cold rain. Tuper headed inside and took a seat at the counter, scanning the room for potential sources of information.

"Good morning, Toop," the waitress said, smiling coyly. She was a woman in her late thirties with hair that was dyed too blonde, nails that were too long and too red. Her face was unnaturally pale, probably from the contrast of her bright orange-red lipstick, but she did her job well.

"Hi, Bonnie. How's my sweetheart this mornin'?"

"I'm good," she said. "What brings you here so early?" She gave him a furtive glance. "Or have you been at the poker tables all night?"

"Nope. I'm trying to find someone who's in deep trouble." He lowered his voice. "My friend was kidnapped, and I think she's in an abandoned building somewhere here in Montana City."

"Oh no! That's terrible. But why are you being so secretive? You know this whole town would come out and help if you asked."

"That's exactly why I can't. It's too risky. If the word gets out, she'll be moved and this is the only real lead we've had so far."

"I won't say a word, Toop. But what can I do to help?"

"I'm looking for abandoned buildings, most likely a barn or a warehouse. Since you've lived here most of your life. I figured you'd know."

"There's the old mill that's been empty since before I was born. And that old warehouse down by Prickly Pear Creek, just off Highway 518." Several customers came in and Bonnie scooted over to serve them. When she returned, she said, "There are several old barns around here. A couple that come to mind are the Stevens' old place on Sawmill Road and the Clark farm on Jackson Creek."

"Thanks, Bonnie, that ought to get me started." He stood to leave.

"Oh, and the Tanner farm has been empty over a year now."

"Is that the one on Lump Gulch Road?"

"That's it, but I heard someone bought it recently, so it may not be uninhabited anymore."

Tuper stepped out of the cozy restaurant into the cold rain. The morning was beginning to brighten, despite the persistent drizzle that hung in the air. He made his way down the street, splashing through shallow puddles on the sidewalk. He called Lana and asked her to check out three farms: the Stevens' place on Sawmill Road, the Clark farm on Jackson Creek, and the Tanner farm on Lump Gulch Road. Then he got into his car and drove to the warehouse by Prickly Pear Creek.

There were no cars around, and no footprints in the mud. But even if someone had been there recently, the rain would've washed them away. He located a rusted door on the side of the warehouse, its hinges creaking in protest as he forced it open. The darkness inside seemed to swallow him whole, and he fumbled in his pocket for a flashlight. With a click, a beam of light sliced through the gloom, revealing dusty crates and cobwebs hanging heavy from the rafters. The air was thick with the scent of mildew and decay.

"Clarice," he called out softly, "You here?"

There was only silence. Tuper made his way through the building but found nothing. No signs that there had been any recent activity.

"Dang it," he cursed, wiping his brow. "Where are you, Clarice?"

Chapter Thirty-Six

Sunday morning

Tuper called Lana for an update, certain she was working in her digital world. "Did you come up with anything?" he asked.

"I've scanned a lot of real estate websites and searched for abandoned buildings of all kinds. I've hacked into several databases, including county property records, searching for something that could lead us to Clarice."

"Anything?" Tuper asked.

"Maybe," she replied, glancing at her screen. "I found a few warehouses that are currently vacant. "There's an old mill on—"

"I know where that is. What else?"

"And a warehouse near Prickly Pear Creek."

"You can cross that off your list. I was just there. No sign of recent life anywhere around."

"I'm still looking into the farms. I'll call you when I have something."

"Okay. I'm headed to the old mill."

It didn't take long to get there. Tuper had been to the mill many times as a child when it was in its full glory. A broken-down truck sat in the parking area, but Tuper didn't see anyone around. He found an unlocked side door and went inside the mill.

Tuper scanned the area for any signs of life. The place was eerily quiet and the air was musty. The metal walls were rusted and paint-chipped, and the windows were smashed inward.

Tuper felt a surge of determination. Floorboards creaked as he walked around the mill, pushing open doors and peering behind old machinery. He was about to turn back when he noticed something strange. In the far corner of the main room, a faint yellow light came from a closed door. Tuper stopped in his tracks and cautiously approached the door, instinctively reaching for the handle. He opened it slowly, then realized it led outside. Another dead end. He pulled out his phone and keyed in Lana's number. "Nothin' at this one. On to the next."

"Got it, Pops," Lana replied. "I'll keep digging, see if I can find anything else."

"Make any headway on the barns?"

"You can skip the Stevens' place on Sawmill Road. They tore it down a few weeks ago. I'm still working on the other two."

"Appreciate it," Tuper said, ending the call. He climbed back into his car and sped off toward the Clark farm on Jackson Creek.

~~~

Meanwhile, Ron waited in Mary Ann's Honda Civic across from the DoubleTree Hotel, his eyes glued to the only parking lot entrance. He'd been watching the place for hours, waiting for any sign of the silver sedan Jack had rented. When he saw it approach, he grabbed his binoculars and steadied his visual on the license plate:
~~~

Y43-MCP. That was him. His pulse quickened and he fumbled for his cellphone sitting on the console. He quickly called JP, without taking his eyes off Jack as the man exited his car and entered the hotel.

"Jack just went into his hotel."

"Alone?"

"Yes."

"I'll let Tuper know. Can you call Lana?"

"Sure." Ron felt a little twinge at the thought. He hadn't had a chance to talk to her yet. There was too much else going on. He certainly didn't want to take up her valuable time or distract her from her effort to find Clarice.

"Let me know right away if he leaves," JP said. "And, Ron, don't approach him, but follow him if he leaves."

"Will do." Ron hung up and called Lana. "Good morning again," he said when she answered. "I wanted to let you know that Jack is at his hotel."

"Good. This might be the break we needed. Hopefully, he'll lead us to Clarice."

"That would be great. Are you making any progress on the search for the abandoned building?"

"There's quite a few in Montana City, but I've found three warehouses of sorts. And Tuper found three more abandoned farms. We can't be certain it's actually a warehouse, so we're trying everything that's empty. We're really just guessing. I think our best bet is you right now. Watch Jack closely. Are you sure you'll see him if he leaves? Because I can send Mary Ann over to watch from a different angle. We can't afford to lose sight of him now. It might—"

Ron interrupted her. "Lana, he can't drive away without me seeing him. Even if he goes on foot, he has to leave the hotel parking lot to get away. I've examined the area, and there's a large fence around the back, so unless he climbs over it, he has to either walk or drive out the front. But if you'd feel better, go ahead and send Mary Ann. Just give her my number and tell her to call me so I can situate her at the best vantage point."

"It'll give her something to do. She can't sleep, and she's driving me crazy."

Ron chuckled. "Sounds like a plan. Just tell her to be careful and not let Jack see her, or it might ruin our only chance of finding Clarice."

A half hour passed and there was no sign of Jack or Mary Ann. Ron waited patiently, his eyes never leaving the front of the hotel. He jumped when his phone rang.

It was Mary Ann. "I'm here. I just pulled into the lot next door to the hotel."

"What are you driving?"

"Clarice's car, the burgundy Pontiac."

"I see you," Ron said. "That's not a good spot though."

"Where should I go?"

Before Ron could give her a direction, he saw Jack step out of the hotel and scan the area prior to walking toward his car. "Oh no! He's walking in your direction. Stay in your car. He's about twenty feet from you."

"I can see him. He's texting."

Just then a shot rang out, and Jack fell to the ground.

Chapter Thirty-Seven

Sunday morning

As Ron got out of the car, a few people in the parking lot ran to the body to offer assistance. Seconds later, others spilled out of the hotel and ran toward Jack's body, lying there lifeless, blood rolling down his cheek. Ron hurried toward the crowd. He heard someone yell, "Call 9-1-1." The onlookers sprang into action, grabbing for cellphones, so Ron didn't bother. Instead, he dashed over amongst the crowd to see if Jack was alive and to check on Mary Ann.

Just as he reached the huddle of people, he saw Mary Ann hustling toward her Pontiac. A man knelt at Jack's side checking for a pulse, while others stood around staring at the body. A little hole was visible in Jack's temple, right above his left eye. Blood welled from it and spilled down his face, with a few drops landing on the concrete.

"Is he dead?" a woman screamed.

"Yes," the man examining him said, with a grim expression. "He was hit right in the head. Whoever did this was a great shot."

Ron sprinted toward Mary Ann's car just as she slammed the door shut. His breath coming in ragged gasps, he asked, "Are you okay?"

"I... I'm fine, just scared." She broke down into sobs. "How will we find Clarice now?"

"Don't worry. Lana and Tuper have other ways."

Mary Ann held out a small black cellphone. Her hand shaking. "Do you think this will help?"

"Where did that come from?"

"It's Jack's. It flew out of his hand toward me when he was shot. I got out and picked it up. I thought it might help Lana."

"That was reckless, Mary Ann," Ron hissed. "You're tampering with evidence."

"I didn't think...I just reacted," she whispered apologetically. "All I could think about was finding Clarice."

"I'm sorry." Ron patted her on the back. "You did a brave thing, and it may help us find your sister." He locked eyes with her for a moment, then glanced around nervously. "Go! Before someone spots you and pegs you as a witness. If the shooter saw you, he may be concerned that there's information on the phone leading to him. Not to mention the cops will be here any minute."

Mary Ann nodded numbly, wiping her tears as she started the engine. But she didn't move.

"Are you okay to drive?"

"Yes."

"Then please go. Take the phone to Lana. I'll wait here a bit to see what happens next, and to find out for sure if he's dead or alive."

Mary Ann drove off just as sirens started to blare. A whole entourage of emergency vehicles were approaching. Ron avoided the crowd, now twice the size, that had gathered around Jack, as he hurried back to his car. He called JP and gave him the unexpected update.

Chapter Thirty-Eight

Sunday afternoon

As Tuper neared the Clark farm, his phone rang again. It was JP calling to tell him Jack had been shot.

"Dag nabbit!" Tuper shouted. "That just made it a whole lot harder."

"There's no need for me to stay here," JP said. "What can I do?"

"Check in with Lana. She can tell you where the Clark farmhouse is. You can head that way. I should get there just before you do."

Tuper hung up and drove the rest of the way to the Clark homestead, his senses on high alert. He scanned the area, noting the rusted metal gates and overgrown weeds that choked the entrance. The wind whispered through the surrounding trees, carrying a faint chill that made Tuper pull his hat down tighter on his head. At least the rain had stopped.

The gravel crunched under his feet as he approached another abandoned building, the late afternoon light starting to fade.

A few minutes later JP arrived. They entered the barn first and came up empty.

"Dang it! I've searched every empty building in this forsaken town. Where the hell is Clarice?" Tuper's heart was strained with worry. He couldn't help but picture Clarice's slender body bound and gagged and shivering somewhere.

JP sighed, running a hand through his thick, dark hair. "I know, Tuper. But we're going to find her. We have to."

As they entered the house, Tuper couldn't shake the feeling of dread that gripped his chest. The air was musty, heavy with the scent of rusted metal and decay. He glanced around the dimly lit space, noting some old furniture and dusty garage bags.

Now that Jack was dead, Tuper was no longer concerned that the man would be lurking in the shadows, so he called out. "Clarice? You here?" His voice echoed off the walls.

"Clarice!" JP shouted, desperation seeping into his tone.

They searched the house top to bottom, their frustration growing with each passing minute. They came across a pile of discarded junk that looked like it had been recently disturbed. Tuper glanced at JP. "What do you think?"

"Let's dig in and pray she's not buried here," JP said.

They frantically threw debris off the pile until they were certain she wasn't there. They both exhaled a sigh of relief.

"I don't know how much more of this I can take," Tuper admitted, rubbing his facial scar. "We're runnin' out of time, and I can't bear the thought of anything happening to that sweet woman."

"Neither can I, Tuper." JP said. "But we can't lose hope. Jack Peterson may be dead, but that doesn't mean we're out of options."

"Options?" Tuper snorted, his age showing in his sagging shoulders. "We've searched high and low, talked to every dang person I dared to in this town, and still no sign of her. I'm startin' to think we'll never find her."

"Come on, Tuper. You know better than that." JP clapped a hand on Tuper's shoulder, his gaze steady and determined. "We're not done yet. Lana said there was another farmstead, the Tanner place on Lump Gulch Road."

Tuper nodded, and they headed for their cars. "Let's get back to it. I only wish Jack wasn't dead, so I could kill him myself."

Tuper's phone buzzed, the screen illuminating with Lana's name. He answered on the first ring, impatient for any news.

"Hey, Pops," Lana's voice crackled through the speaker. "I've got something for you. I hacked into local property records and found a list of houses around Montana City that have been empty a while."

"I'm with JP. Send it to him," Tuper said.

"Already done," Lana replied.

Within moments, a text message appeared on JP's phone, displaying a series of addresses scattered throughout Montana City. Tuper and JP exchanged a glance, the weight of their task settling heavily on their shoulders.

"We still have the Tanner place, so we'll check that out first," Tuper said to Lana. "Did you find anything helpful about it?"

"Nothing unusual, so I guess you'd better check it out. And I have another list of properties that might be worth checking if that first one doesn't produce results. Ron's on his way with half the list. He wanted to help, and since there's nothing more to do about Jack, I sent him your way."

"Good. We can cover more ground. I'll take JP with me. He can follow the list and get directions."

"That's smart," Lana said.

"Let's get to it." JP climbed into Tuper's car.

They went first to the Tanner farm, but it was a bust. Then they drove from house to house. At each location, they were met with locked doors, boarded-up windows, and some suspicious neighbors eyeing them warily from behind curtains. But Tuper and JP were undeterred.

"Dang deadbolts," Tuper said as he struggled with yet another locked door. His frustration simmered like a boiling pot, threatening to spill over. He walked around to the back of the house and broke the window on the door. Then reached in and grabbed the knob and turned it. "Dang lock isn't gonna keep me out."

They searched the house without finding Clarice.

As they stepped back outside, a voice called from across the street. "Hey, Tuper!"

Squinting into the fading light, he recognized an old friend, Royce, leaning against his truck.

"Royce, what brings you here?" Tuper asked, trying to sound casual.

"I live next door, but I was about to ask you the same thing."

Tuper explained about their search for Clarice.

"I'm awful sorry. I'd offer to help, but I gotta get to work. You checked the old mine shaft yet?"

Tuper exchanged a glance with JP, who shrugged. "No. Can't say we have. Didn't think anyone would stash her there."

"Seems like a good place to hide someone, if you ask me," Royce suggested. "Might be worth checking out before it gets too dark."

"Appreciate the tip, Royce," Tuper said, tipping his hat. With newfound purpose, he and JP climbed back into their car and sped off toward the old mine shaft. They still had a few houses to go on their list, and Ron was still working on his, but they decided this might be a better move.

The road leading to the mine was rough and uneven, jostling them in their seats. As they drew closer, Tuper couldn't help but feel a chill run down his spine. The entrance loomed ahead like a gaping maw, swallowing the last light of day.

"Stay sharp, JP," Tuper warned as they approached on foot, flashlights in hand. "No telling what we might find in there."

"Roger that."

As they ventured deep into the mine, the air grew colder and danker. The smell of damp earth and decay hung heavy, making it difficult to breathe. Tuper pushed aside his mounting fear, focusing instead on the hope of finding Clarice alive.

They went as deep into the old silver mine as they dared, but came up with nothing. As they exited, both their phones lit up with messages from Lana.

As they walked to the car, JP called and put Lana on speaker. "I've got something," she blurted. "There's an old farmhouse on Jackson Creek, not too far from the Clark place. It's only been empty a few months, but from the aerial view, it looks pretty damaged. And get this. It was leased last month to a company called Hackerty Enterprises."

"Who's that?" JP asked.

"It's a name Jack has used in the past for a shell company."

"We're on our way. Give me the address."

Lana complied and gave him some basic directions.

"Do you know where to go?" JP asked Tuper.

"I shore do."

"Lana, I don't understand. Why would Jack use a name you know about?"

"I gathered a lot of intel on him that he never knew I had. I thought it might come in handy someday."

"Let's hope today's the day."

Chapter Thirty-Nine

Sunday early evening

Tuper and JP drove to the farm that Lana thought had been leased by Jack. With a sense of dread, Tuper surveyed the crumbling farmstead. Overgrown fields stretched as far as the eye could see, their once-vibrant colors faded into shades of brown and gray, the snow washed away by the recent rain. The dilapidated barn stood like a silent sentinel amidst the desolation, its weathered wood reflecting years of neglect and decay. A low, mournful wind whistled through the rusted machinery scattered haphazardly, a testament to the farm's long-forgotten purpose.

Tuper glanced at JP, who stood tense and alert beside him. "What do you reckon happened here?"

"Hard to say," JP replied, his voice tense. "This was once someone's livelihood, and not that long ago. Now it looks like hell with everyone out to lunch. How could it get so bad in such a short time?"

"Times were bad for some of these farmers. It's probably been years a comin'."

"Let's start with the barn," JP suggested, nodding toward the looming structure. He took a step forward, but Tuper hesitated, staring at the ground.

"Someone was here not too long ago," Tuper said, pointing out the tire tracks, partially washed away by the rain.

Together, they approached the barn, its creaky door hanging open just enough to allow them to peer inside.

"Stay sharp, Tuper," JP warned.

"You too, kid."

As they stepped into the dark interior, it was clear something was amiss. The air hung heavy with the scent of damp earth and rotting wood. They both inched their way along, adjusting to the lack of light.

Suddenly something ran across the floor. Each made a sudden move for his revolver. They both gave a nervous chuckle when they realized it was a rat.

"Dang varmints," Tuper said.

They carefully picked their way through the debris-strewn barn, calling out Clarice's name in hushed tones and listening intently for any sign of movement or response. Even though Jack was dead, they didn't discount the possibility of a partner. Lana had said they needed another person to pull off the deal they were working on, so maybe he or she was in on this too.

"Where are you, Clarice?" JP whispered.

"Did you hear that?" Tuper asked.

JP frowned, straining to listen. "Sounds like... something's moving in that room."

"Probably another rat," Tuper said. "Watch your step."

As they approached the dilapidated room, the strange noises grew louder—a shuffling sound, accompanied by the occasional soft moan.

"Right behind you," JP said, his hand resting lightly on the grip of his revolver. Then he spotted something. "Over here!" JP called out, his flashlight beam illuminating a woman lying on the dirty floor, her hands bound to a chair that had tipped over, and her clothes torn.

"Clarice!" Tuper cried, rushing to her side. Tuper's heart clenched at the sight. Clarice's hair was matted with dirt and sweat, and her face was bruised and swollen, her slender frame trembling. She looked up at them with weak, unfocused eyes, a shadow of the strong woman they knew. But she was alive.

"Dear Lord!" Tuper's heart ached at the sight of his friend. He knelt beside her and began to untie the ropes that held her captive. "Clarice, it's us. We're here to help you."

JP scanned the area for any potential threats.

"Hey... Tuper," Clarice whispered, her voice barely audible. "You found me."

"Damn straight, we did," Tuper said, his voice thick with emotion. "And we're gonna get you out of here, I promise."

"I knew you would," Clarice murmured, her blue eyes wide with fear and confusion. "S-so c-cold," she mumbled, her teeth chattering. "Wh... where's Lana? Jack was using me to get to Lana." Tears streamed down her face. "I didn't know what to do."

"Shh, it's all right now," Tuper reassured her. "Lana is safe and Jack is dead." But he wasn't sure she heard him as her eyelids fluttered closed and her body sagged with exhaustion.

JP reached down and touched her clammy skin. Each shallow breath she took seemed to rattle in her chest. "She's burning up," JP noted, as he pressed his hand against her forehead.

Tuper finally managed to untie Clarice's hands, then he cradled her in his arms. "Can you walk?" he asked gently.

"I think so." Clarice tried to sit up, but her body trembled, and her face contorted in pain.

"Take it slow," JP advised, supporting her as she attempted to stand. But Clarice quickly collapsed into JP's arms. "Toop, call 9-1-1! We need to get her to the hospital—now!"

Chapter Forty

Sunday midnight

Tuper pulled his cellphone out of his pocket. "I just remembered the ambulance service no longer operates in Montana City. It would have to come from Helena." JP and Tuper exchanged a glance, silently acknowledging the gravity of their situation. "We'd better take her ourselves," Tuper said. The two men carried her to the car and gently placed her in the back seat, making certain she was comfortable.

"JP, you drive," Tuper instructed. "I'll stay back here with Clarice."

"Got it." JP slid behind the wheel and started the engine.

As they sped toward Helena, Tuper held Clarice's hand, the weight of responsibility for her safety bearing down on him.

JP quickly called 9-1-1 and put the call on speaker. "We have someone who was kidnapped and held hostage. She's feverish and has chills. We're transporting her to the Helena hospital right now. Is there anything we could be doing for her?"

"Let me transfer you to the medical service department, and they should be able to help you." The operator sounded calm and professional.

Within moments, JP was on the line with a doctor.

"Does she have any open wounds?"

"Not that I can see. Mostly bruises and scrapes."

"It's important to keep her warm and give her plenty of fluids, if you have them," the doctor said. "If you can, cover her with blankets or coats. Do you have any Tylenol?"

"No."

"How far away are you?"

"About ten minutes," Tuper cut in.

"Okay. Do the best you can to keep her warm and get here as fast as you can, safely." The doctor emphasized the word *safely*.

As JP sped down the highway, he shed his coat and handed it to Tuper. "Wrap this around her." Tuper did the same with his coat.

JP called Lana and briefly updated her. "Please call Ron and tell him to quit his search, then all of you need to meet us at the hospital."

~~~

Monday morning, 2 a.m.

The sterile smell of disinfectant filled the hospital room as Mary Ann sat by Clarice's bedside, watching her chest rise and fall with each labored breath. Tuper stood near the window, his brow furrowed in thought as he gazed out at the black sky. The steady beeping of the heart monitor provided a rhythmic backdrop to the tense atmosphere.
~~~

"Damn Jack Peterson for doing this to her." Tuper's voice was hoarse with anger and fear. "I'd like to find the guy who killed him and shake his hand."

Mary Ann looked up. "Any idea who might have done that?"

Tuper sighed. "No. But we need to find out because we could still be in danger."

"The doctors have been pretty optimistic so far," Mary Ann said, trying to keep from crying. "The one I spoke to earlier said he expects her to be okay with some rest. She's dehydrated, but not too bad. Apparently, Jack did give her some water. She is malnourished though. Even if he brought her food, she probably couldn't get much down. She has a hard time eating when she's scared or upset." She swallowed and took a deep breath. "The doc said he doesn't expect any permanent damage, but he'll know a lot more when she wakes up."

Chapter Forty-One

Monday morning just before sunrise

Lana sat at the small dining room table, the house quiet. JP, Ron, and Tuper were still sleeping, and Mary Ann was at the hospital with Clarice. Lana couldn't sleep. She was anxious to discover what was in Jack's phone, which she held in her hand. She stared at the screen. It was cracked, but the phone was still functioning. She owed a debt of gratitude to Mary Ann, who'd had the wherewithal to grab it from the crime scene after Jack was shot.

She laid down the phone and went to the kitchen to put on a pot of coffee. Then she returned, picked it up, and ran her fingers over its smooth surface, feeling both a sense of dread and determination. It was Jack's phone, and she vacillated between wanting to stomp on it and not wanting to even touch it. She hated Jack Peterson! Not only for what he'd done to Clarice, but she also believed Jack was responsible for her father's death. And he'd tried to force her to commit cyber-crimes for his benefit.

Lana took a deep breath. *Let's see what secrets this thing holds*, she thought, swiping the cell screen. But the phone was locked. She would have to figure out his password or find a way to bypass it. She pressed familiar combinations of numbers and letters, trying to guess Jack's password. As her frustration grew, she tried more complex sequences, based on everything she knew about him. Just when she was about to take a break, a shimmering icon appeared on the screen, signaling she had bypassed his security protocol.

She checked his phone calls first to see who his last contact was. He had received a call from someone in Denver, Colorado. The number wasn't in his contacts. She spent a little time on tracking the number, only to find out it was likely a spam call. She continued down the list. There were calls to both hotels and the rental car agency. Nothing interesting so far. But she did have his list of contacts. It would take time to go through it, but she hoped it would pay off.

Tuper walked into the room, his gray hair disheveled. He looked different without his hat, Lana thought. But he mostly looked tired and old. She wondered how much of that was her fault.

"Find anything interestin' yet?" Tuper asked.

"Not yet, Pops," she replied. "But I'm still convinced Jack killed my father, and that it was no accident."

"You're probably right." Tuper went to the kitchen to put the teapot on, then took a seat next to Lana.

Lana scanned through Jack's text messages. Suddenly, she stopped, her eyes widening as the message on the screen hit her like a ton of bricks. There it was, an unsent message from Jack to her: *I did NOT kill your father.*

"Wait... what?" Her heart raced, and the room seemed to close around her.

"What is it?"

"Look," Lana said. She tried to hand the phone to Tuper, but he wouldn't take it.

"Just tell me." He sounded frustrated. "I don't have my glasses on."

"I'm sorry." She read it to him, but she was quite certain it wasn't about his ability to see.

"Are you sure that message is from Jack?" Tuper asked.

"Positive," Lana replied.

"And it was to you?"

"Yes."

"But you didn't get a message from him, so how do you know?"

"He was writing the message to me when he got shot. He didn't get a chance to send it or maybe even finish it. I wonder what else he would've said."

"I still don't get how you know it was to you."

"That's the way it works, Tuper," JP said, entering the room. "When you text, you select the person you're sending it to before you start writing it."

"Dang-fangled machines. I'll never understand 'em."

"You don't really have to. You have Lana for that." JP briefly touched Tuper's shoulder as he walked past. "I smell coffee."

"There's a pot ready," Lana said. "Help yourself."

JP returned with a cup of black coffee. "Good stuff. Thanks, Lana."

"Sure," she said, her mind still on Jack's message. "If he didn't kill my father, then who the heck did?"

"From what I've learned about Jack, you needed to count your fingers after you shook hands with him," JP said.

"What are you saying?" Lana asked.

"Maybe Jack was lying to you in the text message," Tuper said, clarifying JP's comment.

Lana smiled for the first time in a long while. "You two speak the same language. It must be that cowboy thing." She looked at the message again. "You're right. Jack can't be trusted for sure, but why would he write that? What would he have to gain?"

"He wanted your help. Maybe he thought he could get on your good side," JP said.

"I don't think he would bother with that. He knows...knew how much I hated him. That's why he resorted to kidnapping. He knew he'd have to force me."

"But the main reason you hated him was because you thought he killed your father."

"There were plenty of other reasons," Lana said.

JP took a different approach. "Let's assume for a minute that Jack didn't kill your father, but that he was murdered. Who else would want your father dead?"

"Everyone he cheated and stole from. There are so many."

"How many of those people would know it was your father who cheated them?"

"Probably none. He was too good." Lana thought for a second. "You're right. It's a smaller list than I thought."

"It's likely it was personal," JP said. "I can think of one."

"You mean my half-brother, Danny."

"It's possible."

"You know anything about that kid?" Tuper asked.

"Not really. I haven't seen or heard from him in years. I always looked up to him when I was little, but when he left, I felt abandoned. I never really forgave him for that." She touched her laptop. "I'll do some research on him as soon as I have time."

"Here's another thought," JP said. "Jack might have known who killed Charles, and his shooter didn't want you to find out. Jack could've been about to tell you."

"You're suggestin' the sniper knew right then what Jack was writin'?" Tuper asked.

"I don't know," JP said. "Is that possible, Lana?"

She sighed. "It's possible, but it would have to be someone pretty tech savvy."

"So, that's where we start looking," JP said.

Grant Simmons. A cold fear gripped her heart. If Jack wasn't responsible for her father's death, then the real killer was still out there—and she had no idea who they were or when they might strike next.

Ron was the last to get up and join them. His morning hair looked like a Rod Stewart imitation. Lana smiled, thinking it made him look even more handsome. She quickly composed herself. "Where do we go from here?" she asked, not to anyone in particular.

"Here's a better question," JP said. "Who would've been after Jack?"

"That could be a million people," Lana said. "He made a lot of enemies, including my father."

"And they both ended up dead," Ron said. "What about the cellphone Mary Ann picked up? Maybe that could give us some clues."

"I've been working on that." Lana caught Ron up on the text message.

"Maybe we should focus more on the people Lana's been digging up dirt on," JP said. "Someone close enough to know what Jack did to Clarice, like the third person Jack needed to finish his scheme."

"Or someone who was trying to stop Lana from doing Jack's bidding." Ron added.

"If that's the case," Tuper said, "that person could want Lana dead too."

A hush fell over the room. Finally, Lana broke the silence. "That's nothing new. Lots of people have wanted me dead for a long time. Sometimes, I think my own father might have been one of them. I know Jack did for many years, until he decided he could use me instead. There's one man who comes to mind that I'd put pretty high on the list: Grant Simmons, my ex. He showed up in Helena recently."

"What?" Ron bellowed. "Why didn't you mention that?"

"We haven't had time to tell you everything. Sorry." Lana described her encounter with Grant and gave a brief history of their background.

Ron shook his head, remaining silent.

"That guy sounds like bad news," JP said. "Did he know Jack?"

"Yes. And he knew about many of his escapades, but I don't think Jack knew anything about my cybercrimes with Grant. And I don't know what Grant would gain by killing Jack."

"Does Grant's skill set match what Jack needed for his plan?"

Lana thought for a moment. "It does, mostly. Grant is very good technically with what he does, and very fast. The problem is that he's reckless and cocky. His ego won't allow him to realize he has limits, and that's dangerous."

"If Grant is the third person in Jack's little plan, then it may be purely mathematical." JP paused to sip his coffee. "If Grant thought the two of you could finish the job without Jack, that splits the pot only two ways. Greed has a way of motivating people. Or maybe he thought he was protecting you."

"Or maybe there's something else we don't know, and Grant thinks he needs to take you both out," Tuper said.

"Whatever the case, we need to find Grant and talk to him," JP concluded. "Lana, do you know where he's staying?"

"At the Delta Hotel by Marriott on Colonial Drive. He hasn't tried to hide it from me, so we need to be careful. He knows that I know where he is."

"He can tell where you've been looking on that thing?" Tuper asked.

"There are some things that give away a search, but mostly he'd know because he would do the same thing. Besides, he didn't cover his tracks, so he wanted me to find him. He may not greet you with the same open arms."

Ron stood. "I'm going with you."

"I don't think that's a good idea for lots of reasons," JP said. "But mostly because we need you to stay here with Lana and keep her safe. Tuper and I can handle this."

"I don't need a babysitter," Lana objected.

All three men gave Lana a look that said *Really?* She gave in, realizing it would be a chance to spend time alone with Ron, even if they would be working.

"Agreed." Tuper stood and walked toward the door. "Let's saddle up and ride, partner."

Chapter Forty-Two

Early Monday morning

Just as Tuper and JP reached the door, Lana's phone buzzed with an incoming message. Glancing at the screen, her heart skipped a beat. "Speak of the devil." She scanned the message. "Grant Simmons just texted me. He wants to *catch up*."

"Grant?" Tuper raised an eyebrow and turned back. "Tell him to go to hell."

"Not so hasty," JP said. "Maybe you should tell him to buzz off in person. If you set up a meeting, we can follow him, then see where he goes and what he does."

"That may not help. Grant's activity could be mostly online."

"What does he actually want from you?" JP asked.

"To hook up with him again."

"What?" Ron blurted.

"You jealous, pretty boy?" Tuper asked.

"Absolutely," Ron said glibly.

"We're talking about Grant Simmons," JP said, "Lana's old boyfriend and partner in crime."

"Now I'm not only jealous, but worried," Ron said.

"Will you all stop, please." Lana raised her voice. "I'm not hooking up with anyone, least of all Grant. But I need to answer his text."

"Just tell him no," Ron said.

"Not so quick," JP countered. "Remember what we decided earlier. He could be our killer."

"What?" Ron interjected.

"We think it's someone who is very adept at this tech stuff," JP said.

"Then why are we even thinking about this? We're not going to put Lana at risk. She can just tell him no."

"Please stop talking about me like I'm not here!" she shouted. Then she looked at the text message and responded.

Lana—*Not now.*

Grant—*When?*

Lana—*I'll let you know.*

Grant—*Don't take too long.*

"I just told him *not now*. Please let it go."

"I'm sorry, Lana," JP said. "We're all just worried."

"I know."

"Tuper and I are leaving. We'll find Grant and see where he goes."

"Good idea." Lana wrote Grant's information on a piece of paper and handed it to JP. "Here's Grant's hotel room and car rental info. I'll text you a photo of him." She turned toward Tuper. "You remember what he looks like?"

"I never forget a face."

JP looked at Lana. "While we're gone, maybe you can find a current connection between Grant and Jack."

"I will."

JP pivoted to Tuper. "You okay with the plan?"

Tuper gave a single nod of his head. "But only if Ron will stay here with Lana." He winked at Ron.

"Subtle, Toop," Ron said. "But I think that's a good idea. Besides, Mary Ann should be bringing Clarice home today. They may need some help."

After the men left, Lana uploaded the contents of Jack's phone to a special server on her laptop to make the search easier.

"Is it secure there?" Ron asked.

"The way I did it, yes."

"But if someone can take over a phone, can't they take over a computer as well?"

"Ordinarily, but not with the security I have in place. I'd know in time to move the files."

Ron shook his head, obviously amazed at her skill.

Lana printed a list of Jack's contacts and handed it to Ron.

"There's only about fifteen names here," Ron said. "Is that all the contacts he has?"

"He must only use this burner phone for his criminal life. I didn't see any names or notes that indicate those are family or friends. He does have his dentist on here. Lucky for us, we got this phone and not his other one."

"You sure he has another one?"

"Absolutely. I've already checked that out." She smiled. "Did you bring your laptop?"

"I did."

"Then boot it up and research these people."

"What am I looking for?"

"What they do for a living, backgrounds, phone numbers, home and business addresses, whatever you can find. Check social media if they have any. Anything that's readily available out there. I can use that to do a deeper search."

"You got it." Ron dug his laptop out of his suitcase in the living room, set it on the table, and started his task.

Lana checked in with Ravic.

Cricket—*Can you help again?*

Ravic—*Give me 3.*

Lana went to the restroom, then poured herself a cup of coffee while she waited.

Ravic—*Back. What can I do?*

Cricket—*Cover.*

Ravic—*Let her rip.*

"Let's see if there's a connection between Jack and Grant," Lana said, mostly to herself. Her fingers pranced across the keyboard as she delved into the World Wide Web, her mind racing with possibilities.

"Dang it." Lana's frustration mounted as she skimmed through more search results. "Why can't anything be simple?"

She had to tiptoe through Grant's footprint. He was good at covering his tracks, except those he wanted her to see. There was an obvious difference between the two. She had kept tabs on him since they split up, and he had learned a great deal since, but he was still no match for her. She could see places he had hacked into, money he had scammed by hacking into medical records, insurance companies, and credit bureaus. Then he used the information to conduct scams through phishing, trojan horses, and social engineering. He attacked mostly elderly people, stealing their life savings. Grant had deposited them in an offshore account. She shared the information with Ron.

"So, he's stealing from innocent people?"

"Yep. That's what he does."

Ron looked up from his laptop. "Is that what you did?" He held up his hands. "No judgment. I'm just curious."

"Yes." Lana hadn't shared her past with Ron, but she wasn't going to lie to him either. She just hoped it wouldn't affect his feelings for her, whatever they were. "I've since put all the money back that I could. It took time, and it was riskier than taking it."

"Why would it be riskier?"

"Because I had to find innovative ways to return it. Banks are almost impossible to hack. If I could get the account numbers and passwords then I could make deposits, but if they were huge amounts, they would be too noticeable and people would likely get suspicious, so I had to be very careful."

"So, what did you do?"

"I sent some debit cards that looked like they were coming from stimulus money. People don't question it when they get money from the government. I paid a lot of bills online for the victims. I paid medical bills and school tuitions from anonymous benefactors. I had to get pretty creative, and Ravic helped me a lot."

"Wow, who would've thought it would be harder to return than to take."

"I'm sure my actions still hurt a lot of people, but I did the best I could. I'd like to find another way to compensate them and redeem myself, but there's not much I can do. I thought if I ever got into my dad's accounts, I would do just that."

"But didn't he steal from people too?"

"He did."

"Wouldn't it be better if you just return it to the people he stole from?"

"It would, but it would be difficult to figure out where it goes. Most of his fraud and theft was from institutions, like charities and corporations. That doesn't make it any better, I know, but he had a long time to cover his tracks, so I'm not sure I could trace the activity. At least, not without getting caught. It doesn't matter. I'm not going there anyway." She sighed. "Have you found anything yet?"

Just then, Lana's computer dinged. It was Ravic.

Ravic—*Ready when you are.*

Cricket—*Buckle up.*

Chapter Forty-Three

Monday morning

The low-pitched hum of laptop fans filled the dining room as Lana and Ron sat at the table, eyes locked onto the screens.

"Here goes nothing." Lana started keying in familiar strings of code. She caught Ron's eye as he stole a quick glance at her before diving back into his search. His face was illuminated by the blueish glow of his screen.

Ron said, "I've been working on Agnes Blackwood."

"She's an associate of my father's who's been involved in underground hacking rings for decades."

"Sounds like you might already know more about her than I do."

"I doubt it. That was a long time ago. What did you learn about her current life?"

"It looks like she may have gone legit. She doesn't have much of an online presence, but she owns a preschool that has a good reputation and is well liked by parents. Agnes started the school back in the nineties as part of her mission to give children from low-income families better educational opportunities." Ron stood to stretch. "Overall, it appears Agnes had a rich and varied past and has made a positive impact in her community. She's a dedicated educator, a passionate technologist, and an advocate for marginalized communities. How does someone like that get involved with your father?"

"That, I don't know. But somehow, they had a *business relationship*. And since she's in Jack's phone, she must've connected with him after my father died."

"Maybe she's gotten more involved in cybercrime. But what motive would she have for killing Jack or your father?"

"Beats me, but I'll check a little deeper into Agnes and see if there's any connection to Grant." Lana turned back to her laptop and got to work. "Alright," she whispered under her breath, her fingers tapping a staccato rhythm on the table. "What are you hiding, Agnes? What secrets do you share with Grant?"

As she dove deeper into the digital abyss, she couldn't help but chew on her lower lip, a habit born from years of searching for truths buried beneath layers of deception.

"Find anything?" Ron asked.

"No connection to Grant yet." Frustration crept into her tone. "But I'm not giving up. We're close, Ron. I can feel it."

With each new discovery, Lana found herself torn between her longing for answers and her fear of what those answers might reveal.

As she continued her search, Ron called out softly, "Victor Marsh is a telephone lineman. He once saved a kid from drowning while on duty."

"Really?" Lana was momentarily distracted from her hunt. "That's impressive. Look deeper. Maybe there's more to him than meets the eye."

A few minutes later, Ron said, "This is pretty cool. Victor has worked for the telephone company for nearly forty years. He was born and raised in a small town in southern California and has worked as a lineman since he was sixteen. He has no social media presence at all, but he won an award for his bravery in saving that boy. He saw him fall into a pool when he was up on a telephone pole, then scrambled down and ran to get to him. He broke through their fence and jumped in the pool to pull him out. There are YouTube posts of him being interviewed right after. People who know him say he has a reputation for being honest, reliable, and hard-working, as well as helping people less fortunate." Ron shook his head. "How would this guy be involved?"

"Who knows?" Lana said. "I'll see if there's any connection to Grant or Jack." Lana shifted her focus back to the web. "All right, Victor Marsh. Let's see if your heroics hide a darker truth."

Lana continued her search, determined to uncover any connection between Jack's contacts and Grant Simmons.

"Got something new for you." Ron broke the silence that had settled around them. "Owen Unger is a fire marshal in San Diego."

"Fire marshal, huh?" Lana mused, thinking about the fire at her father's home. She hacked into Owen's records and scanned each line of information for any hint of a connection to Grant. "Interesting..."

"Anything there?" Ron asked, intrigued by her reaction.

"Maybe," Lana replied, feeling guarded, unwilling to reveal too much until she was certain of her findings.

"Got one more," Ron said, focusing on his laptop. "Wayne Osborne is a dentist in Del Mar."

"Del Mar?" Lana raised an eyebrow. "Maybe he's just Jack's dentist, nothing more." But she didn't really believe that. She started searching for any trace of a link between Osborne and Grant.

As Ron offered up more intel, Lana felt gratitude toward him. He had proven himself to be a valuable ally in her quest for the truth, even if their relationship was still fraught with uncertainty. The possibility of romance still lingered between them, but Lana couldn't bring herself to indulge in such thoughts—not when her future was still so uncertain.

"Wayne's reputation seems solid," Lana admitted, a little disappointed. "I bet there's more to him than we're finding."

"Owen Unger, Wayne Osborne." Lana committed their names to memory. "You may have hidden your secrets well, but I will find them. And when I do, the truth will finally be set free."

Lana and Ron stopped talking as they searched for the next name on the contact list: Isaac Newton. The silence in the room was punctuated only by the tapping of fingers on keyboards. She searched for Isaac Newton, constantly avoiding the information on the famous mathematician, looking in public records, Reddit threads, and dark web forums, but came up with nothing.

"Anything?" Lana asked impatiently, then took a deep breath in an attempt to keep her frustrations at bay.

"Nothing," Ron said, equally frustrated. "It's like this guy doesn't exist outside of Jack's world."

Lana clenched and unclenched her fists. She couldn't help but feel disheartened by their lack of progress; every lead so far had ultimately come to a dead end. "Maybe it's a code name," Lana suggested. "Or an alias. There has to be something we're missing."

"Could be," Ron agreed, continuing to search. "But for now, this is all I can find."

"Let me finish up," Lana said. There was a stubborn fire in her gut that refused to be extinguished.

Her laptop dinged.

Ravic: *Can you get by without me for a few hours? I have to take care of something.*

Cricket: *Sure. Let me know when you're available.*

Lana switched her search to something less risky, but continued her task.

"He's all yours." Ron leaned back in his chair, his fingers drumming softly on the wooden table as he watched Lana work. "I'll see what else I can find on Marsh and the others."

Lana was deep in thought when Ron said. "Oh, my God."

"What is it?"

"Marsh was killed in a paragliding accident. He was just taking off from Torrey Pines when he crashed."

"When?"

"The day after the fire that burned your house."

"That can't be a coincidence."

Chapter Forty-Four

Monday afternoon

Tuper stopped on the sidewalk, leaned against a brick building, and watched the entrance to the Delta Hotel for any sign of Grant Simmons. When his phone rang, he checked the number: Henry Fenton. "Don't have time for you now, Henry," he said aloud, then returned the phone to his pocket.

"Any word from your contacts?" JP approached Tuper with two steaming cups of coffee.

"They don't have any tea?"

"No tea."

"Thanks, anyway." Tuper took the offered cup, grateful for the warmth against the chill that clung to the air. "Nothin' yet," he replied, taking a sip. "But I know a guy who might be able to help."

JP raised an eyebrow but didn't question Tuper's mysterious sources. "I checked the parking lot for his F-150 and didn't see it. There were several out-of-state license plates, probably rentals, so it's possible he switched cars."

"I suppose that's likely, the way these guys operate." Tuper blew on his coffee to cool it.

"So, what's the plan?"

Tuper thought for a moment. "First, we need to figure out where Grant's goin' around here, who he's seein'. Maybe it'll help us figure out if Grant was the third guy workin' with Jack. Also, we need to keep an eye on him so he can't get to Lana. She ain't safe until we know what Grant's real motives are."

"Sounds good," JP agreed. "What's next?"

"We need to find Grant and follow him without spookin' him."

"Right." JP adjusted his Stetson. "So, how do we do that?"

"We start here at his hotel," Tuper glanced at the building across the street, its glass windows reflecting the afternoon sun.

"I'll go inside and have a look around," JP said. "You need to stay out of sight. He might recognize you and, as you said, we don't want to spook him."

~~~

JP entered the lobby, noticing the polished marble floor and massive chandelier. *Classy.* He scanned the gift shop and seating area, searching for any sign of Grant. Finding none, he approached the front desk, where a young woman with a welcoming smile greeted him.

"Hi there," JP said. "I'm looking for a friend who's staying here. Name's Grant Simmons. I hope you can tell me if he's still checked in."

"I'm sorry, but I can't give out that information," the woman replied apologetically.

"Please, miss," JP insisted, taking on a pleading tone. "It's real important I find him."

"All I can tell you is that he's not here."

"Thanks," JP said, then texted Lana.
~~~

JP—I think Grant is gone from the Delta Hotel. Can you check?

Lana—I'm on it.

JP walked out to where Tuper was waiting. "No sign of him. The desk clerk wouldn't tell me if he checked out, but she made it clear that he isn't there."

"We need to have Lana check."

"I already sent her a text."

It wasn't long before Lana texted back: *Grant checked out this morning. So far, I can't find another hotel for him, but I'll keep looking.*

"So, he's got a head start on us." JP looked up at the sky, where dark clouds were gathering, and felt a chill run down his spine. "But we're not out of options yet. We'll find another way to track him down."

"Like what?"

"We've got to draw Grant out into the open. If we don't make a move soon, he'll likely get to Lana first." JP walked toward the car.

"We could use Lana as bait," Tuper suggested hesitantly.

"Are you out of your mind?" JP snapped. "That's too dangerous. We can't risk her life like that."

"I know it sounds risky, but it might be our only chance," Tuper said calmly, meeting JP's gaze. "We'll be there to protect her, and we'll set the terms of the meeting. Besides, Grant's a punk. Either of us could take him with one hand tied behind our backs."

"Maybe so, but whoever killed Jack was a dang good shot, and he wasn't necessarily close."

"That's a good point, but do you have a better plan?"

For a moment, JP hesitated. Finally, he said, "I guess we don't have many options. She's at risk until we figure this all out. Maybe it's better to play offense."

"Humph," Tuper said, removing his cowboy hat and running a hand through his graying hair.

"It's a plan," JP said, "but only if Lana's comfortable with it."

Chapter Forty-Five

Monday late afternoon

As Lana dived deeper into the digital rabbit hole, she began to see connections forming between Jack's contacts and her father. She had searched but never found anything that connected Victor Marsh to Grant. *And why would Jack have Marsh's name and number in his phone when the man had been dead for three years?*

"Ron, I need you to do some more research on the other names on the list. Find out where they all are today. See if they're still alive."

"Will do. Mostly I was checking for things around the time of your father's death. I'll finish up what I started."

Ding. "That's Ravic," Lana said. "He's back and ready." She typed back to him.

Cricket: *Thanks. Follow me.*

Lana looked into the intricate web of possible relationships between Jack's contacts and Grant, but each strand led further away from Grant. She could feel the truth slipping through her fingers like sand, and it only fueled her determination to keep digging.

"Dang it." Lana sat back, taking a break. "I can connect them all to Jack and even my father, but nothing links them to Grant."

"Maybe we're looking at this the wrong way," Ron offered. "If your father and Jack are the common threads, perhaps they hold the key to uncovering Grant's connection."

"Perhaps," Lana mused. "But for now, Isaac Newton remains an enigma. And until I unravel that mystery, I don't think I'll be able to find the link I need."

They fell silent again as Lana continued her search, each dead end strengthening her resolve and propelling her forward.

The steady hum of the laptops, punctuated by the *click-clack* of keys created a sense of urgency that seemed to mirror the nature of their pursuit.

"You're not going to believe this," Ron said.

"What now?"

"I've checked the entire list to see what Jack's contacts are doing today. Agnes Blackwell is still running her daycare business, Martin Foster is still a funeral director, and Susan Walsh is still practicing medicine, but at a different hospital."

"What's your point?"

"The others haven't been so lucky. Owen Unger was shot in the head about two years ago. He's alive, but he can't take care of himself or even communicate. Osborne is also in a facility with round-the-clock care."

"What happened to him?"

"He had a stroke."

"When?"

"About a year ago."

"And Kent, the attorney?"

"He's dead. A car accident shortly after Unger's stroke."

"That's a lot of coincidences," Lana said.

"And we know nothing about Isaac Newton," Ron added.

"Except this. Have a look."

Ron stood, went to her side, and peered over her shoulder at the screen. "Whatcha got?" he asked, leaning in closer for a better look.

"See this comment on this blog post?" Lana's finger hovered over a seemingly innocuous remark. "It mentions both Isaac Newton and Grant Simmons."

"There's your connection," Ron said. "What's the context?"

"That's just it, I can't tell," Lana admitted. "It's so darn vague. It could be about Sir Isaac Newton, for all I know. There's no context to tell."

Behind her, Ron read the comment out loud, "Grant Simmons and Isaac Newton wouldn't accept that premise." He scratched his head. "What's the article about?"

"It's a political post about Russia," Lana said. "I don't think it's about anyone we know."

"Why would it come up then?"

"Because I keep searching for those two names, and eventually I'll get something about every Grant Simmons or Isaac Newton in the world."

As Lana refocused on her search, she felt the familiar fire of determination surge within her. Somewhere amidst the tangled web of information, there was a vital clue that would lead her to the truth. And with every new discovery, she felt herself inching closer.

Suddenly, everything clicked into place. Lana leaned forward in her chair, her eyes widening as the pieces of the puzzle began to fit together. A triumphant grin spread across her face.

"Ron," she said breathlessly, "I think I've finally found something."

"Really?" Ron's excitement was unmistakable as he eagerly looked over Lana's shoulder. "What is it?"

"Give me a moment to confirm," Lana said, following her newfound lead. The thrill of the hunt surged through her veins, propelling her forward with renewed fervor. She bit her lower lip as she contemplated her next move. The vague connection between Isaac Newton and Grant Simmons was tantalizingly close, inviting and promising, but possibly just another illusion.

She adjusted her position, leaning in closer to her laptop. "I've got my eye on the prize, Ron," she murmured. She delved into the digital labyrinth once again, her fingers a flurry of motion. The comment on the blog post had provided a slender thread to follow, and she pursued it with dogged persistence.

As time passed, Lana's eyes stung from staring at the screen. But she refused to give up. As she dug deeper and deeper, Lana felt that familiar thrill, the sense of purpose that had driven her for so long.

Suddenly Ravic appeared on her screen with an alert. Ravic—*STOP NOW!*

Lana quickly finished the coded task she'd started. Her fingers flew across the keys with a fervor she had never exhibited to Ron before. Ravic repeated his alert. Ravic—*GET OUT!*

Lana punched some more keys, then typed back. Cricket—*I'm out. Later.*

Lana shut down everything she was working on and turned off her laptop.

"What just happened?"

"Someone was on to me," she said, trembling. Lana stood up and started to walk off the anxiety she was feeling.

Ron stared at her, shaking his head in wonder. "That was intense."

"Yeah," Lana said, still breathing heavy.

"Who's Ravic?"

"He's a cyberfriend. He's been with me for years."

"Should I be jealous?" Ron teased.

"I don't know. He could be an old, ugly woman with a huge wart on her nose, or maybe it's a guy who looks like Ichabod Crane, or maybe he looks like George Clooney." She smiled. "That would be nice. But I don't know, and I'll never know because we can't ever reveal who we are. Nor do I want to." She explained how they'd met and how they helped each other.

"You live an interesting life, Lana."

"It's about to get more interesting," Tuper said as he walked in the door. "Agony, we have an idea we want to run by you."

"Shoot."

"Poor choice of words," JP said.

"What's the idea?" Ron asked, his voice skeptical.

Tuper explained what he wanted to do, making it clear that Lana had to be okay with the plan or it was off the table.

"No," Ron said, before Tuper was even done. "That's too risky. Grant is our prime suspect in Jack's murder. We can't take that kind of chance with Lana."

Lana frowned at Ron. She appreciated his concern, but this was her life, her future, and her choice to make. She fluctuated between appreciation for his chivalry and frustration at his over-protectiveness. But in the end, she was the one who had to live with it. She just wished Ron had more faith in her ability to make her own decisions. Then she realized, he was afraid too. Afraid of losing her.

"I didn't like the idea either at first," JP said. "But Tuper has a point. Right now, Lana is a sitting duck, especially if Grant is the shooter. That means he could pick her off any time, and any one of us, as well. He's evading us now, so we have to get him out in the open. That way, we can keep an eye on him, and get Lana and the girls somewhere safe."

"After what we found out today," Ron said. "I don't like it."

"What?" Tuper asked.

Lana and Ron explained what they had discovered about Jack's phone contact list.

"That's all the more reason to stop this guy," Tuper said.

He started to make another argument for the sting when Lana interrupted him. "Stop," she said in a loud voice. "This is my decision." Everyone got very quiet. "If I decide to go along with the plan, when would we do it?"

"It's getting dark, and it's likely to snow tonight. We need daylight and at least decent weather conditions, so we can follow him. So, if we don't get hit with a blizzard, we can do it tomorrow. I say we send the feeler out in the morning and set up a meeting as early as we can in the daylight hours."

Might as well get it over with, Lana thought. "Okay, that's the plan."

Chapter Forty-Six

Tuesday morning

Tuper, JP, and Ron sat around the dining room table arguing about the plan to get to Grant. Tuper suggested a park near the center of town, a place where they could easily monitor the situation from afar. With Lana's help, they sent a message to Grant, specifying the exact lo cation and time of the meeting.

"Are you sure this is a good idea, Pops?" Lana asked hesitantly. Her feet shifted nervously on the floor.

"Trust me." Tuper placed a gentle hand on her shoulder. "We'll be watchin' your back every step of the way. But if you don't think it's a good idea, we won't do it."

"It's not too late to change your mind," Ron said. "We can call the whole thing off."

"No. I'm good," she said softly. "But, Tuper, promise me you'll be careful too, okay? All of you."

"Promise," Tuper and JP echoed in unison. Ron said nothing.

As they finalized their plan, Tuper felt a knot of anxiety tightening in his stomach.

"Let's do this!" He straightened his cowboy hat and steeled himself for the confrontation.

~~~
~~~

The cloud-filled winter morning sky allowed the sun to peek out occasionally, casting shadows across the park where Lana waited for Grant to arrive. The playground was empty due to the cold, and except for a single dog walker and Lana's out-of-sight backup, the park was void of people. She waited near a statue, too restless to sit on the nearby bench, and paced. She was on constant vigilance, being careful not to slip on the icy ground while scanning the area for Grant.

~~~

At one end of the park, Tuper leaned against a large oak tree, keeping a watchful eye on Lana, his fingers drumming restlessly against his denim-clad leg. JP stood at the other end; his Stetson tipped low to shield his eyes as he surveyed their surroundings. Ron drove the perimeter, watching for Grant's red Ford F-150, ready to send a group message when he spotted him.

Prior to setting up in their respective locations, JP had called Tuper and had him leave his phone line open so they could communicate without anyone's phone beeping. That had been Lana's idea.

Tuper stood in the shadows, watching Lana from a distance, his boots sinking into the damp earth as he surveyed the park. The rain had long since subsided, but the cold air hinted at an approaching snowstorm. He looked down to the other end of the park, but JP was keeping out of sight. Lana was stationed in the middle near a statue. He locked eyes on her for a moment to be reassuring.

As they waited for Grant to arrive, Tuper couldn't help but feel a pang of guilt. He hoped he hadn't made a mistake, but it was too late now to second-guess himself.
~~~

"Any sign of him?" JP whispered over the open phone line.

"Nothing yet," Tuper responded, scanning the area with eagle-eyed precision. "I don't expect it'll be long now."

The minutes ticked by, each second stretching out like molasses, thick and slow. Tuper's heart thumped in his chest, his mind filled with what-ifs and worst-case scenarios. Every rustle of leaves sent his pulse skyrocketing, every shadow a potential threat. At least he had a good view of Lana. He could see her moving around and rubbing her hands together, trying to keep warm.

Tuper heard his phone beep, probably a text message he couldn't get to. Just then, JP said, "Ron just sent a message. Grant is on his way into the park."

"Here we go," Tuper whispered.

~~~

Lana received Ron's text saying Grant was coming in the west entrance, leaving no surprise when he appeared. His eyes narrowed as they locked onto Lana.

"Hey there, Lana," Grant said smoothly, his voice slick like oil. "I've missed you."

"I haven't missed *you*," she responded.

He stared at her for a moment, looking her up and down. "You still look good, even in all those layers."

"What do you want?" Lana asked. "Because whatever you're selling, I'm not buying."

"Can't I just want to catch up with an old friend? Or maybe a little more than that?" He smirked and closed the distance between them. "We used to be quite the team. We could be again. All you have to do is come back to me, or at least help me out with a little online venture I've got going."
~~~

"What venture?" Lana had no intention of helping him, but she did want to know if it involved Jack. "What's it about, and who else is involved?"

"I can't tell you unless you're in all the way."

"How do I know if I want in if you don't tell me what it is?"

"That never used to matter to you. You were always game if it was a challenge, and believe me, this is a challenge."

Convinced he wasn't going to give her the information she needed, Lana tried a more direct approach. Her jaw set in defiance, she said, "Not gonna happen, Grant. I'm not interested in your schemes or whatever else you're peddling. Speaking of which, were you working with Jack and my father on their *big project*?"

He swallowed but quickly regained his composure. "I don't know what you're talking about."

"Of course, you do. Here's what I think. You, Jack, and my father were planning the heist of a lifetime. A real power grab. Then my father died in the fire, and you needed me to fill his spot. I know about the cybercrime because my father had been working on it for years. That's one of the reasons I left. I didn't want any part of it. It's politically and socially dangerous."

"Come on, Lana," Grant pressed, his voice taking on an edge. "Don't you miss the thrill? The power? You can't tell me you're happy playing house with these hillbillies."

"Leave my friends out of it," Lana shot back. "They've been kinder to me than you ever were. I won't go back to that life, Grant. Not with you, not with anyone."

"Is that so?" Grant's anger bubbled to the surface. "Maybe I'll just have to persuade you a little more. Let's go."

"No," she said defiantly.

"Look, Lana." Grant leaned in, his voice low and cajoling. "This conversation is getting us nowhere. Let's go somewhere more private, where we can talk this out properly."

"First, tell me who Isaac Newton is."

A brief pause, but long enough for Lana to know she had hit a nerve. "He was an English mathematician, physicist, theologian, astronomer, and alchemist. Did I leave anything out? Oh yeah, he was also an author. He was brilliant and known as a philosopher. Best known for his theory about the law of gravity."

"You know that's not who I'm talking about."

"That's the only Newton I know. The only Isaac too."

Grant's smug expression was starting to irritate her.

"Come on, Lana. We made such a good team. Together, we can conquer the world."

"I don't want to conquer the world." Lana crossed her arms, her feet planted firmly. "I told you, I'm not going anywhere with you." He took a step closer to her in an obvious attempt to intimidate her. She stood her ground. "What part of 'no' don't you understand?"

"Damn it, Lana!" Grant spat, his frustration boiling over. "You always were so stubborn. But I didn't come all this way for nothing."

Before she could react, Grant lunged forward and grabbed her arm, his grip like iron.

Shocked by the sudden move, she tried to yank herself free. "Let go of me!" she snarled; her feisty spirit undeterred.

As Grant attempted to drag Lana away, her resistance seemed to infuriate him further. She dug her heels into the ground and twisted her body, trying desperately to break free from his vice-like grip.

"Stop fighting me! You're only making this harder on yourself," Grant growled through gritted teeth.

Lana's thoughts were a whirlwind of fear and determination. But if she couldn't break away from him, she was confident Tuper or JP would come running.

"Never!" Lana spat back. He was pulling her toward an opening in the trees where Tuper was stationed. She looked for Tuper but couldn't spot him. She looked back over her shoulder to where JP was supposed to be but couldn't see him either.

Why couldn't she see either one of them? Had something gone terribly wrong?

Chapter Forty-Seven

Tuesday morning

Tuper stepped out from behind the tree and shouted, "Let her go!"

Grant looked up and laughed. "Who do you think you are, old man?"

His cockiness grated on Tuper's nerves like nails on a chalkboard. Tuper clenched his fists, hoping the punk would give him a reason to use them. "Yer messin' with the wrong person," Tuper warned. "Let her go!"

"Or what? You'll hit me?" Grant released Lana's arm long enough to shove Tuper back. Lana wrenched free and stumbled away.

Tuper regained his footing and growled, "Big mistake," as he swung his fist. The force of the blow caught Grant by surprise and sent him staggering backward, eyes widened in shock.

"Ya should've listened." Tuper's pulse pounded in his ears as he prepared for round two.

Grant recovered quickly, lunging at him with a vicious punch that narrowly missed Tuper's face. Their fists flew, connecting with flesh and bone in a dance of violence.

"Come on, old man!" Grant taunted, but his voice wavered, betraying his unease.

Tuper caught him with a left hook, followed by a knee to the groin. When Grant doubled over, Tuper slammed his palm into the back of Grant's head.

JP arrived at the scene, his breath coming in short gasps and his hand hovering near his holster. But he made no move to stop them.

"Ya done yet?" Tuper snarled, panting slightly. Grant slumped against a tree, his face contorted with pain. "Stay away from her." Tuper pointed a threatening finger at the defeated man. "Next time, you won't get off so easy."

JP approached Tuper, looking concerned, but Tuper waved him off, not wanting to admit he'd suffered any pain. His pride wouldn't allow it. He glanced around to make sure they were still alone.

"Don't worry, I'm keeping a vigilant eye out for on-lookers. So far, the park's empty," JP said. "By the way, you're doing a great job with that punk."

"Dang right." Tuper couldn't suppress a wry smile. "I don't like being called an old man."

Just then Grant came at him again, but Tuper swung fast and hard, his fist connecting with Grant's jaw, sending him staggering backward. The force of the blow stunned Grant for a moment, but his eyes blazed with fury and he lunged at Tuper again.

Grant aimed a punch at Tuper's face, but with uncanny agility, Tuper dodged and countered, landing another solid blow to Grant's ribs. The younger man grunted in pain, but rage seemed to fuel him.

Grant tried to land a kick to Tuper's midsection, but he sidestepped it effortlessly and grabbed Grant's extended leg. He used the momentum to knock him off balance, causing Grant to crash heavily to the ground. Tuper gave him a good, swift kick with his cowboy boot.

"Boy, you don't know when to quit!" Tuper pinned Grant beneath one knee. "Now, stay down."

Grant struggled futilely, his face contorted with frustration. There was no denying the truth: Tuper had bested him in this fight, and Lana wasn't going anywhere with him.

"Let me go," Grant grunted under the weight of Tuper's knee.

"Not before we get some answers," Tuper said. "What do you know about Jack? And don't play coy. We know you've been up to no good."

"Jack who?" Grant frowned, feigning ignorance. "I don't have anything to say."

"Wrong answer, boy," Tuper pressed his knee harder. "You'll talk, or I'll make you regret ever laying a finger on Lana."

"Fine," Grant spat, glaring daggers at them. "I don't know Jack. I just wanted Lana back, that's all."

"Like hell you did," Lana cut in, her voice ice-cold. "You always have an ulterior motive. What are you really after?"

"Believe what you want," Grant retorted. "But I don't know anything about a guy named Jack."

"Jack Peterson. Maybe you knew him by another name. He was shot in front of his hotel yesterday."

"Let me up, and I'll tell you what I know."

Tuper glanced at Lana and then at JP. JP took a step closer and pulled his jacket back to expose his shoulder holster.

Tuper checked Grant for weapons, then let him sit up.

"What is this, Lana? You have your own thugs to keep an eye on you?"

"Just answer the question. How do you know Jack Peterson?"

"I don't."

Lana swung a heavy combat boot, landing it on Grant's already bruised knee.

Grant moaned and grabbed his leg. "You're crazy."

"A little," Lana said.

Tuper smiled at her admission and at how well she was handling this.

"I swear, the first time I saw that guy was on the news. I don't know him."

"You're telling me that two guys from my past who both live in San Diego just happened to show up here in Helena at the same time?"

"I guess."

"You're lying! I can see it in your eyes. We're not leaving until you tell us everything." Lana squatted to Grant's level. "You keep saying you don't know him, but he was my father's business partner, and you know that. So cut the crap."

"All right." Grant took a deep breath. "I started watching Jack online after your father died. I knew he'd try to find you because he needed you to replace your father. It took him a while, but he finally led me to you. I just want your help. I figured if you were getting back into the business, you'd be better off with me than with that parasite."

A quiet moment while they all processed that possibility.

Then Lana demanded, "What do you know about my father's death?"

"Just what I read in the papers. I never talked to your father after we broke up. I wasn't one of his favorite people."

Lana stared at Grant for a moment, then stood and said, "I'm done."

Tuper yanked Grant to his feet. "Get out of here! And if I ever see you near Lana again, I won't hesitate to put you down for good."

"Sure." Grant hobbled away, then stopped and turned. "Lana, you know this isn't over."

Tuper started to go after him, but JP grabbed his arm. "Let him go."

"Something doesn't add up." Lana's brow was furrowed in thought. "I don't know what to believe, but if Grant didn't kill Jack, then the sniper is still out there. I know Grant's lying because his lips were moving. I just don't know which part he lied about."

"Is it possible he's just a pawn in someone else's game?" JP asked, watching Grant as he left the park.

"Could be," Lana conceded. "But one thing's for sure. He's right about this not being over."

"And you're not out of danger, from Grant or whoever else is out there," Tuper said. "I can't believe he thought he could just grab you in a public place and drag you off."

"The man thinks he can do whatever he wants, and he believes he's invincible. He's a legend in his own mind."

"I'll tail Grant and see where he goes," JP said shaking his head. "Ron has his eye on him now, so I'll take over."

Chapter Forty-Eight

Tuesday afternoon

Snow fell like a silent whisper, blanketing the streets of Helena. The cold bit through JP's leather gloves, but he kept his focus on the car ahead. He was determined to keep Lana safe, and that meant staying on Grant's tail.

"Damn," JP muttered under his breath as he watched Grant's taillights disappear around a corner. "This guy's slippery as a hog on ice."

Grant eventually pulled into a hotel parking lot. JP found a discreet spot nearby to observe. As he waited, his thoughts wandered back to when he was five and witnessed a shooting involving his father. He hadn't told anyone for twenty years.

Secrets, JP thought. Everyone had 'em, but Lana's might just get her killed. He wondered whether she truly understood the danger she was in. According to Ron, she felt remorse for her previous life choices, and she was trying to make amends for them.

When Grant finally left the hotel, JP's pulse jumped with anticipation. He started the Hyundai and began tailing Grant again, his eyes locked on the man who posed a threat to his friends. He followed him to The

Jesters Bar. The place didn't look like much from the outside, but JP googled it on his phone and read the reviews. It was apparently a jumpin' place for the local millennials. JP waited outside and watched for him to come out. Grant stayed inside for a good hour and a half and when he walked out, he appeared a little unsteady.

JP followed him, and with each turn it became increasingly apparent where Grant was headed: Clarice's trailer. JP knew no one was home, so his concern was minimal, but it did confirm that Grant hadn't given up on getting to Lana. He was as arrogant as Lana had said, and with a few drinks in him, likely far more dangerous. He was certainly more stupid.

JP parked across the street and watched as the icy wind whipped up Grant's collar as he stepped out of his F-150. Grant approached Clarice's home, and glanced around, but he obviously didn't see JP.

"Where are you, Lana?" Grant called out loud enough for JP to hear. The man paced outside Clarice's door for a while, but soon the bitter cold drove him back to his car. Grant got in and waited. He eventually gave up on Lana and drove off. JP followed him to a Taco Bell, where he got in line at the drive-through. The smell of food made JP's stomach rumble, but he couldn't get anything yet. Tuper would relieve him soon. He would eat then.

JP continued to follow Grant around town until he finally went back to his hotel. Once he left his truck and went inside, JP picked up his phone and reported to Tuper what Grant had been up to, emphasizing his idiotic trip to Clarice's trailer in search of Lana. "I think that boy's got two brains—one's missin', and the other is out lookin' for it."

Chapter Forty-Nine

Tuesday afternoon

At Tuper's insistence, Lana rode with him and Dually to the Hutterite colony, where he thought she would be safe. He trusted the members, and it was an unlikely place for anyone to look. The wheels of Tuper's old car kicked up mud as they slowly wound through the rolling hills, past fields sprinkled with snow. Lana found herself again captivated by the beauty of the landscape. She'd stayed in the colony before on an earlier case, but this time of year was special. She watched as snowflakes floated slowly toward the ground. Everything seemed so peaceful.

Everyone had agreed that Mary Ann and Clarice would be safer here too, so they were behind them in Mary Ann's car with Ron driving. Poor Clarice was still recovering from her ordeal. Lana worried she would never be the same and that it was her fault.

Tuper finally came to a stop in front of a collection of unpainted buildings. As she climbed out, Lana could see people scurrying around, their faces curious.

Tuper and Lana walked over to the others, who were standing near Clarice's car.

"What now?" Ron asked.

"I've already spoken to Jacob," Tuper said. "He's expecting us. They don't have a lot of extra room, but they've arranged for Clarice and Mary Ann to stay with the older girls. Ron, you and Lana can stay in the loft in the barn. She can use her computer from there."

"They have internet?" Clarice asked, a little surprised.

Lana's thoughts went back a few months to when she was here helping Tuper find a couple of girls who were missing from the colony. She remembered she had WiFi but the connection was slow. She'd been grateful to have it then and was thrilled to know it was still available.

"They do." Tuper said. "And they have one computer that stays in Jacob's house." He picked up Clarice's overnight bag. "They grow their own crops, raise their own livestock, even make their clothes. Unlike the Amish, they do believe in machinery, as long as it's used to better their life as it is." Tuper started toward the buildings. "Don't worry about stickin' out like a sore thumb. They're welcoming folks, and they'll keep you safe while we figure out what the heck Grant wants with Lana."

As they neared, a man in his seventies with a long, gray beard came out to greet them. *"Willkommen, Brüderlein."*

"Danke," Tuper said. "You know Ron and Lana, but I'm not sure if you've ever met my friends Clarice and Mary Ann." Tuper looked at the women. "Jacob is the *Haushalter*. Excuse me, the leader of the colony."

"The Lord has blessed anyone who has a friend in Tuper," Jacob said. "Welcome to our home. Clarice, I'm sorry to hear of your ordeal. I hope you can get some rest here and heal quickly."

"Thank you," Clarice said.

"Do you need some help?" Jacob asked.

"No. I'm weak and I move slowly, but I can manage on my own."

Mary Ann and Ron acted as bookends as they walked her to the door.

"Come in, come in." Jacob held the door open stepping back to let them all enter.

Even though Lana had been here before, she experienced the same nostalgic feeling she had the last time. The room resembled an old movie set from the silent era, with only the bare essentials. The wooden table and chairs were simple and functional, but finely finished. It shouldn't have been a surprise to her. These people lived a simple, religious life, focused on farming and community. Worldly goods were not important to them. It was such a contrast to her father and the way she'd grown up. She felt a little ashamed.

"Sit, sit." Jacob motioned them to the chairs.

As they did, Jacob's wife, Mary, entered and offered hot tea and *Strudel*. They all declined.

"Mary," Jacob said, "I think it's best to take Clarice to her room. She needs rest." Jacob turned to Ron. "I'm glad the Lord has brought you back here. You, as Tuper, are welcome any time. You and Lana can stay in the barn. You know where it is."

"Thank you," Ron said. "I appreciate your hospitality."

"I'll get them settled in the barn," Tuper said, standing. "Then I'll come back and visit before I leave."

"*Danke, Brüderlein.*"

Lana made a mental note of the German words they'd used.

After they left Jacob's house, Tuper's phone rang. He listened for a few seconds, then hung up.

"Dang!" Tuper exclaimed, as they walked to the barn. "This Grant fella's like a bad penny and just keeps turnin' up. JP said he followed Grant right to your house."

"Did he try to get inside?"

"No. He's sitting outside, probably waiting for you to get home."

Such strange behavior. "At least we know where he is."

As they made their way through the colony, Lana was again struck by the stark contrast between this place and her life back in Helena. The people here dressed simply, in dark, modest clothing, with no trace of modern fashion and no one carried cellphones. They moved with purpose, tending to the crops and animals with a quiet determination that spoke of generations of tradition.

"What now?" Lana asked.

"I'm leaving to go help JP," Tuper said. "We can take shifts keeping an eye on Grant. You've stayed here before, so you know the ropes. This is their home, their rules, even though they may seem strange."

"Got it, Pops."

"Humph." Tuper turned back toward Jacob's house.

Lana shivered and went inside to get warm. The barn was surprisingly warmer, the heat no doubt provided for the animals. When she went back outside a half hour later, Tuper's car was gone. She stood outside the barn, watching the snowflakes dance gently through the air. The quiet serenity of the winter landscape was a stark contrast to the unease that hung heavy in her heart.

Chapter Fifty

Tuesday evening

Clarice and Mary Ann stepped into the dorm room, a small space with four double beds in a row for the eight girls who slept there. Patchwork quilts covered each bed and homemade rugs were scattered on the floor. The walls were bare. The Hutterite girls smiled as they welcomed them in, offering pillows to make their stay more comfortable. Two of the girls had given up their bed for Clarice and Mary Ann.

"We don't want to take your bed," Mary Ann said.

"It's not a problem," one of the girls said. "We're used to sleeping tight. Until we moved to this room, we had three in the bed every night."

Clarice lay down, wincing at the pain. Her bruises were still prominent on her face and arms, and the memory of spending thirty-six hours alone in a cold, dark barn made her shiver.

The oldest girl said, "We heard you were kidnapped. Is that true?"

"Yes," Clarice said.

"Would you mind telling us about it? We don't hear many stories from the *Welt Leut.*" When Clarice didn't respond right away, the girl added, "If you're too tired, it's okay."

Clarice was tired, but the girls were all standing around her bed in anticipation. They were so anxious to hear stories from the *outside world* that she couldn't say no. She knew they'd had some problems a few months back when some girls had been enticed to leave the colony, but most of them had no idea what life was like outside their realm. Clarice sat up and started with her date with Jack, wincing again at how naïve she'd been.

The girls listened in rapt attention, their eyes wide, as she recounted the events, while trying not to make her story too graphic. A few of the more adventurous girls found it very exciting. Most, however, seemed to have a new appreciation for their colony and their safe way of life. When Clarice finished her story, the room was silent except for the occasional sniffle.

"I'm fine now, or at least I will be soon. I really appreciate you giving us shelter."

"Do you think he'll come after you here?" one of the girls asked.

Another cut in. "Weren't you listening? Someone shot him. He's dead."

"But maybe he wasn't alone," the first girl said.

"You needn't worry," Mary Ann assured her. "We're all safe here. Tuper wouldn't let anything happen to us." Mary Ann forced a smile. "We better let Clarice rest. She's very tired."

~~~

As Lana entered the warmth of Jacob's home, she pulled off her gloves and shook the snow from her hair. The Hutterite elder stood by the stove, stirring a pot of
~~~

steaming soup, the scent permeating the air. She felt comforted by the sight.

"It sure smells good in here," Lana said.

"Mary makes a fine vegetable-beef soup," Jacob said.

"Can I talk to you about something?" Lana asked hesitantly, taking a seat on a wooden chair.

"Of course." Jacob's eyes crinkled with kindness as he turned to face her. "What's on your mind?"

"Did you know Tuper when he was younger? Like, really young?" Lana fiddled with a loose thread on her coat.

"Ah, Tuper." A nostalgic smile crossed Jacob's face. "I've known him as long as I can remember."

"Really?" Lana leaned forward. "What was he like?"

"Fun, smart, generous, a rule-breaker—not much different than he is now."

"Got any good stories about him when he was young?"

Jacob considered her request for a moment, then nodded. "Many stories." He took a seat beside her. "Tuper never liked going to school. He'd sneak away and go hunting with his sling shot. His mother would get very angry at him, but then he'd do something sweet, like bring her wild raspberries, which she loved, and she couldn't stay mad at him."

"Please tell me more," Lana pleaded.

"Let me share a tale from our childhood."

Lana nodded eagerly.

"Years ago," Jacob began, "there was an incident in our community. Some money had gone missing, and everyone was suspicious of each other. It was a dark time, full of distrust and accusations."

Jacob paused, his eyes clouding. "One day, Tuper overheard some men talking about the theft. They were convinced they knew who the thief was and planned to take matters into their own hands."

"Did Tuper know the accused?" Lana interjected.

"Indeed, he did," Jacob confirmed. "And Tuper knew the accused person was innocent. So he decided to take the blame himself. He couldn't stand the thought of that child being hurt because of a false accusation."

"Wait, so Tuper let everyone think he was the thief?"

"Exactly," Jacob affirmed. "He took the punishment and suffered in silence, never once complaining or trying to clear his name."

"Why would he do that?"

"Because I was the one the men had accused, and Tuper knew he could take the punishment easier than I could."

"But you didn't do it?"

"No. Eventually, they discovered the thief, but Tuper's reputation was forever tarnished."

"But if people knew he wasn't the thief, why would it hurt Tuper's reputation?"

"Because he lied and, in our community, that's as bad as stealing."

Lana's heart was heavy with the weight of this revelation. She had always seen *Pops* as a pillar of strength and unwavering loyalty, and now she realized he had been that way even from the start. He was apparently always loyal to those he cared about.

"Thank you for telling me, Jacob."

"Lana," Jacob said gently, "as a child, Tuper spent a lot of time in trouble, but he always had a good heart. He grew up to be a good man with lots of faults, but with at least as many virtues. Tuper had to make a difficult decision long ago, and it changed his life forever. We all have our secrets, and sometimes they're best left buried. He'll share his secrets with you when, and if, he's ready."

"Tell me this, Jacob." Lana was quite certain she knew what he was talking about. "Do you think he made the right decision?"

"He made the right one for him. That's the only thing an honest man can do."

Chapter Fifty-One

Tuesday night

Lana sat in the barn loft, the glow of her laptop screen the only light in the room. The scent of cow manure mingled with the cold winter air that seeped through the window cracks, but Lana barely noticed as she tracked Grant's online footprint.

Frustration mounted as she tried to make sense of the trail of breadcrumbs he'd left behind. Her fingers moved with practiced precision, a testament to her skills as a hacker. She was determined to uncover the connection between Grant, her father, and Jack Peterson. The truth was out there, hidden within a tangled web of secrets and lies, waiting for her to find it.

She finally stumbled upon a series of encrypted messages between the three men. Lana's heart raced as she decoded the mishmash of numbers and letters, a code meant to hide their intentions from prying eyes. The code resembled a series of strange symbols, a foreign language that made no sense. Compiling the encrypted messages using common words and a substitution cipher, Lana studied the decoded messages on her worksheet, desperately trying to make sense of them. Her breath quickened as she read the chilling words.

"Gotcha," she whispered, wavering between triumph and disbelief at what she was uncovering. Grant, her father, and Jack had been working together to carry out her father's original plan—manipulate the stock market and skim millions from unsuspecting investors. Their twisted conspiracy involved politicians in several countries, including the US. Lana had known about her father's plan, but she'd never believed he could actually carry it out, and she didn't know the details until now. It had been so far-fetched, but no matter how unsuccessful he was, he would've still destroyed a lot of people. He had expected her to help him. That was the main reason she'd left.

Had Jack and Grant figured out that they needed her instead of her father? Was that the reason her father had been killed? She was sure now that her father's death was no accident. And now, Grant had plans for her as well. She felt a chill run down her spine as she read their words again and again, until the truth of their intentions became clear.

She slammed her fist against the table, her thoughts tumbling over each other like a violent storm. The knowledge felt like a heavy weight pressing down on her, threatening to crush her from the inside out.

She heard Ron climbing the steps to the loft, then he stuck his head through the opening. "You okay?" Ron took the last few steps into the room.

"I just found the connection between Jack and Grant. They both appear to be involved in my father's death."

"I'm sorry about that, but not surprised."

"First, they planned to kill me, so I couldn't stop their grand crime. But then they had a falling out with my father and got rid of him, which meant they needed me for one last job. And they still do."

"So, they tried to persuade you from both angles. Jack tried, and when that didn't work, Grant tried," Ron said. "Do you think Grant decided he didn't need Jack anymore, so he got rid of him?"

"That's what it looks like. With Jack out of the way, Grant would get all the money and more importantly, all the power."

"I'd better call Tuper and JP and update them."

"Thanks," Lana said. "I still have some unanswered questions, so I'll stick with this awhile."

Ron disappeared down the steps.

Trust no one. She repeated the mantra that had guided her through the darkest times of her life. She hated that she still needed to live that way, with the exception of her Helena family. She knew Grant couldn't be trusted. He'd proved that long ago, but seeing in black and white his and Jack's motives had been frightening. The worst though was her own father's involvement. She had exposed the sinister motives of those closest to her. With that sobering thought echoing in her head, Lana dove back into the digital shadows. A moment later, she remembered JP's suspicions of Danny. It seemed pointless to look into him now, but she had some time.

She searched everywhere for information about Danny Atterbury. She found his birth certificate, his high school graduation diploma, and his driver's license. But she didn't find any social media or online presence of any kind, not even an email account. If he had one, it was under another name. She called JP to let him know.

~~~

Ron descended the steps of the loft, allowing Lana to work uninterrupted. He pulled on his coat and went outside to get some fresh, winter air. He liked the cold weather, at least as a change from the steady warm weather that San Diego offered. He'd spent a few years in Washington and really enjoyed the seasonal changes.

As he walked toward the main building, the snow drifted slowly to the ground over the Hutterite Colony. Ron suddenly caught sight of a shadowy figure approaching out of the darkness. The intruder moved stealthily, clearly intent on remaining undetected. Ron's pulse quickened, and he steeled himself for a confrontation. He crept forward, determined not to let this interloper get closer to Lana.

"Hey!" Ron barked, his voice echoing through the night. The figure froze for a moment, then bolted, their footsteps leaving a trail of disturbed snow.

Ron went back into the barn, hoping it had just been a teenager from the colony trying to sneak out. He climbed the stairs to the loft.

"Who was that?" Lana asked.

"I couldn't get a good look." Ron positioned himself by the window where he could keep watch. "But don't worry, it wasn't Grant. JP's got eyes on him in Helena."

In the dimly lit room, Lana hunched over her laptop, digging deeper into the web of secrets that had ensnared her. Ron occasionally took his eyes off the compound outside and glanced over at Lana. The cool air from the window seemed to prickle at her skin. He
~~~

couldn't help but admire her; she was so smart, but so troubled. He got up and walked over to her.

"Have you found anything more?" Ron asked quietly from behind, scanning her screen.

Lana shook her head. "Not yet. But I'm close. I can feel it."

"Be careful," Ron warned, still worried about her.

"I am, but I'm so tired of running."

Ron sighed, knowing there was no use trying to argue with her. Instead, he went back to his watch.

As the night wore on, Lana's eyes grew heavy, but she refused to give into sleep.

"Maybe we should call it a night," Ron suggested, noting Lana's exhaustion. "You won't find anything if you can't focus."

"Fine," Lana conceded, rubbing her eyes. "But only for a few hours." She closed her laptop and crawled into the makeshift bed in the corner.

Ron sat vigilantly at the window where he could see if anyone approached, hoping the intruder wouldn't return. His mind raced with thoughts of what could be lurking in the shadows – *Was Grant getting closer? Was JP able to keep him at bay? Was there someone else out there they hadn't counted on?* He wondered as he watched sleep finally claim Lana.

A few minutes later, Ron saw a shadow move along the edge of the property. The faint sound of crunching snow echoed in the night. He wondered if someone from the colony was out for a stroll, which didn't seem likely, or if someone was looking for Lana. He wished Tuper or JP were there with a sidearm.

Chapter Fifty-Two

Wednesday morning

The meeting room at the Hutterite colony was small and austere, with a single light bulb illuminating rough wooden walls. Lana and Ron sat on sturdy, handmade chairs around a well-built table. With her unusual style of dress and brightly colored hair, Lana felt out of place amongst the simple surroundings.

"We're connected," Lana announced as she set up FaceTime on her laptop. JP, cowboy hat and all, appeared on the screen. He looked focused, his eyes squinting against the sunlight that streamed through the window.

"I'm still on Grant's tail," he said. "But he just entered his hotel room, so hopefully, he'll stay there awhile."

"You look exhausted," Ron said. "Were you up all night?"

"No. Tuper relieved me most of the night. I just had a little trouble sleeping. Too much on my mind, I guess."

"Where is Tuper?" Ron asked.

They heard a car door open in the background, and Tuper got inside, partially appearing on the screen. He shivered and rubbed his hands together in front of the heater vent. "I'm here."

"Let's get started," Lana said. She pulled out Jack's phone from her pocket and held it up. "I found some evidence that I believe points to my father's death."

"Go on," Tuper said.

"Okay," Lana began, taking a deep breath. "I found a lot of damaging information last night. Without going into detail, we now know for certain that Grant, Jack, and my father were working on my dad's big power move. Basically, their plan was to control the world, or at least a huge part of it."

"That's pretty ambitious. Could they do that?"

"No. But he could've done lot of damage, and hurt a lot of people along the way. My father was a dreamer. He had convinced himself he could do it all, have it all, and be king of the world."

"What do you think happened?"

"My take on it is that Jack and Grant either couldn't get along with my father, or they decided they didn't need him and they killed him. I haven't sorted that all out yet." Lana sipped her coffee, taking a moment to compose herself. It was difficult to discuss her dad's murder so casually. "With my father gone, they realized they couldn't pull it off without him, and therefore, they needed me. Or maybe, they just decided they could control me better than him, and that's why they got rid of him. Or, they figured out my father didn't know as much as they thought, and they needed me to do his job instead." Lana continued without taking a breath. "Whatever their reasons, they killed my dad, then came after me. They planned to use me and then get rid of me. I'm guessing Grant figured out that Jack had done all he could do, so he shot him. Which means, I'm the only one left who can help carry out the plan. Well, me and maybe Isaac Newton."

"Who's Isaac Newton?" Tuper asked.

"I don't know. I'm still working on that."

"Dang, Agony, you're exhausting me," Tuper said. "Where are you goin' with this?"

"Here's a few of the messages I found." She brought up a screen so they could see them. Then she scrolled through the messages, showing the men the incriminating chat. "Look here." She pointed at one message. "Jack wrote, *Charles gone dark, but we've got everything in place*."

"Here's another one," Lana continued. "Grant replied, *As long as no one finds out, we're in the clear. His daughter won't suspect a thing*."

Tuper exhaled sharply, his jaw clenched.

"Do you think both Jack and Grant were involved in your father's death?" JP asked.

"I haven't quite figured out how it all happened, but I know they both wanted my dad out of the picture, and I'm not sure about their motives. I also know they were scamming a lot of money and putting it in off-shore accounts. But let's get down to the nitty-gritty." Lana set Jack's phone on the table. "This little gem has provided us with tons of information. I dug deep into Jack's contact list. Every person in Jack's phone had a connection to my father, with the exception of Isaac Newton. But I'm thinking that's not a real name. I'm still working on that. We managed to uncover some pretty damning evidence about his contacts." She glanced at Tuper, who looked perplexed.

"What kind of connections?" Tuper asked.

"Many, if not all, were involved in my father's death. Some, in his life."

"Who are these people?" Tuper scowled.

"Okay." Lana inhaled deeply as she prepared to lay out the intricate web of deceit she'd uncovered. "You know my father died in a house fire that was deemed an accident."

"Of course," JP replied. "I remember it from the time it happened. The fire was all over the local news."

"I don't believe it was an accident at all," Lana said. "I think the fire marshal, Owen Unger, was part of the coverup and was working for whoever killed him, which I think was Jack and/or Grant. Owen claimed it was accidental when it was actually arson."

"Son of a gun," muttered Tuper. "Who else was involved?"

"Victor Marsh, a telephone lineman, helped my father somehow. I'm sure of it. I just don't know how. Then there is Agnes Blackwell. She was also a hacker, so I'm guessing she helped my father with things he couldn't do when he was *unavailable*. Just a guess. There are four more names in his contacts, including Martin Foster, Susan Walsh, and Philip Kent. I think they were all involved in the cover-up of the arson. Some of them may not have known what he was doing. My father was very good at compartmentalizing. He would have people do pieces of things so even they didn't know how it all connected."

Lana kept her tone precise and methodical as she laid out the facts. "Martin Foster is the funeral director who handled my dad's arrangements. I can't quite figure out how he plays into it, but I'm still searching.

"Then there's Susan Walsh who was once my father's doctor. But I can't find any connection to his death, so I don't know why she's in here."

"Finally," Lana said, her voice barely concealing her anger, "there's Philip Kent, an attorney who specialized in estate law. He helped my dad transfer all his assets to a shell company two weeks before he died."

"Good Lord." Tuper rubbed his weathered hands over his face. "This just gets stranger and stranger."

"Don't forget Wayne Osborne and Isaac Newton," Ron said.

Lana shrugged. "Wayne Osborne was my father's dentist. I don't see how he fits into the scheme yet, but I've been able to establish that he was also Jack's dentist."

"Maybe he was doing some dental work for Jack," JP said. "Sometimes a possum is just a possum."

"That's possible," Lana said. "But that would make him the only personal contact on his phone. The rest all seem to be involved in some way in his shady business."

"Even Isaac Newton?" JP asked again.

Lana hesitated. "I'm not sure about him yet, but he's likely connected to this as well. His name popped up a few times in the encrypted messages, but I'm sure it's an alias."

"Which explains why we can't find an online presence for him," Ron said.

The FaceTime group fell silent as they absorbed the information Lana had shared.

"All right." Tuper broke the silence. "We've got our work cut out for us."

Lana nodded, then looked at Jack's phone as if it held the answers. "There are more texts, emails, and even some encrypted files I haven't been able to crack yet. But one thing is clear: My dad, Jack, Grant, and several other people were all working together. The question is—what went wrong that got four of them killed?"

Chapter Fifty-Three

Wednesday night

Lana had been stuck inside her tiny sanctuary for too long. So, when Ron went to see Benjamin, one of the men he had gotten to know previously at the colony, Lana stepped outside and inhaled the cold night air. Her feet crunched piles of snow as she took a few steps away from the barn.

Lana heard footsteps and turned toward the sound. Out of nowhere, a man lunged for her. Lana gasped, barely managing to pull away before his hand could clamp down on her wrist. He tried to cover her mouth, but she yanked her head to the side and shouted, "Get off me!" Lana tried to pull away, kicking and fighting the hooded man.

"Ron! Help!" she yelled, panic rising like bile in her throat.

A moment later, Ron came around the corner of the barn and charged the attacker. "Let her go!" Ron roared, tackling him to the ground. The two men grappled, fists flying. Curses spewed from Ron. But the assailant was silent. Lana's heart was racing as Ron fought off the kidnapper. There was something familiar about him, but she couldn't pin it down.

"Ron!" she screamed, watching helplessly as the attacker nearly overpowered him. Suddenly, several men came running from a colony dormitory. The stranger scrambled to his feet, gave Ron a hard shove, and sprinted away into the darkness.

"Are you okay, Lana?" Ron asked, panting heavily as he rose to his feet.

Lana stared at him, her chest heaving with each breath, struggling to process what had just happened.

"Y-yeah," she stammered, her voice shaking. Ron pulled her in and hugged her. She suddenly felt so vulnerable. She hated that feeling of helplessness, and it morphed into anger.

Several of the young men raced after the assailant, but he had vanished into the woods. The darkness seemed to swallow him whole, as though the night itself had conspired against them.

Just then Jacob walked up. "Are you two okay?"

"We're fine," Ron said.

"We'll get our flashlights and look around," Benjamin offered.

"No," Ron said. "Don't. It's too dangerous. He could be armed, and he may not be alone."

"Ron's right," Jacob said. "Benjamin, you get three others and station yourselves where you can watch the perimeter and warn us. Let's hope he's just getting as far away as he can."

Lana leaned heavily on Ron, as they trudged back toward the safety of the barn. Her eyes darted around, searching for any signs of danger. Once inside, Ron pulled her closer, trying to make her feel safe. But it only irritated Lana. She was still angry that she couldn't protect herself and was putting others in danger.

"Any idea who that was?" Ron asked.

"No. Although there was something oddly familiar about him. I just can't put my finger on it."

"Could it have been Grant?"

"It definitely wasn't him. Wrong size. Grant is much taller and huskier." Lana shook her head. "Besides, unless JP or Tuper lost sight of him, Grant can't be in two places at once."

"You're right. But I'll check with JP." Ron placed the call and put him on speaker.

"Hey," JP said. "Everything okay?"

"Not exactly. Can you see Grant?"

"Tuper is on him. We just traded spots. Why?"

"Because someone just tried to grab Lana," Ron said.

"Oh no. Any idea who?"

"No. But I have to call Tuper." Ron ended the call.

"That's it," Lana said. "We're leaving here tomorrow. I'm not bringing any more danger to these people."

"Let's go up."

Once inside the loft, Ron stood near the window where he could keep watch. Lana called Tuper, put him on speaker, and explained what had happened.

"It sure wasn't Grant. I'm watching him right now eat burgers and fries. Never saw a guy who ate so much." Tuper made a sound in his throat. "So, unless he has an identical twin brother..."

"He does not," Lana said. "Besides, I could tell it wasn't him."

"Neither of you got a look at the man's face?"

"No. He wore a ski mask," Lana said. "All I know is we can't stay here any longer. He knows where I am, and it's not safe for us or these people."

"You're right," Tuper said. "It also means that either Grant has an accomplice or someone else is after you. Which puts us completely in the dark, because we don't know who or why."

"I know," Lana said quietly. "I'm so sorry."

"You got no reason to be sorry. Just let Jacob know you're leaving. Clarice and Mary Ann can stay if they want. Whoever this is wants you, and Clarice can't keep moving around. They're already wearing the Hutterite garb and have blended in. They should be safe there, and there's no way we can watch everyone."

"Where should I go?" Lana asked.

"Head toward Helena. Call me when you're on your way, and I'll let you know. And be careful. Make sure you're not being followed."

Lana and Ron hurriedly packed their belongings, thanked Jacob, and said goodbye to Clarice and Mary Ann.

Under the cover of darkness, they got on the road, checking for headlights behind them. Ron called Tuper, putting him on speaker so Lana could hear. "We're moving and no one seems to be following us."

"Good. You're goin' to Jerome Johnson's house," Tuper said. "He's a good friend who lives in East Helena. You'll be safe there for now."

"I've been there, but I'm not sure exactly where he lives."

Tuper gave him the address.

As they drove through the night, checking constantly behind them, Lana couldn't help but feel the weight of uncertainty pressing down on her chest. She glanced over at Ron, who sat silently behind the wheel, his expression unreadable. She wondered if he felt the same gnawing dread that clawed at her insides.

Ron seemed to sense her thoughts. Without a word, his hand found hers, offering a touch of reassurance that she desperately needed.

They arrived at the new safe house just before midnight.

"Make yourselves comfortable," said Jerome, a blond, blue-eyed, muscular man in his early fifties, who welcomed them with open arms. "You're safe here, I promise. This home is protected by my good friends, Smith and Wesson."

"Thank you, Jerome." Lana forced a small smile.

Lana visited with her host for a few minutes, then excused herself. She was beat. She lay on the bed in the guest room trying to fall asleep. When she couldn't, she got up and looked out the window. Ron and Jerome sat on the porch, talking in low voices. A noise, coming from the side of the house near Lana's bedroom, suddenly pierced their conversation. The men jolted to their feet and sprinted around the corner of the house, with Jerome brandishing a gun. She heard the intruder yelp and saw him take off into the trees. Jerome chased after him. Just then Ron came into Lana's room.

"Are you okay?" he asked.

"They know where we are." Lana stood there for a second staring at Ron. "That means they've been tracking us. Somehow, they've been following our every move."

"But how?" Ron asked.

"It must be our phones." Lana shook her head, despair on her face. "One of us must have a tracking device. I'm pretty sure it's not me, but I'll check to see if my security has been breached. In the meantime, we need to be very careful about what we say and what we text."

"Someone can monitor all that?" Ron asked.

"For techies, almost anything is possible. There is no privacy in this world anymore."

Jerome came into the room. "Sorry, but he got away. I'm fast with my weapon, but not my legs."

"So, how do we communicate?" Ron seemed baffled.

Lana looked at Jerome. "Can we use your phone to call Tuper?"

"Of course." He handed it over.

"What if Tuper's phone has been breached?" Ron asked.

Lana couldn't help but laugh. "Have you seen Tuper's phone? It's an ancient flip phone. He's lucky he can still get a signal on that thing. It's highly unlikely there's any spyware attached to it. There just aren't any openings to access."

Lana called Tuper. When he answered, she said, "Can you come to Jerome's? We've got a problem. He's found us again." She told him briefly about the attempt to get to her, but she didn't want to discuss much else on the phone.

"I'm still tailing Grant, but JP will be here to relieve me about five. Do you think you're safe until mornin'? If not, I'll call and wake JP up."

"I think we'll be fine. Jerome is pretty diligent."

"Good. Get some sleep. I'll be there by five-thirty."

"Thanks, Pops."

Lana went back to bed, but she couldn't sleep. Every sound put her on edge, and the darkness of her room seemed alive with unseen forces. Who was after her?

Jack and Grant had always been her biggest fears, but was this someone else? Someone not even connected to them? Her mind flooded with thoughts of who it might be and why.

Chapter Fifty-Four

Thursday early morning

"Dang it! This guy is good." Tuper slammed his fist on the table, startling Lana. Ron flinched too, but Jerome was unfazed. They were all sucking down coffee after a restless night.

"You're right," Lana said. "We need to figure out which phones we can safely use. I think yours is fine, Pops, because it's too old to hold any sophisticated spyware. And I've checked mine for every possible breach and can't find anything. Besides, if he was into my phone, he would've had lots of chances to get to me before now. That leaves Ron's phone as the likely problem."

"Great." Ron ran a hand through his hair. "What exactly can they do with this breach?"

"That depends on what they've attached to it. They may be able to follow us like a GPS signal or just see where we are. That's easy to do. It would be similar to those apps families use so they can tell where others are. A lot of parents use them to keep track of their kids. And the kids use them to keep track of their friends. But that's all voluntary. This one is involuntarily attached to your system."

"So, he can't tell what we're saying to each other?"

"That depends. He could set up something so he can read your text messages, which again is pretty easy. And if he's really good, he can actually hear your phone calls. That's much more difficult though."

"Geez," Tuper said. "That's scary. I'm sticking to my flip phone. I don't want anyone knowin' where and when I'm comin' and goin'."

"So," Ron said, worry etching lines across his face, "if they've tapped one of our phones, they could know everything we've been saying."

"That's possible," Lana said.

Tuper's eyes narrowed, but he didn't speak.

"All right, then," Lana said. "Ron, hand me your phone. I'll check it for any signs of a breach."

Reluctantly, Ron handed over his sleek smartphone. Lana moved deftly through the device, knowing where to look for signs of hacking or intrusion. "This would be easier if I could connect the phone to my laptop with a USB cable, but I don't want to give him access to that too. So, I'll have to do it the hard way."

"But it can be done, right?"

"Just takes a lot longer. You all might want to find something to keep you busy for a while."

"I can make some breakfast," Jerome said.

"Thanks, Jerome," Tuper said. "I think I'll lay down for a bit and get a little shut-eye."

After Jerome and Tuper left the room, Ron watched over Lana's shoulder as she accessed the inner workings of the phone. "What are you looking for?" he asked.

"Spyware or malware, any suspicious activity logs, unauthorized access points, anything that screams 'someone's been snooping around where they shouldn't be,'" Lana explained.

The deeper she dove into the phone's digital entrails, the less patient she became. *Come on, come on*, she thought, anxiety gnawing at her insides. *If we've been compromised, we need to know now.*

Jerome brought eggs and bacon to the table. Ron encouraged Lana to eat, but she didn't want to stop. The men went ahead without her, then cleared the table, leaving a plate for Tuper who had fallen asleep.

Finally, Lana shouted, "Got something."

"What is it?" Ron moved to her side.

"The phone has traces of a remote-access trojan horse."

"Speak English," Tuper barked as he joined them at the table.

"Someone's been listening to Ron's conversations and tracking his movements. They've had access to everything."

"Dang it," Ron hissed, clenching his fists.

Tuper's face paled. "That's how he knew we were at the Hutterite Colony, and now here."

"I'll bet when we check JP's phone, we'll find the same thing."

"This place ain't safe anymore." Tuper turned to Jerome. "Sorry, man. I hope we didn't bring you danger."

"I'm not worried. Anyone comes around here, they'll wish they hadn't."

"Where do we go next?" Lana asked.

"I know a guy who can help," Tuper declared. "He's got a secure place we can use. Name's Brad Bergstad."

"Who's that?" Ron asked.

"Old friend of mine." Tuper's tone was nostalgic. "Known him since he was a kid. His father and I were good friends, and when they fell on hard times, I took 'em in. Brad's got a heart of gold, and he owes me a favor or two. He runs a DNA lab now, so security is top-notch."

Lana nodded in agreement. "Let's go see this Brad guy."

Ron picked up his phone. "I'll call JP and tell him what's happening."

"No." Lana and Tuper said it at the same time.

"Oops." Ron turned to Jerome. "Can I use your phone?"

"That won't work either," Lana said hastily. "We don't know about JP's phone yet."

"I'll go see JP after I escort you guys to Brad's," Tuper offered.

"We have to get some burner phones for JP and Ron," Lana said, "but for now, we know yours and mine are safe."

"Can the culprit tell that you found the breach?" Tuper asked.

"Since I disabled Ron's phone, the hacker will suspect something I'm sure. But he can still read texts and listen to phone calls. I didn't disturb that in hopes he'll either think it's a glitch and the GPS went down, or that we don't know about the rest of it."

"Do you think that'll work?"

"Wait a minute," Ron said. "So, he can't tell where I am, but he can still read my texts and hear my calls?"

"That's right. So, don't use it unless we want him to know something," Lana said. "I think we should leave the tracker on JP's and then he'll think we don't know about that phone, or that yours was a fluke. It might help throw him off."

"But then he'll know where we are from JP's phone."

"Not if he leaves it somewhere."

"He can bring it here, if Jerome doesn't mind," Tuper said. "He already knows about this place anyway."

"No problem," Jerome said.

"Good," Lana said. "We'll have JP send a message to you saying he's going to lay down for a few hours. That'll explain the inactivity."

Tuper shook his head. "I hope this works."

Chapter Fifty-Five

Thursday morning

"Brad's place is about fifteen minutes away," Tuper informed them, his voice gruff in the quiet morning. "The culprit knows where we are right now, so I'll take the back roads. You just follow me. If you see anything suspicious, let me know."

"We'll watch carefully," Lana said.

The sun was rising in the sky, casting a golden hue across the horizon as Lana, Tuper, and Ron stepped outside. The air was crisp, carrying a scent of dew-streaked grass and damp earth.

Lana shivered, zipped her jacket, then climbed into Mary's Honda that Ron was still using. He seemed lost in thought as he followed Tuper.

They drove along winding, unpaved roads, and Lana kept a vigilant watch. When she was confident they weren't being followed, she stared out the window, watching the passing landscape and wondering if she would ever truly be able to escape the relentless pursuit of her past.

"Watch out!" Ron shouted.

Lana's heart leapt in her chest as Ron threw his arm over her to protect her. Tuper's vehicle skidded to the side as a large deer sprinted onto the road. Ron braked and jerked the wheel to narrowly avoid crashing into Tuper's rear end. As quickly as it had appeared, the deer was gone, melting silently into the underbrush.

After a few moments of tense silence, Ron chuckled. "Well, that was close!" He rubbed Lana's arm reassuringly.

Lana gave a nervous laugh. "After everything we've been through, I'd hate to think a deer would take us out."

"That would be a shame."

A few minutes later, a modest house came into view, nestled among the trees. A sign near the gate proudly proclaimed *Bergstad DNA Lab* in bold letters. Tuper slowed and pulled onto the property.

When they exited the vehicle, Lana felt a vague sense of security wash over her. The home was well-kept, surrounded by towering pines that provided ample cover from prying eyes. A series of security cameras were attached to the tree trunks dotting the perimeter, their unblinking lenses scanning for signs of intrusion.

"Good to see you, Tuper." Brad greeted them warmly as he stepped out of his front door with an outstretched hand. His prematurely graying hair and kind eyes put Lana at ease.

Tuper clasped Brad's hand firmly. "Got ourselves a bit of a situation. Someone's been poking around where they shouldn't be, and we need a safe place to figure things out."

"Say no more," Brad replied, nodding. "You're welcome to stay as long as you need. Let me show you inside."

The warm light filling Brad's living room brought a sense of comfort the group hadn't experienced in days. Lana sank into a plush armchair, and her tense muscles finally started to relax. Brad excused himself, then returned with a pot of coffee and a handful of cups. Lana reached for hers eagerly.

"Thank you for taking us in, Brad," Lana said sincerely, cradling a steaming cup of coffee.

"Of course." Brad's voice was reassuring. "You're safe here."

Tuper leaned back in his seat, letting out a long sigh. Ron remained standing. He'd volunteered to go meet with JP so Tuper could rest.

"You should stop at Walmart and pick up a couple of prepaid phones," Lana said. "And explain everything to JP."

"Will do."

"Ron," Tuper added, "you should stay on Grant's tail and send JP back here. I'd feel better with another man with a gun."

"Good idea." Ron headed for the door.

"Be careful," Tuper called out. "Make sure no one is following you."

The door closed behind him and Lana got up to lock it.

"We've bought ourselves some time," Tuper said, "but we need to figure out our next move. This ain't gonna stop just 'cause we're hidin' out."

Lana nodded. "We need to use this time to our advantage—turn the tables on whoever's spying on us. Maybe we can feed them false information and lead them into a trap."

Tuper's phone rang. He looked at the number but didn't answer it.

"Who is it?" Lana asked.

"Henry Fenton. I'll call him later."

"You can't put him off forever, Pops."

"I know." Tuper nodded. "About your trap. It's a good plan, but how do we make sure they buy it? And where do we set the trap?"

"We set up some fake plans, send the guy where we want, then capture him. We can sound panicked, like I'm fleeing. That should bring them out."

"Sounds risky," Brad spoke for the first time, his brow furrowed. "What if they come with backup?"

"We'll be ready," Lana declared. "It appears he's come alone twice now, but at best he might have one other person to help."

"I don't know." Brad shook his head.

"Where should we have the fake meeting?" Lana asked, determined to move forward. "It should be somewhere isolated. We don't want innocent by-standers getting hurt. And it has to be somewhere we can see him approach without him seeing us. He won't just drive up and walk in. He'll try to sneak up and take us by surprise. Maybe even wait until he thinks I'm leaving by myself. And he—"

"Are you done jibber-jabberin'?" Tuper cut in. "I know just where to meet."

"Where?"

Tuper looked at Brad.

Brad nodded and smiled. "That'll work."

"Where?" Lana said louder.

"Brad's family owns some property a few miles from here. It has the perfect setup, with a little tower that will let us see all around the perimeter without being seen."

"We need to set the time," Lana said. "I think late afternoon, around four-thirty. It'll still be light enough to see, but not too bright that we can't hide."

"Sounds good," agreed Tuper. "Now, let's work on the message."

"I'm sure they're expecting to hear from us soon since we've been radio silent for a while. Hopefully, they think we're getting some much-needed rest. We need to make it look like nothing has changed. Like we're hiding out and watching Grant, and we're a little scared and a lot angry. We need to keep that tone." Lana got up to pace. "I think the best way is for me to send a group message. He'll be able to see that I sent it to everyone. When the responses come back, he'll be able to read them on Ron and JP's phones."

"Agony, stop your jibber-jabber and create the messages. I'm going to take a nap." Tuper walked out of the room.

Chapter Fifty-Six

Thursday afternoon

When JP showed up at the house, Lana ran his phone through the same drill as she had with Ron's. Not surprisingly, it had the same security breach. Lana updated JP on some of the details then called Ron on his new phone and told him the plan. Then she sat down with her cell and the two compromised phones and began her messages. She didn't need Tuper's because he never sent texts. She started with the message from her own phone, deciding to only send it to Ron. She hoped that would sound like a more convincing setup.

Lana—*I appreciate all you've done for me, but I can't keep putting people in danger. I need to leave before someone is killed or seriously hurt.*

Then she picked up Ron's phone and responded.

Ron—*We're here because we want to help. We'll keep you safe.*

Lana—*Look what happened to Clarice. Whoever is doing this will not stop. I need to go.*

Ron—*I need to see you before you do.*

Lana—*I'm afraid to go out in public, so I want to just head out of town from here.*

Ron—*Where will you go?*

Lana—*I haven't decided yet. And it's best you don't know.*

Ron—*Please! Please!* (followed by an emoji of praying hands) *I need to hold you one last time.*

Lana paused for a few minutes, as if she needed time to consider the proposition.

Lana—*OK. Let's meet at 4:30.*

Ron—*Fine. Where?*

Lana—*I'll text you the address later.*

She entered a thumbs up emoji on Ron's phone.

"There," Lana said aloud. "The stage is set."

The two hours of waiting were agonizing for Lana. Tuper and JP were both trying to rest, but she couldn't bring herself to sleep. She called Ron on his burner phone.

"Do you still have an eye on Grant?"

"He's having lunch at Burger King," Ron said. "I haven't let him out of my sight. If he heads your way, I'll let you know immediately."

"It can't be him, right? He was being watched when the intruder showed up last night."

"He might still be involved as back up. In that case, I'll be right behind him, and JP and Tuper will be ready for him."

"Sorry," Lana said. "I'm just getting anxious."

Finally, the time had come to go. On the way to the family property, Lana rode with Tuper, and Brad rode with JP in Clarice's car, which he was still driving. They needed time to look around and get into position. The sun was beginning to dip below the horizon, but it left plenty of daylight in the crisp air.

After they arrived, they all got out and surveyed the area, noting the tall trees and thick brush that provided cover. The dilapidated farmhouse, the tower, the swing, the piles of junk, and the configuration of the yard. This was the perfect place for them to lie in wait.

The structure had been built as a storage shed with a lookout to see the animals on the farm. Initially, they could see in all directions. Now, the trees on the west side had grown too tall. It still provided a good view in three directions. Lana climbed the wooden stairs to look around. "This is amazing," she shouted down. "Can you see me?"

"Nope," Tuper responded.

She moved to another area. "How about now?"

"Nope."

"This is great." She dashed down the steps.

"The only way someone could see inside that tower is if they are up high, like in a helicopter or something," JP said. "It's a good lookout point."

"Who's going to be in the tower?" Lana asked.

"I will," Tuper said. "JP and Brad are both faster if they need to chase him, and I'm a better long-distance shot. I'd love to take the jackass out, if it comes to that."

"It's settled then," JP said.

Lana was certain JP hoped it would go that way too.

"Where do you want me, coach?" Brad asked JP, who as an ex-law-enforcement officer, had the most experience.

"If you go over there, you'll be hidden by those bushes, and you can see if anyone approaches from the west." JP pointed to a clump of bushes beyond the swing. "Just watch your back in case he sneaks in from that way."

"I will."

"Where will you be?" Lana asked JP.

"That depends. I think you should sit in that swing, as if you're waiting for Ron to show up. I'll be by the side of the house behind that junk pile. That'll put you halfway between Brad and me. I checked it out and I get a good view from there, and he won't be able to see me. I can shoot from there, if I need to. And I'll be close enough if I have to rush over."

"Okay," Lana sighed before she realized it. "I think I should send a message from Ron saying he's running a little late. That way the stalker will think he has time to confront me alone."

"Good idea," JP said.

"Are you sure you want to do this, Lana?" Tuper asked. "It's not too late to pull out."

"I have to. I can't keep living like this."

"Then it's time to send the message with the address." Tuper's gaze met Lana's.

She opened the text conversation with Ron and typed in the address for the property, mentioning that she was already there. Her hands trembled slightly as she pressed *send*. She knew that once the message was in play, there would be no turning back.

"Now, we wait," Lana announced softly.

Lana watched as the three men took their positions. She worried this could be a mistake, but she had to do it. And it was too late to back out now. She just hoped they didn't have to wait too long.

About a minute later, she sent a response from Ron's phone.

Ron—*You're further away than I thought, and I hit traffic. I'll be there in about forty minutes. Can you wait?*

Lana—*Sure. It's not bad here. It'll do me good to relax for a bit. But please don't take too long. I don't want to be here after dark.*

Lana parked herself in the swing and waited. As the minutes ticked by, Lana's tension grew. Each rustle of leaves or bird call made her jump, her eyes darting around for signs of movement. Lana could feel her heart pounding in her chest.

Lana thought she heard an engine purring in the distance. She waited. She texted JP and Brad to let them know. It wasn't long before she heard the rustling of leaves and the crunching of footsteps. She took a deep breath, bracing herself for what was to come. Her heart raced and her hands shook.

Suddenly, a tall figure emerged at the edge of the clearing. Lana's breath caught in her throat as she strained to get a better view. She could see his silhouette. His movements were precise and deliberate, as if he were on a mission. Lana felt a strange sense of both anticipation and dread as the figure stepped into the clearing. The figure stopped. He had noticed her. Time seemed to stand still as he peered in her direction. Lana felt like she couldn't move, couldn't breathe, as if she were frozen in place. As he moved closer, Lana's eyes narrowed, and she gripped the ropes of the swing tightly.

"Trust the plan," Lana whispered to herself.

As he reached the center of the clearing, everyone remained in position. The middle-aged man with graying hair looked around nervously, then walked in her direction. She suddenly felt the familiar sting of the man's gaze and knew without a doubt who he was. She couldn't believe what she was seeing. She recognized that walk. *It couldn't be.*

"It... it's you," Lana gasped.

Chapter Fifty-Seven

Thursday, late afternoon

Lana sat there, mouth agape. She didn't know whether to laugh or cry. Then the anger surfaced. "You're supposed to be dead."

He was within ten feet of her now.

"That's far enough," JP's voice boomed. He was off to her side, gun pointed directly at the intruder. Brad was on her other side, his rifle aimed at him as well. Tuper remained in the tower. The plan was to make sure he was alone.

The man stopped and raised his hands. "I'm not armed."

By then, JP was moving in quickly. "I don't plan to take your word for it."

"Check for yourself."

Brad kept his rifle aimed at the man, while JP patted him down for weapons. "He's clean."

"Why did you do this?" Lana demanded, noticing the large bruise on his face. She wondered if that was from the fight with Ron at the Hutterite colony.

"Please, Lana," her father whispered, his eyes begging her to understand. "I know I've made mistakes, but I want to make things right."

"By hacking into our phones and spying on us? By coming after me and terrorizing me?" Lana spat, her voice dripping with venom. "You have a twisted way of showing your love!"

"I didn't mean to scare you. I just wanted to talk." He looked ashamed.

"What about everything in the past?" Lana's hands clenched into fists.

Lana's face contorted with a mix of disbelief and rage. She took a deep breath. "Start explaining, or I'm leaving," Lana said.

Charles's eyes darted between Lana and JP, as if searching for the right words. Finally, he sighed, looking defeated. "I didn't want any of this to happen." He grimaced. "But I had no choice. I did it to protect you, Lana."

"Protect me?" Lana scoffed. "By disappearing and letting me believe you were dead?"

"I hated leaving you like that." Charles seemed earnest. "If there had been any other way, I would've taken it. But I had enemies, dangerous people who wanted me gone. And they would've come after you to get to me."

"Why come back now? Why risk everything for some stupid, grandiose scheme that could never work?"

"That's where you're wrong. It can work," Charles insisted. "But I needed to get close to you, to make sure you were safe. The only way I could do that without putting you in more danger was by staying in the shadows and watching from afar."

"Excuses," Lana said bitterly. "You abandoned me, and now you expect me to accept your pathetic explanations?"

When Charles took a step toward Lana, JP moved between them. "Back up. You're close enough."

Charles complied but stayed focused on Lana. "Please, Lana," her father pleaded, his eyes welling with tears. "I know I can never make up for the time we lost, but let me try to be part of your life again. Let me help you."

"Help me?" Lana repeated, her voice dripping with disdain. "I don't need your help. I've survived all these years without you, and I'll continue to do so."

"Damn it, Lana!" Charles snapped. "Can't you see I'm trying to make things right?"

"Make things right?" Lana echoed, her voice raw with emotion. She stared at him for a moment, then shook her head, as if dismissing the idea. "You can't fix this, Dad. You can't erase the past or take back the pain you caused. This—" she gestured between them, "—is beyond repair."

Charles's face fell, and she witnessed the weight of her words crush him. Now that she could see his pain, she wanted to take it back. She vacillated between anger and love for her father. When she was young, he had been a good father.

"Fine," Charles said quietly. "If that's how you feel, then I won't force myself into your life. But know this, Lana: I never stopped loving you, and I never will."

Lana flinched, her eyes glistening with unshed tears. For a brief moment, she thought she might relent, might allow her father to reach out to her. But then she blinked her tears away and reverted to cold anger. "I can't trust you."

"Look, Lana. We can be a family and go away together. We can live anywhere we want. C'mon, baby, remember how it was? It was always you and me against the world. It can be that way again."

Lana sighed. She looked down at her feet and swallowed. Her father seemed to read the signs and kept pushing. "We used to do everything together. Now we can travel the world with new identities and we won't have to look over our shoulders."

"And how will we live?" Lana asked.

"I have money in offshore accounts. And we can get more if we need it."

There it was. Lana finally heard what he was really saying. "That's it, isn't it, Daddy? You need me."

"Of course, I need you. You're my baby girl. I will always need you."

"But right now you need me to get you out of a jam. Just for once, Dad, tell me the truth. Because I'm not going anywhere with you if I can't believe you."

Charles hesitated. "I could use your help with something." He must've seen Lana's shoulders tighten, because he quickly added, "But that's not why I'm here. Please, just come with me and let's try."

"I have more questions. And I expect honest answers."

"Okay."

"Why did you fake your death? I know you said there were bad guys after you, but it was more than that, right?"

"Yes. It was people close to me."

"Like Jack and Grant?"

"Yes."

"Why?"

"We had been working together for a while and things were going great—until they decided they could run the scheme without me. I made the mistake of teaching them too much, so they thought they could do everything without my skill set. Perhaps they even planned to kill me. I don't know, but I got wind of it and decided the only safe way out was to make them think I was dead."

"So, you planned the whole thing. You got Unger to declare the fire an accident. You got Osborne to falsify your dental records, Agnes to do some technical work for you, and Philip Kent to move your assets to a shell company, which meant I wouldn't inherit anything, and you would have funds to live on. How am I doing so far?"

"You're spot on, as usual. I knew you would eventually figure everything out. You're smarter than any of them. You're smarter than me."

Lana ignored the flattery. "So, whose body was in the fire? Who burned up in your place that night?"

Charles looked down at his feet, either ashamed or feigning it. Lana couldn't be sure.

"A homeless guy."

"What did you do? Invite him in for dinner, then set the house on fire?"

"It wasn't like that."

"I'm sure you had help with that too. Let me guess, Victor Marsh, the lineman with a criminal record?"

"He provided the body. I don't know who the corpse belonged to, but he fit my general description."

"And then you killed Marsh?"

Her father's silence answered that question.

Lana shook her head. "You must've paid these people a lot of money."

"More than I should have."

"Did you shoot Jack too?"

Again, no response.

Lana asked again. "Just tell me. I need to understand."

He took a deep breath. "Jack had figured out that I was alive. As you know, he had information on everyone who helped me. He knew everything and would've killed me if he had the chance. I couldn't let him get any closer."

"And Grant? How long was he in on the scheme?"

"Ever since you two broke up. He saw some of what we were doing when you two were dating. That was your fault. He forced his way in, but he was actually a real asset until he joined forces with Jack."

"Who else's life did you destroy? Unger? Osborne? Kent?"

"Lana, let's just go. We can talk about all this later. I promise to tell you everything I know."

"I've heard enough, Isaac Newton."

Charles gave a half smile. "You got that, huh?"

"When I heard it, I wondered about you for a split second. You always claimed to have a higher IQ than Sir Isaac Newton. But since you were dead, it had to be someone else, right?"

"You're very smart, baby girl."

"One more thing," Lana said. "What does Grant want with me? Does he want to kill me because I know too much about him?"

"No. Grant's an idiot. He doesn't think you can squeal on him without implicating yourself, so he's not afraid of you. He needs your help to score in the big leagues."

"But that's where he's wrong. If I turned state's evidence and brought down a couple of big offenders, I'd likely avoid jail time, wouldn't I?"

"C'mon, Lana. You don't want to do that. Remember how much we meant to each other. Remember how I took care of you after your mother died."

"I remember." Lana's thoughts rushed back to her childhood and those long, lonely days after her mother committed suicide. He had spent a lot of time with her, but looking back, she realized it was always for his benefit. Her father was ruthless. Why hadn't she seen it before? *No wonder my mother committed suicide.*

"If you can't see us working together right now, then just let me go, and I'll stay out of your life forever, or until you're ready. Your call."

Lana heard the operative words again—working to-gether. That's what he really wanted. She took a deep breath. "Goodbye, Charles," she said flatly, turning her back on him. And with that, she strode away, leaving her father standing there, disappointment etched into every line of his face.

Chapter Fifty-Eight

Thursday, late afternoon

Tuper stood on the porch of Brad's abandoned family home, the worn wooden planks creaking beneath his cowboy boots. He pulled out his phone, squinting at the buttons as he dialed his friend Pat Cox's number. The wind whispered through the trees, bringing with it the scent of pine and the faintest hint of impending rain.

"Hey, Tuper," Pat answered, his voice raspy with age. "What can I do for you?"

"I'm standing here looking at a guy who committed murder."

"Murder?" Pat sounded incredulous. "Are you certain about this, Tuper?"

"Nothin's ever certain in this life," Tuper replied, rubbing his scar. "But I've got some pretty good evidence for you."

"Where are you?"

Tuper gave him the address.

"I'll be right out there."

It wasn't long before sirens echoed through the sleepy community as police officers swarmed the old Bergstad estate.

As officers cuffed him, Charles whined, "Is this really necessary? I haven't done anything!"

"Sorry, Mr. Storm," one of the officers said. "We have reason to believe you're involved in a murder case. You need to come with us."

"Murder?" Charles scoffed. "This is preposterous! I've never harmed anyone in my life!"

"Then you'd better get a lawyer," another officer warned, pushing him into the back of a squad car.

Lana watched as they drove her father away. She knew he would do everything he could to protect himself, even if it meant throwing her under the bus. She discussed her options with Tuper and JP, then decided what she had to do.

She took a walk around the yard, working up her courage, then called Sabre, Ron's sister, an attorney in San Diego. The line rang for what felt like an eternity, then a familiar voice picked up on the other end.

"Hello, Lana."

"Hey, Sabre," she began hesitantly, her heart pounding. "I need your help. I need legal help."

"I'll do whatever I can."

Lana gave her a brief rundown of what happened. "Can you help me?"

"I'm not sure I'm the one you need."

"I don't know anyone else I can trust. Please. I'm willing to turn myself in to the feds, but I want a favorable agreement in exchange. Can you make that happen?"

"Lana, this is a big step," Sabre said cautiously. "I don't know much about this kind of law, but let me make a few calls and see if something can be negotiated. If not, I'll find you someone who has the right experience."

"Thanks, Sabre. I appreciate it." Lana let out a shaky breath. "I'll be waiting for your call." She hung up and stared at the screen, her mind consumed with uncertainty about her future. She couldn't shake the feeling that the world around her was closing in.

The four of them drove back to Brad's house to regroup and wait for Sabre's call. Over an hour passed before Lana heard from her.

"Look, Lana," she said, her voice a mix of caution and concern. "I can try to negotiate a deal with the feds, but I need you to understand something. They won't make any promises until they see the evidence. They'll want to know what you've got before they agree to anything."

"Understood." Lana glanced around the room, taking in the exposed wooden beams, the bright rug, and the faint scent of pine. The sensory details grounded her, helping to chase away the creeping panic that threatened to overwhelm her.

"Give me some time to get things moving on my end. I'll contact you as soon as I have any news," Sabre said.

"Thanks, Sabre." Lana tried to keep the desperation out of her voice. She hung up and turned to Tuper. "Now what?"

"Let's go back to Clarice's and get out of Brad's hair. It'll put us closer to Ron and Grant too."

"Good idea," JP said. "I can relieve Ron for a while. We should still keep an eye on Grant until we figure out our next step."

"One of us can pick up Clarice and Mary Ann in the mornin'. I'll call and let them know what's going on."

By the time they arrived at Clarice's and settled in, the sun had long since set. Lana stared at the darkness through the window, her fingers drumming on the dining room table. She felt a chill that had nothing to do with the rapidly approaching night.

They hadn't been home long when Sabre called. "I was able to reach a colleague, who knows an attorney who handles this kind of thing."

"How often does *this kind of thing* happen?" Lana asked.

"More often than you would think. The attorney's name is Quade Goldstein. He was a federal prosecutor for ten years, and now he does defense work. He's worked with the feds on both sides. He really knows his stuff."

"Did you talk to him?"

"I did. And you need to hire *him*, not me." Lana started to object, but Sabre was adamant. "He knows who to talk to and what to ask for. You need him to negotiate the deal. You'll be a lot better off."

"I don't know how comfortable I'd be opening up to Mr. Goldstein."

"Look, I understand your concerns," Sabre said, her voice a comforting presence amidst the chaos of Lana's thoughts. "But if you want the feds to take you seriously, you need to show them something they can't ignore, and he knows just how to do that."

Lana clenched her fists. "I know. I know." She sighed, trying to quell her fear. "It's just... what if it's not enough? What if they don't believe me?"

"Quade will know how to deal with that," Sabre replied, her tone resolute. "Why don't you talk to him and see how you feel about it. If that doesn't work, then we'll find another way. You're resourceful, Lana. You've made it this far by relying on your wits, and I have no doubt you can keep going. But you need to trust someone eventually."

"Trust is a luxury I can't afford, Sabre," she whispered, her voice laden with regret. "Not anymore."

"Sometimes, you have to take a leap of faith. We can't always know what awaits us on the other side."

"Faith," Lana murmured, the word feeling foreign on her tongue. "I've never been good at that."

"None of us are," Sabre said softly.

"All right," she whispered. "I'll do it. I'll call your attorney, and I'll turn myself in."

Chapter Fifty-Nine

Friday morning

Last night Lana had shared the highlights of her story with the attorney, explaining that her father had taught her how to hack and had used her to help steal a lot of money. She gave him the names of her father and his business partner. She also told the attorney that her father had a master plan that could destroy a lot of peoples' lives. Quade was about to catch a plane and didn't have a lot of time to talk, but he had promised to call her back this morning. She hadn't slept well.

When her phone finally rang, Lana's heart skipped a beat. "Hello."

"Lana," came the attorney's deep voice on the line. "I just got off my plane, and I wanted to give you an update."

Lana shifted in her seat, anxious for whatever news he had to share. "Yes?"

"It turns out your father has been planning this for quite some time."

"Ever since I was a teenager," she cut in.

"So, longer than investigators thought," Quade said. "He was smart enough not to leave any paper trails and very little digital evidence of his actions. Unless you have some hard evidence, it'll be hard to prove anything."

Lana kept listening.

"However," the attorney continued, "we've been able to gather some information that might be useful in building a case against him and his partner." He went on to explain that they were already working with law enforcement and intel agencies from around the world to try and stop her father's scheme before it could be put into action. "The feds have been onto him for a long time, but he's slick. Any insight you can supply in that regard will go a long way."

"What do you want to know exactly?"

"Tell me what he was planning and how he was going to do it."

"They wanted to take over the U.S. government, manipulate the stock market, and gain control of major banking institutions. I know it sounds extravagant, and it is, but he believed he could do it. As a kid, I believed in him and thought it was possible. As I got older, I realized he wasn't going to be successful. But I also knew what he could do on the dark web, and how good he was at scams. He was an expert at obtaining money. With enough money, he believed he could manipulate certain government seats, and with political power, he could gain a lot of control. I know it was grandiose, but the destruction he'll leave behind if he ever gets the chance to implement more of his plan could be catastrophic.

"However, money wasn't enough for any of them. They wanted power. As I said before, my father started this when I was still a teenager. I ran away five years ago because I refused to be a part of it, but they've been hunting me ever since." Lana took a deep breath, then continued. "A few years ago, my father died, supposedly, in an accidental fire. I thought Jack Peterson might've killed him, but I have recently learned that my father faked his own death. I can give you everything you need—names, addresses, and phone numbers of everyone involved, from the name of the guy who provided his replacement corpse to the dentist who falsified his dental records."

"Details would certainly be good. How much do you know about their plan?"

"I know all the technical procedures and many of his scams. I don't know his exact plan of action. I can show you exactly what he was doing on the web. At least enough so an expert can trace his footsteps."

"The guys investigating this are masters, and they haven't been able to track him." The attorney sounded skeptical. "What makes you so certain you can do it?"

"Because I was the real hacker. Jack and my father needed me to finish the job. That's why they've been looking for me all this time."

"You?"

"Yes."

"I knew you were involved, but I didn't realize you were the mastermind."

"I'm not the mastermind. It was all my father's idea. I was just the technician. He taught me what he knew, then I surpassed him. He was stuck, and I wouldn't tell him what I had learned."

There was a moment of silence. Finally, Quade asked, "Can you provide names, dates, and specifics?"

"More than you can imagine."

"Excellent. I spoke with a federal agent who said they've been trying to catch them for nearly a decade. The feds also know there is a third person working with them, and if you give him up, you'd make the prosecutor very happy. Do you know who it is?"

"Grant Simmons." She gave him his phone number, home address, and the hotel he was staying at, plus the license plate of the car he was driving.

"You certainly are thorough."

"I learned from the best," Lana scoffed. "We have a tail on Grant right now because he keeps trying to get to me. He wants me to help him finish the scheme my father started. Do you think they'll arrest Grant?"

"I'm sure he'll get a visit from the feds right after I make the call."

"Quade." Lana hesitated to ask. "Can you help get me out of this mess?"

"I'm sure of it," Quade said. "I'll set up a meeting in the next few days, and I'll fly to Helena to be present at that meeting."

Lana sighed. For the first time, she felt like she had a chance.

When she hung up, she explained the gist of the conversation to her worried friends, then said, "I'm going to see Grant."

"What?" Tuper exclaimed. "You can't. You'll mess up the whole plan."

"I'm just going to give Grant a piece of my mind."

While they all shook their heads in protest, Lana called Ron. "Where's Grant?"

"He's eating breakfast. Why?"

"Call me when he goes back to his hotel." She hung up before he could ask more questions.

Lana took a quick shower, then joined Mary Ann in the kitchen. Clarice was sitting on a barstool near the counter. JP and Tuper were at the dining room table.

"Do you want some breakfast?" Mary Ann asked.

"Just a cup of coffee, please."

Mary Ann poured the coffee, and Lana took it to the table and sat down. Before she got a sip of it, her phone rang.

"Is he at his hotel, Ron?"

"He's back in his room."

"I'll be right there."

"What?" Ron said. "No."

Lana hung up.

Tuper and JP went with Lana to meet Grant. They wouldn't take no for an answer, and Lana didn't argue much.

She knocked on the door of Grant's room.

"Who is it?"

"It's Lana. Please let me in."

He opened the door and Lana barged in with the three guys behind her.

"You really thought I wouldn't figure everything out?" she demanded.

"Listen," Grant began, taking a step closer. "I know I messed up, but we can still work together. We're stronger as a team. You know that."

"Work with you?" She scoffed, crossing her arms. "You're an idiot if you think I'd ever trust you again after what you've done!"

"Please, just give me a chance to explain—"

Lana cut him off. "You're a liability, and I don't need that in my life."

"Fine. Have it your way." Grant glared at her. "But when the feds come for you, you'll wish you had someone like me on your side."

"Never," Lana hissed. Lana brought her leg back and was about to plant it in Grant's crotch when JP grabbed her and spun her around. She tried to object, but JP led her toward the door. Tuper opened it, and two men in dark suits walked up. "Looking for Grant Simmons?"

"Yes."

"You're just in time," Tuper said.

JP pointed inside to Grant. "He's right over there. Tie a quarter to him and throw it away, and you can claim you lost something."

Chapter Sixty

Friday afternoon

Tuper and Lana sat across from Henry Fenton in a small café. As Tuper prepared to deliver the devastating news about Angel's cancer, rain pummeled the building, casting a somber backdrop for the occasion.

"Did you find anything?" Henry asked anxiously, his voice tinged with desperation. He glanced around the café as though afraid someone might overhear their discussion.

"Sit down, son," Tuper said gently, gesturing to the seat across from him. "We need to talk."

As Henry settled into the chair, Tuper could see the fear and suspicion swirling in his eyes. The man loved his wife deeply, and the thought of her being unfaithful was tearing him apart. It pained Tuper to know that the truth he was about to reveal would hit even harder.

"Angel's not cheating on you," Tuper said. "But there's something else going on, and it's serious."

"What is it?" Henry glanced from Tuper to Lana and back again.

Lana remained silent.

"First, you must understand that Lana and I only found this information because we were trying to help you," Tuper explained, his tone cautious. "It wasn't our intention to invade Angel's privacy, but we couldn't ignore what we discovered."

"Please, just tell me," Henry pleaded, gripping the edge of the table.

"Angel has stage two breast cancer," Tuper revealed. "She's scheduled for a mastectomy."

The color drained from Henry's face, as he struggled to comprehend the news. "Are you sure?" He choked out, tears welling in his eyes.

"I'm afraid so," Tuper replied softly, his heart aching for the man. "I reckon she didn't tell you 'cause she was scared it would affect your relationship and her career. Of course, she knew she would eventually have to come clean, but she wanted to buy as much time as she could without you thinking she was a freak."

"Damn it," Henry wiped away tears. "I don't care how many breasts she has. I love her. We could've faced this together."

"You need to tell her that," Lana said.

"I need to talk to her. I need to be there for her." After a moment he said, "Thanks," and stood.

Tuper turned to Lana. "I wish I'd never taken the case. People are so darn untrusting."

"Speaking of trust, Tuper," Lana said. "Why don't you ever tell anyone about your childhood? Where you grew up? I'll bet it's an interesting story."

Tuper stared at her for a minute. "You think you know somethin', don't you?"

"I think you have family very close by. Jacob and Peter are your brothers, aren't they?"

"Not much gets past you, does it, Agony?"

"Not much. But I don't understand why you wouldn't embrace that. They are wonderful men. Why do you hide it?"

"For their sake. It's one thing for them to have a heathen for a *friend*. It's another to be related. I was an embarrassment to the whole colony when I was young. They were better off without me."

"But you came back. Didn't people know then?"

"I was thirteen when I left. I returned as an adult. No one recognized me except my brothers and a few elders. But by then, Jacob was their leader and the elders really liked him." Tuper scowled. "Are you done with the third degree?"

"Just tell me one more thing."

"What's that?"

"I know you can't read. How have you managed all this time without people knowing?"

"A few people know, like Clarice and Mary Ann, and my brothers, of course, but the rest have been easy. Most people are too interested in themselves to really pay much attention to others."

"You've always been obstinate, haven't you, Pops?"

"That's two things."

Lana laughed. "Your secrets are safe with me."

Chapter Sixty-One

Monday morning

The stale air in the government building hung heavy, as if the walls had absorbed years of whispered secrets and desperate pleas. Lana's heart hammered in her chest as she walked down the corridor, her boots feeling like lead weights with every step.

Her attorney strode confidently beside her. "Remember," Quade advised, "just be honest and trust that I'll do everything I can to get you the best deal possible. And if I interrupt you or touch your hand, stop talking. No matter what you're saying, just stop. I'll take over."

Lana nodded. They soon reached a conference room. Lana paused and steeled herself, then pushed open the door, her feisty personality overshadowed by nerves and fear.

"Have a seat, Ms. Storm," a stern voice greeted her from across the table. The room was devoid of warmth or comfort, and a single window offered only a sliver of sunlight.

Lana sat, her legs feeling like jelly, and Quade took his place by her side.

"I'm Agent Valdes, and this is Agent Long," said the man in his early forties with salt-and-pepper hair. He wore a navy suit that seemed to have been tailored precisely for him. His partner, a woman with auburn hair pulled back into a tight bun, wore a crisp white blouse and a matching navy skirt. Lana focused on the ticking clock on the wall, trying to regain control of her breathing. She knew this was her best chance at finally moving on from her haunted past. But at what price?

"Ms. Storm?" Agent Valdes said. "We need you to be completely honest with us. Can you do that?"

"Y-yes," she stammered, her voice a whisper. "I can do that."

"Good," he replied, his face impassive. "Let's start with Grant Simmons. What can you tell us about him?"

"Grant and I... We were together for a while," she admitted, her voice surprisingly steady despite the knot in her stomach. "We used to hack into systems together, but he started to take things too far. He's always been obsessed with power and control."

"What systems?" the female agent asked. "We need specifics."

Lana spent the next forty minutes detailing their money laundering and fraud schemes, explaining how they funneled illegal funds through shell companies to avoid detection.

"How did you meet Grant?" Agent Valdes asked.

"He was a friend of my dad."

"Your father is Charles Storm?"

"Correct," Lana confirmed.

"Who else was involved?"

"Jack Peterson. He was my dad's business partner. They ran an investment firm."

"Jack Peterson," Agent Long looked up from her notepad. "That's the man who was shot in front of his hotel, correct?"

"That's right. And I think my father killed him."

"Why do you think that?"

"Jack and my dad were once close, but they had a falling out. They committed a lot of cybercrime together, and my father taught him everything he knew. I think Jack decided he didn't need his partner anymore, and my dad got wind of it," Lana explained, her voice shaking slightly as she remembered his chilling blue eyes." Jack also tried to use me for my hacking abilities. He wanted me to help him with my father's plan for power."

"Can you be more specific?" the male agent pressed.

"I don't know all the details of the actual plan," Lana admitted, her hands fidgeting in her lap.

"If you were the one who was doing the high-level hacking, how could you *not* know the plan?"

"I know how to get into accounts and places most people can't go. I know how to cover my tracks. I know how to move things around and make it impossible to follow. I can show you all that. I can create a roadmap for you. What I don't know is how he planned to manipulate certain people and offices for his benefit. Perhaps when I lead you down the path they've taken, you can figure out the rest."

"So, you know how to get the information, but not how they would use it?"

"For the most part that's true. I know it involves fraud on a massive scale. I know they wanted to go after a couple of big banks. They thought they could take over the federal government and Wall Street."

Before she could say any more, Agent Valdes cut in. "Tell me exactly what you mean by that."

Lana paused for a moment, considering her words carefully before speaking. "They had a plan – a well-crafted and comprehensive plan. They wanted to use their connections to powerful people in the government to gain access to information and resources that would give them an advantage in the markets. Once they had enough money and influence, they hoped to manipulate the stock markets and affect political decisions for their own benefit. My father was always talking about how he'd *change the game,* whatever that meant."

"And Charles Storm was involved in the whole thing, correct?"

"It was his plan from the beginning." She paused. "I also have a list of the companies that I know he stole from in the past."

"How do you know that?"

Lana looked at Quade again, then said, "Because I helped him do it."

"And where is the money now from those companies?"

"I hacked back into them and put my part back."

Quade glanced at Lana with surprise when she said that. Lana realized she hadn't shared that part with him.

"What?" the female fed said. "You say you returned some of the money?"

"I returned every cent I ever took, with the exception of what we stole from organized crime. Some of that I had already spent, the rest I gave to a charity for abused children. My father, on the other hand, walked with far more than I ever got."

"Do you realize that if we pursue this, your boyfriend will do prison time?"

"As he should. And he isn't my boyfriend. Hasn't been for years."

"And your father could be put away for life?"

"I believe my father has killed several people, and hurt many more. He deserves to be put away, if not for stealing, then certainly for that."

The interview went on for several hours, with Lana spending much of the time answering the same questions asked in different forms.

"Thank you, Ms. Storm," Agent Long finally said, closing her notepad. "Your cooperation is greatly appreciated."

The male agent stood, as if he were leaving, and Lana's heart skipped a beat. *Was there not going to be a deal? Had she messed up somehow?* She looked at Quade, her eyes pleading. Before he could respond, the agent said, "We're going to take a break. When we return, we'll talk about the terms of the deal I discussed with your attorney." His face remained a stony mask as he walked out.

Chapter Sixty-Two

Monday morning

Lana made a quick trip to the restroom, then paced the conference room until they returned, steeling herself for what was to come. The agents filed in with the same stony faces, sat down, and immediately started the discussion.

"Based on the information you provided, we believe you can be useful in our ongoing investigation into your father, Charles Storm, and his conspirators, Grant Simmons and Jack Peterson," Agent Valdes said. "In exchange for your cooperation in providing further intelligence and assistance when needed, we are prepared to offer you complete immunity."

Yes! She almost cried with relief.

"However, should you choose not to testify at any of the hearings regarding either your father or Grant Simmons, the deal is off. You will need to keep us informed of any change of address or phone number. Someone will be assigned to your case, and you will have direct contact with that person. You must keep in touch. Do you understand?"

Lana nodded, relief still washing over her. The deal was far better than what she'd expected.

"Keep in mind, Ms. Storm, that any violation of the terms will result in immediate revocation of the deal, and you will be prosecuted," Agent Long warned, her eyes locking onto Lana's. "We expect full compliance and honesty from you at all times."

"I understand," Lana assured them, nodding her head vigorously. "I accept the terms."

"Very well," Valdes concluded, closing the file and standing up. "Your attorney can work out the remaining details and provide you with the contact information you'll need."

"Thank you," she whispered.

As the agents filed out of the room, Lana felt a strange mix of emotions. She knew her life would never be the same, but at least she had a chance now, a shot at redemption.

"Are you all right, Lana?" Quade asked gently, placing a hand on her shoulder.

"Yeah," she said, offering a small smile. "I didn't really think I would get no jail time. Thank you."

Quade told Lana he had to work out a few details with the agents and left the room.

Lana sat alone in the dimly lit conference room, staring at the empty chairs where the federal agents had been moments earlier. The silence was both comforting and unnerving, a stark contrast to the tension that had filled the air during their meeting. She knew she should be relieved, grateful even, but her father's face haunted her thoughts, an ever-looming specter of her past.

"Your father would be so disappointed in you," her mind whispered cruelly, echoing the cutting words he'd often hurled at her throughout her childhood. Lana shuddered, feeling the weight of those memories settle heavily on her chest.

"Hey, Lana," Quade said, jolting her from her dark thoughts. "Are you ready to leave?"

"Yeah," she said with a renewed confidence as she rose from her chair. "Let's go."

As they walked down the sterile, hushed hallways of the government building, Lana's emotions whirled like a storm within her. Fear still gnawed at her insides, insistent and unrelenting, but mingling with it now were tendrils of hope and relief.

"You're going to be okay," Quade said.

"I know," she admitted. "I'm terrified to testify against my father. But I can do it. I've done a lot of things far more difficult."

Chapter Sixty-Three

Monday night

Lana stood in the doorway of the cozy kitchen. The comforting aroma of Clarice's homemade beef stew filled the air as the sisters bustled about, setting the table and pouring tea.

"Come on in, Lana," Mary Ann called out. "We're almost ready to eat."

Lana couldn't help but feel a swell of gratitude for the two women. The weight of the day's events still hung heavy on her shoulders, but within the walls of this humble home, she felt a sense of belonging.

"Looks great, you two," Lana said. "I'm starving."

"Good, because there's plenty to go around." Clarice flashed Lana a warm smile. "After today, I think we could all use some nourishment."

"Agreed," Lana murmured, taking a seat as Mary Ann placed a steaming bowl of stew before her. Lana stared down at the fragrant dish, her thoughts drifting back to the federal agents and the deal she had made.

"Hey," Mary Ann said gently. "We're so proud of you for having the courage to face your past head-on."

Lana blinked back tears. "Thank you," she whispered, her voice thick with emotion. "I don't know if I could've done it without you both."

Clarice smiled at her. "You're stronger than you think."

Tuper and Ron came in the front door after dropping JP off at the airport. Ron had chosen to remain behind for a while.

"Join us for dinner," Clarice said. "There's plenty."

The men sat down, with Ron taking the chair beside her.

"You done good today, Agony," Tuper said gruffly.

"Thank you, Pops."

Ron reached for her hand and gave it a gentle squeeze. "You're incredibly brave, Lana."

"Thanks, Ron." The warmth of his touch radiated through her.

Clarice held up her glass of wine and clinked it against Lana's. "To new beginnings and the family we choose."

"To new beginnings," echoed Mary Ann, raising her own glass.

Lana raised hers as well. "To all of you—my family." She paused. "Speaking of family. I'm thinking about connecting with Danny, if he's open to it. I never really gave him a chance."

"Keeping in touch with your brothers is a good thing." Tuper winked at Lana, and she smiled knowingly. He stared at her for a long minute, then shook his head and said, "Storm? That's your last name? No wonder you never told any of us. But it certainly suits you—Agony Storm."

Lana smiled. "I'm thinking about changing it. Maybe I'll take your last name, Pops. What is it, anyway?"

"Never mind. Eat your stew."

From the Author

Dear Reader,

Thank you for reading my book. I hope you enjoyed reading it as much as I did writing it. Would you like a FREE copy of a novella about JP when he was young? If so, scan the QR code below and it will take you where you want to go. Or, if you prefer, you please go to www.teresaburrell.com and sign up for my mailing list. You'll automatically receive a code to retrieve the story.

SCAN ME

Teresa

Author Bio

Teresa Burrell has dedicated her life to helping children and their families. As an attorney, Ms. Burrell has spent countless hours working pro bono in the family court system. She continues to advocate children's issues and write novels, many of which are inspired by actual legal cases.

Please send an email to Teresa and let her know what you thought of this book. She'd love to hear from you. She can be reached at teresa@teresaburrell.com. If you like this author's writing, the best way to compliment her is by telling your friends. Reviews are nice too.

Made in the USA
Middletown, DE
27 October 2023

41382984R00179